Sealed In Silence

Sealed In Silence

Desaree Armand

Sealed In Silence

Desaree Armand

Vintage Petal Publishing

Vintage Petal Publishing

I dedicate this book to my husband, Merrick, and my sister, Hannah. Both of them believed I could write this story that has been living in my head for almost twenty years and believed I could get it out into the public sphere.

"Look for me in the white forest
Hiding in a hollow tree (come and find me)"
Amy Lee/Ben Moody/ David Hodges

Contents

Chapter One

The school bell sounded loud and clear. It was the end of the school day at the end of the week. I let out a sigh of relief. It was time to go home. As a grade schoolteacher, I spent five days a week with about thirty fourth graders, teaching them everything from English grammar to math and science all while also having to play disciplinarian to keep them in line. They weren't bad kids don't get me wrong. But a few of them liked to constantly try my patience and made me thank God for the rest of my students who came to school every day ready to learn.

Now it was the weekend and just like my students, I was ready to go home and enjoy it. It was my third year of teaching and while the styles of hair and clothing may have changed slightly during that time, the kids themselves did not. At nine and ten years old, the boys are always still more focused on playing sports and video games than on the girls who are always starting to look at them a little differently. The girls are still in that in-between stage where they are starting to care about fashion and music but are still holding on to their childhoods at the same time by making friendship bracelets and necklaces made of gum wrappers. Sometimes I envied them their innocence. They had no idea of the joys and heartbreaks yet to come.

I waited until every student was packed up and out the door before gathering my own things and heading out. I waved to my students who were waiting for their parents as I walked to my car. It was late March in this small South Carolina town and the weather was nice and cool. In just another two months, the kids would be out for the summer, I thought. I drove home anticipating my evening. I walked inside and shouldered off my teachers' bag and purse onto a nearby chair. I walked into my small kitchen and poured myself a glass of red wine, turned on some relaxing music from my phone and connected it to my Bluetooth speaker. Then I slid off my shoes and collapsed on my couch.

I loved my little cottage. With just one bedroom and a full bath with a large luxurious tub, a medium sized sitting room and a small kitchen, it was just big enough to be cozy without feeling cramped. It was over 100 years old with all original wood floors and new vinyl siding on the outside painted a lovely butter yellow with white trim. It had moss green shutters and moss green flower boxes hanging from the windows. I had only just begun looking for a place of my own when I found it and had fallen in love at first sight. I had gotten a great deal on it too which made me feel like it was meant to be. After adding my own personal decorating touch, it became my heaven on earth.

I sipped my wine slowly, relishing each taste. This was my Friday ritual. It was my way of welcoming the weekend. During the week, I spent my home time grading homework assignments and tests and fielding calls and emails from parents about their children. I did everything I could so that by Friday, there was nothing left to do but relax. I closed my eyes and tuned into the music. My muscles began to relax as I felt that familiar warmth from my glass of wine begin to fill all of my senses.

All too soon I had finished my glass. My plan tonight was to call my sister, Allie, and talk to her for a bit before climbing into my tub with a second glass of wine then getting cozy in my bed, watching a little bit of television, and falling asleep early. I tried to keep up with my sister at least once a week but that wasn't always possible since she wasn't always available to talk when I was.

I was the older of the two of us with Allie being three years younger and we were as different as night and day. Allie had olive skin, deep brown eyes, and dark brown, almost black, hair. I had medium toned skin that tanned gold, hazel eyes, and chocolate brown hair. Where I lived my life planned out and organized, she lived her life by the seat of her pants and never seemed to know from one moment to the next where she was going or with whom. At 22 she was still trying to find herself and had no problem taking off at a moment's notice if an invitation arrived for her to do so.

When Allie was eighteen, I had already been out of our parents' house for a few years leaving her alone with them. Just like me, she was ready to run as soon as she graduated high school. But where I had gotten out by going to our small local college and moving in with some girls I'd known since grade school, Allie had moved in with a guy that she barely knew and claimed that she was in love with him. She believed that he was the one for her and that she didn't need college. Needless to say, it didn't work out.

This led her to living alone in a small apartment that she could barely afford from one month to the next. She also always had a hard time keeping a job. In the four years that passed since Allie graduated high school, she kept a steady stream of one new boyfriend after another, none of them ever sticking around for very long. There was a good chance that if I called her right now, she wouldn't answer or that she would answer just long enough to tell me that she was out with some new guy that I'd never heard of. But it was the thought that counted and so I got up, grabbed my phone, turned off my music and called. She answered on the third ring.

"Hello Emily!" she said in a very sing song voice.

"Hey Allie, what are you up to?"

"Take a guess!" she said sounding very excited.

"Okay sure. You figured out what you want to do with your life and are ready to settle down."

"Close. Very close. It's just the second part. I met a guy and I think he may be the one."

Oh no not again I thought. Out loud I said "Great. So, tell me about him. What's he like? Where did you meet?"

As Allie reeled off her story to me about meeting him at a party at a co-worker's house (he was the cousin of the co-worker) I listened intently while hoping in my heart of hearts this guy would turn out to be better than all the ones who came before whom she had equally deemed to be "the one". Fat chance of that though. My sister seemed to have a knack for drawing the losers of the world to her who had no intention of treating her with any kind of real respect.

Within a matter of weeks, I predicted, or maybe even months, she would probably call me crying. Yet again it would turn out that the guy that she had been so in love with turned out to be married or making his money through shady means or was just not ready to commit to one woman. Nothing ever really seemed to change.

"He's so great" she was saying now. "Not like all the others. I really think this time that it's going to work out."

"Well, I hope so" I told her now. "I'll be crossing my fingers for you. Hey maybe you could bring him around some time, and I could get to know this wonderful new man in your life."

"Emily, I don't want to scare him off when I only just started dating him. Not that you'd be anything but cordial to him it's just, I don't want him to think I'm trying to move too quickly by already having him meet the family after just a few weeks."

"Yeah, I totally understand. Maybe in a few months if you're still together then."

"You have so little faith in me! I really do think that in a few months, not only will we be still together, but very happy as well."

"Well, that's great to hear. In the meantime, how's your job going?"

"I knew you'd ask me that. We can't ever seem to talk without you asking me that."

"Well, I can't help it if I want you to finally have a job that you're happy enough with that you want to stay there for more than a few months. So, don't change the subject. I want to know how it's going."

"I don't know. It's just a job. Sure, I make commission on sales of clothing and shoes, and I *am* good at it don't get me wrong, it's just, is it really so horrible to just want to find a good guy with a strong career that will give me a few beautiful children and who makes enough money for the both of us? That's what I really want. I'm hoping this may finally be the one."

"Great guys are hard to find though Allie. You know that. I mean look at mom and dad. Couples like them are becoming more and more common unfortunately. The best thing you can do is to be able to take care of yourself and be happy doing it. If the right guy comes along one day, then all the better. But you can't live your life around the hope of finding someone to make you happy. You must make yourself happy first."

"You always tell me that and I always tell you that you sound like someone who's hiding. You need to get out there and meet people once in a while. Not all relationships are destined to be as bad as our parents' relationship. You can't use them as an excuse forever for why you never go out and try to meet people or why when you do, you always find some miniscule problem with them after just a few dates and end things with them."

"I am too busy with my happy and fulfilling life to go out and meet people. You know that. If the right guy were to ever come along, I would make time for him. I believe if it's meant to happen then it will. But if not, then that's fine too because I am happy with my life without a man in it and I'm not about to spend my time running around looking for one. You need to learn how to make them come to you."

"Like how they flock all over you?" Allie sighed. "I'm sorry. I didn't mean that. I'm just feeling defensive I guess."

"It's okay. I'm sorry too. Who knows, maybe this one will really be 'the one' after all."

"Maybe he will." Allie said now. "And maybe one day you'll give Alex a real chance and find out once and for all if all this time, he's been the one you need, and you've just been keeping him at arm's length by telling him that you just want to be friends."

Here we go again I thought. For some reason my sister seemed to think women couldn't have male best friends. Especially not for the length of time that I'd been friends with Alex, over 15 years.

"How many times do I have to tell you?" I said exasperated now. "It's not just me. Neither one of us like each other that way. I have never told him I just want to be friends. I don't have to. We *are* just friends. Just because a man and a woman are friends does not mean that they have to get involved. That is just a Hollywood fantasy that is perpetuated in television shows and movies. Just like how fairy-tales tell us that our existence should revolve around finding a prince charming to take care of us and that our lives cannot possibly be fulfilled until that happens.

Look at what that belief has done to you. You're 22 years old and still running around barely able to pay your rent while I am comfortably paying a mortgage on a beautiful cottage and still able to put away money into savings for a rainy day. If you ever had an emergency where you needed money, you wouldn't have it."

"It sounds more to me like you've given up on finding someone to love without ever even really trying to begin with. But what do I know? I'm just the family screw-up, right? But one of these days, I *will* really find the one I'm meant to be with, and we *will* live happily ever after, and you will grow old alone with no one to take care of you. Alex is in love with you. I'm not the only one who sees it. He won't wait around for you forever Emily. Eventually he will find someone else and then you won't even have him around anymore as a friend. But let's agree to disagree."

"You're not a screw-up. I never said that. And yeah, I agree, we are two very different people with different points of view. But we *are* sisters and I love you. I'll always be there for you when you need me no matter what happens."

"I love you too. I've got to go now. I was actually in the middle of getting ready for a date with my wonderful new man when you called. He said he was taking me somewhere fancy but wouldn't tell me where. He said it's a surprise. I'm so excited."

"Well alright then. That sounds great and I look forward to hearing all about it another day."

We said our goodbyes and I hung up the phone. I didn't like to think about our parents but now it was stuck on my mind. Our parents were still together, yes, but they were *not* happy. There's was a tragic case of staying married just to be with someone even though they made each other miserable, presumably out of the fear of being alone.

I grew up taking care of Allie like a surrogate parent. There was never a shortage between our parents of yelling and fighting and even throwing things sometimes. This usually resulted in my dad storming out and not coming back for days at a time. God only knows what he was doing when he wasn't at home but that was never our greatest concern. Our greatest concern was how our mother reacted to him being gone and the fear of our dad never coming home. She would typically get drunk and rage about how no good of a husband he was to us before passing out either in her bed or on the couch.

On more nights than I could remember, I would be the one feeding Allie and myself dinner and helping her with her homework. We went to school every day as if nothing were wrong and no one ever suspected a thing. I made good grades and while Allie didn't, she didn't act out like some other troubled kids. We had friends but we kept them at a distance. I decided early on that I would NEVER end up like my parents who to this day, still have the same fights with the same results. The only difference was that now, me and Allie were all grown up and we didn't live at home anymore.

Now my thoughts turned to Alex Coleman, one of my best friends in the world. I met him in the fourth grade. He had just moved to town with his parents and was assigned by our teacher to sit next to me in class. I said hello to him as he took his seat and he smiled back in a shy kind of way. Later that day, at lunch, he walked up to me as I was sitting down at a table with my tray and asked to sit with me because he didn't know anyone. I said yes. He told me all about himself, how he was an only child, and how he had moved around a lot because his dad was in the military. He said that his father had retired to our small town and had taken a job as a police officer while his mother had taken a job at our local public library.

Then he asked me about myself, so I told him that my father worked construction and that my mom didn't have a job. He said that must be nice to have a mom who was home every day when I got home from school, and I just shook my head in agreement not knowing what else to say. If he registered that there was more to my story than I was saying, he didn't let on. He asked if we could be friends since he didn't know anyone, and I said yes. We've been good friends ever since.

At first, the boys poked fun at him for being friends with a girl but he didn't seem to mind. We'd sit around at recess and just talk about stuff like our favorite junk food, and which was the best. His was extra buttered popcorn and Oreos while mine was sour cream and onion chips and fudge rounds. We'd talk about books we'd read and movies we'd seen and our favorite video games. He liked games with war themes and sci-fi movies while I liked Mario games and dramatic shows like Law and Order. He was fun to talk to and we developed a pretty good friendship.

A few years later, in middle school, one day when school was over, Alex asked to come to my house. It was then that I knew that I had to open up about my parents. We were sitting outside on a bench and were getting ready to get up and start walking home in separate directions. When I told him, it didn't scare him away, which is what I'd been most afraid of. He just sat there for a few moments staring at me intently like he was thinking of what he should say, and then he put his arm around my shoulders as if to say, it's all going to be okay.

He didn't have to say anything. His gesture of friendship was enough. After that day, anytime we wanted to hang out after school or on the weekend, I went to his house where, if his mother was home, welcomed me like the daughter she never had. Sometimes we just walked around the neighborhood instead.

Then we went through high school and college together and dealt with all the teen angst that it entailed. I went out with boys, and he went out with girls, and even though our dates had a hard time dealing with it, me and Alex were always still friends. The girls he dated would get jealous of our friendship and the boys I dated felt the same, but it never mattered to either of us.

We were there for each other through all the heartbreaks. He listened to me cry over one boy or another, always ready with a pint of ice cream, and I listened to him complain about one girl or another saying how he just wished they'd tell him what they were really thinking. While a lot of women find him attractive at 6'2 with sandy blonde hair, bright blue eyes, and a smile that could light up a room, he was just my good friend Alex.

Now, I climbed into my big, beautiful tub with built in jets that I had saved for a full year for and sipped on my second glass of wine. I leaned back and let the hot water relax me. Once again, I had my phone playing jazz music set up on the sink counter where it could not get wet while I was in the tub. After about half an hour, I climbed out and got comfortable in my nice soft pajamas and got settled into bed. I was just about to turn on the television when my phone rang. It was Alex.

Chapter Two

Alex was calling me. It was odd because he knew how I liked to spend my Friday evenings. Saturdays were for being social with friends and sometimes reluctantly, family, while Sundays I spent making sure I was prepared for the next week of school by getting my lesson plan together. It must be an emergency, I thought, so I answered the phone.

"Hey, Alex, what's up?"

"Well, honestly, I'm just sitting here with nothing to do at home tonight and so I thought, why don't I see what Emily's up to?"

I laughed. "Alex, you've known me for more than fifteen years. You know what I'm up to."

"Let me guess. You're in bed watching TV."

"Close. I just got into bed, but I haven't turned on the TV yet. I was just about to when I was thwarted by my phone ringing."

"Well, I'm not interrupting anything you were watching then. How would you like to go get a bite to eat somewhere?"

"But I'm already in my pajamas" I whined.

"I know but there's something I want to talk to you about." said Alex.

If I didn't know any better, I would've said he sounded a little bit nervous. But about what? Out loud I said, "Is it really serious? Are you absolutely, positively sure it's something that can't wait till tomorrow? Maybe we can go get lunch or something."

Alex sighed and said, "It's kind of important. I'd rather not have to wait till tomorrow."

The way he sounded bothered me. Maybe it was serious after all. "Okay I guess I'll get up and meet you somewhere. Where do you feel like going?"

———————

Thirty minutes later I pulled up at a little Italian Bistro we both loved. It wasn't too fancy that you had to dress up to fit in there but just fancy enough that you didn't feel like you might as well be down the street at the corner deli. I had thrown on a pair of my nicer jeans and a nice dressy top with a pair of stilettos. I threw on some basic makeup and was out the door.

The sky was kind of a purplish pink as the sun was just going down below the horizon. As I walked up to the restaurant, Alex was standing right outside the door waiting for me. Well of course he would beat me here, I thought as I walked up to him. He hadn't had to get out of bed and super comfortable pajamas for that matter. He looked good in a dark grey suit. Why a suit though, I had no idea. He wasn't really a suit kind of guy and certainly didn't work anywhere that required him to dress that way.

Alex was a physical therapist for our small local hospital. He spent his days helping people who had been physically injured and needed to get back on their feet. Even for this restaurant, a full suit was kind of pushing it.

"I'm here" I said raising my hands in mock surrender.

"I knew you wouldn't stand me up" he said with a smile on his face. "I already put in my name for a table. The hostess said it would be about ten minutes." Just as he said this, the little black disc they gave him to let us know our table was ready vibrated. "Well perfect timing" he said now. "After you" he said as he ushered me through the door.

The hostess brought us to a little corner table by the windows. We sat down and looked at our menus. Every table had a little candle surrounded by a small metal lantern along with maroon linen tablecloths and linen wrapped silverware. They played Italian music through the stereo system that was just loud enough to hear without being intrusive. I liked to imagine I was really sitting in a small little bistro in Italy every time I came here.

It was as I was thinking this and looking at the menu, that our waitress came and took our drink orders. I ordered water and was surprised when Alex ordered an alcoholic drink. It's not that there was anything wrong with that. God only knew we'd thrown back our share back in college. But it was the way he ordered it. His voice cracked as he ordered a double whisky on the rocks, and it was then that I noticed his leg was shaking as if he were anxious about something. The waitress noticed none of this though if the way she wrote down our drinks and walked off was any indication.

"Is something wrong?" I asked now in a hushed tone.

He looked at me with such an intensity that it made my heart jump into my throat. The best way to describe what I saw in his eyes when he looked at me was anguish. I gasped. Yes, something was definitely wrong.

"Yes and no" Alex said. "I do have something important to talk to you about, but I'd rather wait until I've gotten my drink if that's okay."

"Sure. If that's what you want…"

I went back to looking at my menu, but it was hard to concentrate on the words I was reading now. He was making me feel anxious and I didn't know why. I took a deep silent breath and focused on making my choice. By the time the waitress had come back with our drinks I had decided that maybe I shouldn't order anything heavy with the way it felt like butterflies were flying around in my stomach.

I ordered a salad. Alex ordered a shrimp ravioli dish and off the waitress went again. Alex took a huge gulp of his drink and turned his eyes on me with that same strong intensity that I'd only ever seen a handful of times in the years that I'd known him. It really unnerved me. I cleared my throat a little and fidgeted in my chair.

Finally, after what seemed like forever although I'm sure it had only been a few seconds he said, "Do you remember that one party we went to back in college at Jenna Thompson's house?"

Of course I remembered that party. Jenna was a friend of mine that had chosen to live at home while going to college. One weekend during our freshman year, her parents were gone, and just like any other self-respecting college student, she had thrown a party. I'd gotten so drunk that I passed out in the cab I'd shared with Alex to get home that night. He'd had to bring me inside my apartment that I shared with my best girl friend Samantha and put me in my bed before getting back in the cab and having it bring him home to the apartment that he was sharing with his buddies from high school. I was hungover all the next day and only left my bed to run to the bathroom. I never drank that much again.

"Yeah, I remember it" I said. I relayed my memories of being so sick the next day to Alex before saying, "As I recall, you were pretty drunk yourself."

"Yeah...yeah, I was" he said his face turning a little red as he rubbed the back of his neck with his palm. "Do you remember anything I said to you that night?"

"I don't remember anything specific that *anyone* said to me that night. To be honest, if it wasn't for you making fun of me the next day for passing out in the cab, I wouldn't even have known that you had been the one to get me home."

Alex took another large gulp of his drink in response to this and was still piercing me with that intense stare before saying "I told you that I was in love with you that night."

Suddenly every sound disappeared. The sounds of people talking around us, the music playing, everything was silence. What had Alex just said? No way he just said those words, I thought. Unfortunately, my unconscious reaction to my mounting panic was to laugh nervously. Even as the sound came out, in my mind I was already chastising myself for reacting that way.

"You were drunk" I said nervously. "Everyone says things like that when they drink as much as you and I *both* did."

"Maybe so" said Alex staring down at his glass for a moment. When he looked back there was a different look in his eyes. One that I'm not sure I'd ever seen before. Then he said, "But I meant it."

Talk about dropping a bomb. I didn't know what to say. All the sounds within the restaurant seemed to fade away again. I knew that this was just my imagination and that no one was paying any attention to what was going on at our table. The silence between us was palpable. I must have looked like I was in shock because he waited a few moments before he continued.

"I have been in love with you for almost ten years" he said looking down at his drink. "For years, I told myself that it was just because we were so close and that I was mistaking feelings of friendship for love." Alex took a sip of his drink. "I used to get so jealous when you'd go out on a date with other guys in high school. I tried to ignore how I felt by going out with other girls. But it just never seemed to work. I'd tell myself that I was silly for feeling so jealous and I'd get so *angry* at myself for even feeling that way in the first place."

I stared at Alex. I wasn't exactly sure where he was going with this, but I was scared. "Alex..." I spoke.

"Let me finish! Please" he said cutting me off. He took another gulp of his drink and continued.

"By the time we got to college I decided my feelings for you were real and I was tired of pushing them aside. So that night, at that party, I'd decided to tell you how I felt. Unfortunately, I'd gotten too drunk trying to gather the courage to say anything, and you were too drunk to remember me saying it. But I did say it. The next day, I woke up, and realized what I'd done. I was so worried about what you were going to say to me the next time I saw you that I avoided you for a few days. Which as it turned out, wasn't so hard. I had a big test coming up and I used that as my excuse."

"So that's why you avoided me. I remember feeling so ashamed, like maybe you were embarrassed about how drunk I gotten and how you had to bring me to my room."

"No, that wasn't it and I'm sorry I made you feel that way. Anyway, after a few days, I decided I couldn't avoid you forever, so I decided to call you and test the waters. Once I realized that you didn't even remember what I'd said, I felt such relief and I chickened out on trying to tell you again."

"So why did you decide to tell me again now?" I asked not knowing what else to say. "I mean, that was more than six years ago."

Alex sighed loudly and took another drink. "I'm tired Emily. I'm tired of sitting around getting older, and I want to settle down before it's too late. I'm also tired of wanting to be with you and not doing anything about it. I want to know how you feel. Is there any way you could ever give us a real chance to be together?"

My brain seemed to buzz even though I, unlike Alex, had not had any alcohol. I was shocked. To say I felt like the ground had suddenly disappeared out from under me was an understatement. My heart began beating wildly. I didn't know what to say. I didn't feel that way about Alex at all. But I also didn't want to hurt his feelings and ruin all our years of friendship.

On the other hand, he had just thrown this out there and was now asking me to make a huge life-altering decision on the spot about something that I had previously not known anything about. How could he put me in that position? I guess that's what made me feel so upset at that moment. That must've been what prompted me to start shaking uncontrollably and to say what I said next which was, "I can't believe you would do this to me!"

Alex's expression turned from a look of hope mixed with anxiety into a look of confusion. "I'm not sure what I did" he said now in a low and calm voice as if by talking that way, it would calm me down by extension. No chance of that. I was really upset.

"You tell me this life-altering information and then you just expect me to have an answer like that?" I snapped my fingers for emphasis. "This is a big deal and I need time to process it. I mean, I'm just in shock. This is completely nuts! I... I need to go home and lie down."

Alex looked concerned now. "Emily, I'm sorry. I didn't mean to make you feel like I was putting you on the spot. There really wasn't any way that I could tell you that wouldn't have felt out of the blue. That's why I asked you out to dinner. I figured it was better than just coming to your house, or even worse, over the phone. Go home and think about it. I'll get the tab and maybe see you in a few days."

With that I got up from my chair and walked numbly out the door. I didn't even say goodbye. I couldn't. I was just that upset. I could feel my face turning red and once I was back in my car, alone, the flood gates opened. I cried. Hard. I'm sad to say it was a pretty ugly affair. I just had all these mixed emotions. I felt confused and angry and scared all at the same time. And now, as I drove home. I was getting a headache. Great.

What a night. I just couldn't believe it. How could I not have known? He's been in love with me for ten years?! I just couldn't process that. So, in ten years, in almost all the time that we spent together as friends, he was thinking of me completely differently than I was thinking of him. Through every single moment, good and bad, he was in love with me. When I broke up with my first boyfriend in 10th grade, he was in love with me. Wow.

I pulled up in front of my house and suddenly felt so very tired. My arms and legs felt like jelly climbing out of my car. I managed to get inside my house and back into my bed. I didn't even want to think about what had just happened. I didn't even bother changing back into my pajamas or washing the makeup off my face. I sank down underneath my comforter and pulled it up over my head.

When I finally crawled out of bed the next day, about noon, I felt completely distressed. I'd dreamed about Alex, but not in a good way.

In my dream, we were standing in front of each other, and he just had such a sad look on his face. Then out of nowhere, a small breeze started to blow and as it blew towards us, Alex's body started turning to sand and blowing away! It started at his feet and kept going until he was gone. The last thing I saw was his sad face. Then I woke up. I gasped as I sat up in bed. What a horrible dream! I had to take a few deep breaths and make myself calm down. It was just a dream, I told myself. Nothing to be upset about. Alex is fine.

I suddenly felt like I had to talk to somebody. Not my sister though. For one thing, she had just been out on a date the night before and was probably passed out cold right now. For another thing, she'd apparently always known that Alex was in love with me, and I didn't feel like having her rub it in my face that she was right. But I absolutely could not sit inside my house the rest of this day and dwell on this situation. Nor could I go visit anyone and not say anything to them about this. Who to call though?

Samantha Gables was one of my very best friends. I'd known her practically my entire life. Since kindergarten anyway, and she was the one that I lived with in college. I wondered if she had ever had any inkling that Alex was in love with me? I had to know if I was just tuning out obvious signs or if like me, she would be stunned by my news. So, I reached over, grabbed my phone off the nightstand and called her.

Samantha picked up on the third ring. "Hey Emily. What's up?"

"Well, something completely crazy happened to me last night and I was just wondering if you were busy because I really need to talk to somebody about it."

"Well, I just fed Tyler lunch and we are about to head out to the park. If you want to meet us there, you can tell me all about it."

Tyler was Samantha's two-year-old son. He had Samantha's fair skin and natural white, blonde hair with beautiful baby blue eyes and a big smile. Although he could be a handful sometimes, he really was a sweet kid. I was like an aunt to him that was kind of grandfathered in. I bought him a present for his birthday every year and recently,

Samantha had talked about possibly making me his godmother should the unthinkable ever happen to her or her husband, James.

My mind was in such turmoil that I wasn't really able to think before I spoke. "Alex told me he's in love with me last night" was what came out of my mouth as I sank back down into my bed.

"Wow. Well... come meet us at the park and tell me all about it. I really want to hear this story!"

After I hung up with Samantha I crawled out of bed and made my way to the bathroom to get cleaned up to leave the house. I looked worse than I thought. My hair looked like someone had put both hands on my head and shaken it all up. My mascara had run down my cheeks and had flaked off a little while I was sleeping, and I had lipstick smeared all around my mouth. I looked like a drunk clown.

I started with my face, washing all the old makeup off with nice hot water and a soft washcloth. God, it felt so good. Then I took my brush and went to work on my medium length, brown hair. Then I brushed my teeth. Once everything above my shoulders was cleaned up, I went to my closet and pulled out a pair of denim cropped pants and a random yellow t-shirt.

Once I felt like I looked halfway decent, I realized I was starving. I grabbed a breakfast bar out of my cabinet on my way out the door and ate it on my way to the park. Once there, I relayed the whole evening to Samantha from Alex calling me as I had been climbing into bed, to the way he was acting at the restaurant, to his revelation, and finally to how I'd reacted and came home. "I honestly never suspected a thing" I said now. "Did you?"

"Well... yeah I think everyone who knows both of you kind of always knew how he felt about you. You really never suspected at all?"

"No!" I practically screamed, prompting another mother sitting on another bench to look over at us before turning her attention back to her own little boy playing on a jungle gym. "How could everyone see it but me? And how could I be so blind *not* to see it?"

"We see what we want to see, I think. The way I see it, it's kind of an unconscious thing. I don't think you purposely turned a blind eye to his feelings. Our minds just automatically try to block out things that might cause us distress so that we don't have to deal with them. In this case, I guess that would be Alex's feelings for you."

"Yeah, maybe you're right. But I don't like the idea that everyone has known about this forever. He told me he's been in love with me for ten *years!*"

There was silence for a minute before Samantha said, "Yeah, that sounds about right if you think about it. Ten years ago, we would have been just starting high school. It seems like just yesterday sometimes. It's crazy how time flies." Samantha got a faraway look in her eyes for a moment before looking back over at Tyler who was playing in the sandbox.

"Can I ask, when did you first notice anything?"

"I think it would have to be when Robbie Monroe asked you to the homecoming dance in 10th grade. I remember Alex kind of skulking around for a while after that. He just always seemed like he was in a bad mood. It was only after the dance was over and Robbie decided he like Sherrie Cooper instead that Alex went back to acting normal again, like nothing ever happened. That's when I think I first noticed it."

"I remember going to the dance with Robbie, and I remember feeling crushed on Monday morning at school, when he found me in the library and told me that he liked Sherrie and was going to start dating her. But I don't remember Alex acting any differently than normal at all. How could I have missed that?"

"Probably because he told you that he was really busy with a science project that weekend and that he wouldn't really have time to talk to you until he was finished with it. It just so happened that he finished his project in record time by lunch on Monday. Just in time to comfort you over Robbie breaking your heart. You never suspected a thing."

"Wow. I don't remember any of that" I said. "I really don't know what I'm going to say to him the next time I talk to him."

"Well, how do you feel about him, knowing what you know now about how he feels about you?"

"Honestly? I don't feel anything different. I don't feel like I have any kind of romantic feelings towards him at all. He's my best friend, no offense. He's always been my best friend. I really don't want anything to jeopardize that."

"No offense taken, so don't take this the wrong way, but are you sure there's not a different reason he reaches best friend status over me? I mean, you've always kind of had a hard time letting yourself get close to anyone you've dated, what with the way your parent's relationship has always been and all. Maybe calling him your best friend is just the closest you can let a man get to you."

"Allie basically said the same thing to me just yesterday. She said I was hiding. I haven't told her anything about dinner last night with Alex by the way. That was just a coincidental conversation. Do you really think I'm just keeping up a wall between me and every nice man I meet?"

"I hate to say it because I don't want you to get upset with me, but yeah, I do. There have been a few great guys that you've dated who were great for you. But after just a few dates, poof, you always seem to find a reason to break up with them. Remember Mike Garrison? And what about Dean Parker?"

Both Mike and Dean had been great guys. Both had good jobs and owned their own home and were looking for a nice girl to settle down with. Mike was a computer genius I'd met at the school my first year there as a teacher. He'd been hired to fix a virus problem that we'd had on our school's computers and to set up our new firewall. I was ushering my students into the cafeteria for lunch that day when he stopped me in the hallway. He complimented my smile and asked me out for coffee. The coffee date went well, and we had a few real dates after that. But as it turned out, Mike was all about computers and other forms of tech and I just had no real interest in that kind of stuff. He had a hard time talking about anything else. We both agreed that it wasn't meant to be and moved on. No hard feelings.

Dean I met one weekend about a year later, when I was out at a local bar with Samantha and James. Dean, who was tall, dark, and handsome, walked right over to our table and introduced himself. Then he asked me to dance, and I said yes. As we danced, he told me a little about himself. He was a foreman for a local construction company, and they were currently doing very well with various projects in and around our area. I told him that I was a teacher and he complimented me by saying that I seemed very suited to such a noble profession.

We went on a few dates as well and although I loved the idea of him, I just never got butterflies when he called me and asked me out. I just didn't feel anything. I let him down as gently as I could, but he didn't take it well. Apparently, he had really liked me and didn't understand why when our dates had all gone so well, I didn't feel the same. It was awkward for a while anytime we ran into each other in town. But he eventually moved on and now it was like we never even dated.

"I'm not upset" I told Samantha now. "I don't necessarily agree, but I'm not upset with you for just being honest. I've just never felt that tingle, you know? That feeling that I was with someone that I wanted to be with forever. Yeah, Mike and Dean were both great guys. But I didn't feel anything with either one of them and I didn't want to lead them on."

"Well, you know Dean just married that girl that works down at the hair salon. What's her name? Mandy something? They seem happy so I guess it all worked out for the best. I don't know whatever happened to Mike."

"Mike moved to some big city in California, I forget which one. See, I would've been holding both of them back if I had stayed with either one of them. I could never move away from this place. And like you said, Dean is happy with his new wife. It all worked out."

"It worked out for everyone but you Emily. I just want to see you happy with someone. Are you sure you wouldn't want to give Alex a chance?"

"No, I really don't. We're such great friends and I'd hate to ruin that. I know there's someone out there for him, it's just not me. He's always been my go-to buddy, you know? I really don't want anything to change that."

"Well then, you're going to have to tell him how you feel. But, be prepared because that may be all the push he needs to really start looking for someone else. And if he finds someone, no matter what you say, I'm telling you now as a friend, that your relationship with Alex will never be the same. Can you handle the idea of him really ever being serious about another woman?"

"I guess. I mean, I've never really had to deal with that before because he's never gotten that serious with anyone. I guess that should have been another sign for me to see, but neither have I, and that's not because I have hidden feelings for him."

"Are you sure? I think you should really think about it before you let him down. Subconsciously you could actually have those feelings and just be afraid it won't work out. It would such a shame if you only realized it when he moved on to someone else and it was too late for you."

"I really don't have those feelings at all Samantha. I don't secretly fantasize about being with him or even just kissing him. I've never even thought about what that would be like. I would know if I had those feelings, and I don't. I just, don't know how I'm going to let him down."

But was I really going to let him down? I felt a niggling of doubt in the back of my mind remembering that dream I'd had the night before. It felt so real, the emotions that I felt as he turned to sand and drifted away were still present in my mind.

No, I told myself. I'm just being silly. There was nothing to worry about. This was Alex. The worst that could happen was that he'd be hurt, and it would be awkward for a while. But he'd eventually get over it and let himself find someone great. Then the awkwardness would melt away and everything would go back to normal.

I decided later that evening after I'd gotten back home from the park that I would just have to tell him the truth. That I didn't have those kinds of feelings for him. I wasn't eager to talk to him though. I decided it would be best to wait for him to seek me out and ask me what I had decided. I didn't have to wait long. That talk came all too soon bright and early the next morning when my doorbell rang.

Chapter Three

I woke up with a start at the sound of my doorbell ringing. My head was pounding as I looked at my phone to see what time it was. It was only 6:30 in the morning. Who would be knocking on my door so early? I sat up in bed at the sound of a second set of knocks. At the third set of knocks, I got up out of bed and headed for the door.

I hadn't slept well the night before either. I couldn't stop thinking about having to eventually talk to Alex and I couldn't stop worrying about how it would all turn out. My stomach twisted and turned with anxiety as I tossed around every possible scenario I could think of several times through my head. I finally fell asleep, if me being woken up by the knocks on my door were any indication. But I had no idea when I had actually passed out. I felt like it couldn't have been asleep for more than a few hours.

Why did someone have to be waking me up so early? And who could it possibly be? I pondered this as I made my way slowly to the door. Maybe it was Samantha, coming over to check on me. Maybe it was my sister, wanting to tell me about her date from Friday night.

That was unlikely seeing as she'd never get up willingly at this hour of the morning. I didn't think it would be Samantha this early either. So, who was it?

Whoever it was continued to knock. Finally, I made it to the door and opened it. I was surprised to find that it was Alex, standing on my doorstep. He was wearing khaki pants, loafers, and a sky-blue polo that matched his eyes almost perfectly. His hair was combed neatly to the side, just like the other night. He usually wasn't too concerned about his hair. As long as it didn't look like he'd just woken up, he was usually good to go.

"Wow. Sorry, I didn't mean to wake you up" he said now with a slight look of anxiety crossing over his face.

I stood there for a moment just staring at him, my heart suddenly feeling like it had jumped up into my throat. I didn't know what to say. I was not ready to talk to him yet. But then again, could I ever really be ready?

"Aren't you going to let me in?" he asked now sounding nervous. He put his hands in his pockets and rocked back and forth on his heels.

"Oh. Yeah. Sorry. It's just really early. I guess I'm not really all there yet." I stepped back to let him through the door.

"Yeah, I can see that. Again, sorry, it's just, well I've been so anxious ever since the other night that I guess I just couldn't wait anymore."

"Are you going to some sort of meeting or something?" I asked looking at how nicely he was dressed.

"What?" he asked totally lost for just a second before raising his eyebrows as it dawned on his face what I was talking about. "Oh, you mean this" he said as he pinched his shirt between his fingers. "No, I don't have anywhere else to be today. I just thought, you know, that I'd dress nicely to talk to you because maybe it would help your decision a little." At this, his cheeks turned red.

He cleared his throat now and said, "Really, you know Emily, I'm just asking for you to give me a chance. I'm not asking you to marry me or anything. Although, if it works out... Um, but anyway, I just wanted to look, I don't know, hopefully irresistible?"

Any other time, it would have been normal for me to make a joke about him saying that he wanted to look irresistible to anyone, but now everything had changed. It was awkward and I didn't really know what to say. I'd never had that problem with Alex before, EVER. Everything just felt upside down and inside out and I was very uncomfortable with it.

"Well while you do look very nice, it is *very* early for me this morning and I'm really not ready to talk about this yet" I said as I turned to put on a pot of coffee. Clearly, I wasn't going to get to go back to sleep this morning.

"I know and I'm sorry about that. But even for 6:30 am, you really do look tired this morning. I mean, I just thought for someone that has to get up this early during the week you might already be up."

"I get up earlier than 6:30 during the week Alex. So yeah, maybe I just like to be able to sleep in a little on the weekends you know?"

I knew I sounded irritable and defensive, and I wanted to stop myself, but I just couldn't seem to do it. I could only imagine what I must've looked like. If I had to guess, I would've said my hair was probably sticking out at all angles and just looked like a complete mess. Thanks Alex, I thought to myself. Thanks for showing up here looking like a million bucks while I look like I've just been through a windstorm.

Alex put his hands up in a defensive gesture. "You're right, I understand, and I'm sorry. If you'd like me to go, maybe I can come back later this afternoon. I guess I just didn't expect you to look so...tired...in the morning."

"Well, Alex, maybe that's because I spent the whole last two nights tossing and turning over your revelation. Did you really think I would just go home and be able to sleep like a baby after being told something like that?"

"No. I don't know. I guess I don't know what I thought" he said now looking down at the floor.

I felt a little guilty about biting his head off now. Stop talking to him like that, I said to myself. Do you *want* to make him run away and ruin your friendship?! Outwardly I said, "Well, since you're here I guess, I'll go get cleaned up."

I walked down the hall and back into my bedroom. I closed my door behind me and leaned against it. It took everything in me not to slide to the floor and curl up into a ball. What do I do, I thought to myself? I'm not ready for this. I looked around my room at my bed that was all messed up from how I'd had to throw back my comforter to climb out of bed and answer the door. Then I looked at my nightstand where my phone was still sitting, plugged into the charger. Quickly, I walked over to it and put in a call.

"Hello?" said Samantha absentmindedly into the phone. I could hear the sounds of bacon frying in a pan and of Tyler trying to get his mom's attention by saying mom over and over again.

"Hey it's Emily. I'm sorry if you're busy but I'm kind of in a panic right now."

"Tyler, go sit down. Breakfast will be done in a minute. Emily, what's wrong?" she said as I heard the sound of her scraping the bacon up and flipping it in the pan.

"Alex is here. He just showed up and woke me up. He's in my kitchen all dressed up waiting for me to come back out and give him an answer. Meanwhile I'm looking like I just rolled out of bed because, well, I did. But that's beside the point. Alex is here." I said this all in a rush and had to take a huge breath at the end and blow it out.

"Okay. Well take your time getting cleaned up and think very clearly about what you're going to say. You don't want to tear his heart out but at the same time, as you already said, you don't have the kinds of feelings for him that he's looking for. Tell him, that you're sorry but you really just want to be friends. He may get upset and he may walk out, and you may not hear from him for a few days. But I think, as long as you're honest and direct with him about how you feel, it'll all work out. Just... be nice."

"Honest and direct. Got it." I repeated back to her.

"And be nice! That's the most important part. Think about how he feels and try to imagine yourself in his shoes. You wouldn't want him or anyone else to act flippantly as if your feelings don't matter and they don't care about how you feel. Be careful with what you say."

"I would never act flippantly about this. This is Alex we're talking about. He's been my best friend for over fifteen years, and it would break my heart to lose what we have. If I didn't care about that then I wouldn't be so freaked out and I wouldn't be calling you. But yeah, no, I understand what you're saying. Thanks for talking to me. I can tell you're busy this morning. But you've helped me anyway and I feel a little better now."

"You're welcome. That's what friends are for. Now, go get cleaned up. It won't be as bad as you think."

With that, I hung up the phone and walked into my bathroom. I splashed some water on my face and looked at myself in the mirror. "Get it together" I said to my reflection. "It's not a big deal. Alex is a grown man and he can handle this. Besides, he would be better off finding someone who loves him. No reason why we can't still be friends."

With that, I took a deep breath, let it out, and started getting dressed. I put on a pair of jeans and a green t-shirt. I pulled my hair back into a ponytail. I didn't bother with makeup. Then I surveyed myself in the mirror before dropping my hands to my sides and saying "Well, here goes nothing".

I walked back down the hall to my kitchen. As I walked in, Alex had coffee made and he handed me a cup with an ounce of milk and two teaspoons of sugar, just the way I like it. Why did he have to be so nice? He gestured toward the kitchen table and we both took a seat across from each other. We sat there for a moment in silence, each sipping our coffee. Finally, I just jumped in.

"So, Alex, here's the thing. I...I spent the last day and a half thinking about everything you said. I honestly haven't thought of anything else. I even talked to Samantha about it. I hope you don't mind."

"Yeah, I kind of figured you would" he said, looking up from his coffee. "She's been your best friend forever, besides me anyway. It doesn't bother me."

"Well, she did have a few things to say. She told me that she thinks I always find an excuse to break up with the guys I date, even the great ones, because I'm afraid to get too close to anyone. She thinks I'm afraid to give you a chance for the same reason. And apparently, I'm the only one in the world who didn't know how you felt about me all this time."

Alex's neck turned bright red as the color made its way up to his cheeks. "I guess I really wasn't all that good at hiding it" he said as he pointedly cleared his throat. "So, I guess the question is, how did you respond to what she had to say?"

I took a deep breath and let it out. It was now or never. I set down my cup of coffee and slowly reached across the table, taking Alex's hands in mine. I looked up into those impossibly vivid blue eyes and spoke.

"Alex, the thing is, I've searched my soul these last 36 hours. I know I already told you that, but I feel like I can't stress it enough." I could see in his face that he was trying to register what I was saying. I hesitated for a moment.

"I hear a 'but' coming on" was all he said.

"But..." I sighed deeply, "I don't think that I'm afraid. I just don't have those kinds of feelings for you. When I picture you in my head, I see my best friend in the entire world. I tried to picture another scenario, believe me I tried, and I just couldn't. But Alex, I care about you very deeply and you know I would never want to hurt you."

At that, his face hardened just slightly. His eyes grew more intense. It wasn't anger really, that I saw on his face. But it wasn't a look that I recognized either. I was suddenly very unsure of what was about to happen. Alex took a deep breath and released it while letting go of my hands and slowly sliding them back to his side of the table and down by his sides.

"I was afraid you'd say that" he said now as he looked down towards his lap. "Unfortunately, Emily, I don't think that I can go on being friends anymore."

I felt my pulse speed up now. My mouth was going dry, and I could feel my heart starting to hammer in my chest. My stomach started twisting and churning slowly.

"So, what are you saying Alex?" I asked, panic creeping into my voice.

"I'm saying that…this is really hard for me but, I got a job offer up in Maryland to be a physical therapist for a major hospital. It's got a great reputation and state of the art equipment, and they're offering to pay me a lot more than I'm making here."

My mind was numb. I wanted to scream "don't go!" But all that would come out was, "How did this hospital hear about you all the way down here?"

"Well…the thing is…I actually started looking for jobs to move away from here. It's just…when I decided to tell you how I feel, I wanted to have a backup just in case, you know, you said no because I don't think I can handle sticking around here and seeing you all the time. So, I decided to wait until I heard back from any of the hospitals that I reached out to before telling you how I feel."

"How many hospitals did you reach out to?" I asked unable to keep the pain out of my voice. I couldn't believe what I was hearing. Alex was going to leave. Was I ever going to see him again? I remembered my dream from the other night. How he just slowly disappeared, and I felt that deep ache in my heart all over again. Had my subconscious really been trying to tell me something after all?

"A lot" Alex said. "All over the country. I was starting to think no one was going to call me and then the hospital in Maryland did. Remember last month when I took that trip to Virginia to visit that civil war museum?"

"Yes. I remember."

Of course I remembered that. Alex had always been into wars and guns and things like that because of his dad, so it wasn't a shock that he had wanted to take that trip. At the time, my only thought had been that I had wondered why he wanted to make that trip by himself? I reasoned to myself that since both of his parents had passed, he wanted to go by himself to remember the good times he'd had with his father going to things like that.

"Well, I actually went up to Maryland for an interview. I got a call Thursday that they were offering me a job. I was shocked. I wasn't really expecting to hear back from them. I told them I needed a few days to decide, and they said they understood. So then, I spent all day Friday psyching myself up to talk to you."

"But you didn't tell me about the job at all on Friday. Why didn't you?"

"Because I didn't want it to interfere with your decision. I didn't want you to decide to give me a chance just to keep me around. It wouldn't have been right for me to do that to you and it would've eventually led to resentment between us."

"So, you were willing to turn down this job offer if I had said yes? Is that what you're telling me?"

"Yes. It's not that I really want to move. For the most part, I grew up here and all of my friends are here. I've always been happy with my life here. Except when it came to how I feel about you."

I felt a burning building up behind my eyes as I forced back this overwhelming sadness that was threatening to overtake me. "When do you leave?" I asked.

"Well, first I have to call them back and let them know I'm accepting their offer. But they told me that they would be ready for me to come as soon as possible in the event that I said yes. So, I guess, I'll be spending the rest of the afternoon and maybe tomorrow packing up my stuff, then I'll be gone."

"Wh...what? That soon? What about your house?" I asked. I could hear the panic creeping into my voice, but I couldn't stop it.

"I'm putting it up for sale. Brendan said he'd take care of all the details for me so that I'll only have to come back, maybe, for the final paperwork."

Brendan was one of Alex's best friends and a realtor. Of course he would help Alex sell his house. Stupid Brendan.

"But where are you going to live? It's not like you have a place ready to move into once you get to Maryland."

"Actually, I do. See, as soon as I got the job offer, I started searching around for a temporary apartment, just in case I took the job. I found one in my price range that would be just fine. It's not the best place, but once my house sells, I'll be able to find somewhere a little more permanent. I told the guy who owns the place that I'd let him know today if I wanted it. If not, he had someone else lined up ready to take it."

"But what about the job you have here? You can't just up and leave it."

"I was honest with my boss that I had been looking for another job. I didn't really get into the details as to why, but I did let him know Thursday when I got that call, that I might be saying yes to it, and if so, it would mean leaving pretty quickly. He seemed a little disappointed, but he told me that I'm one of his best employees and he trusts that whatever the reason I might suddenly have to leave, it's for the best and that I will always have a job to come back to, should everything not work out for me."

This was really happening. Alex, my best friend for more than fifteen years was leaving and there was a good chance that I would never see him again. All of my best memories were with Alex. Alex, who had been there for me through every breakup, starting with that no-good Robbie Monroe. Alex had always been there with a smile and a hug and a pint of ice cream to share.

We went to movies together and concerts and when we were in college, we even went out dancing together. He always knew what I was thinking, and I had always thought I knew what he was thinking. Apparently, I was wrong. That burning behind my eyes intensified and I felt like I was going to be sick.

"You can't leave!" I practically screamed. "I...I...this is too much. Please don't leave!" I knew I sounded like I was begging. In fact, I was begging. But I didn't care. He couldn't leave like this. I had too much history with him.

"I'm sorry Emily. This is the way it has to be. I can't stay here. I have to go. I know you're upset, and I'm sorry for that, but this is just how it is." With that, he pushed back his chair and started to stand up. "I have to go. I have some phone calls to make. Please, don't try to call me. I think it's for the best."

"No!" I screamed, grabbing his hand as he started to walk past me towards the door. I couldn't help it. I started crying. I didn't care what I looked like. It felt like my chest was being ripped open and someone was reaching in and wrenching out my heart.

"I...I'm sorry Emily. I have to go now." He looked anguished as well and with those last words he pulled his hand out of mine and walked briskly to the door. He pulled it open, pulling it closed behind him, climbed in his truck, and just like that, he was gone.

I suddenly felt the silence around me. It was too much to bear. The next thing I knew, I was running for the bathroom and spilling my guts into the toilet. Once I was done, I sat there on the floor for a few minutes in silence. My mind raced back over everything that had just happened. The pain in my chest felt like it was going to explode. And then, in the silence, sitting there, tucked away in my bathroom, I started crying again. I cried harder than I've probably ever cried in my entire life.

Eventually, I got to a point where I felt completely raw, like I couldn't cry anymore even though that's all I wanted to do. I knew I needed to get up and start getting my lesson plan for school set up and ready to go for the week, but I just couldn't bring myself to do it. I pulled my phone out of my pocket. I called the school principal and told her I was sick and that I wouldn't be able to come in for a few days. Next I called a few of the subs I knew to be reliable until I found one not already working for the week and secured her as my replacement. Then I slowly climbed up off the floor, walked into my bedroom, turned off all the lights, and climbed back into bed pulling the blanket back over my head.

I slept off and on the rest of that day. I had a hard time sleeping, what with the nightmares that I kept waking up from. Every dream I had in one way or another consisted of Alex disappearing. One in particular really hurt the most. In it, Alex told me that he didn't care about me at all and never had. Then he laughed cruelly in my face. I woke up crying with every dream.

Finally, when evening came crawling in and the darkness surrounded me, I got up and realized that I was not going to be able to sleep through this night. I wanted so badly to call Alex and beg him not to leave. I had to stop myself from doing that though because I knew it wouldn't make a difference. All it would do is bring me even more pain when he didn't answer and bring more pain on himself. I imagined that I would be sitting here, knowing that he was right there looking at my number and choosing not to answer. My chest felt hollow.

I distracted myself by calling Allie. I had burdened Samantha enough for one weekend and besides, it was after midnight. I knew there was a good chance that Allie would still be up. And at this point, I just needed to talk to someone, even if they decided to give me the 'told you so' lecture.

"Hello?" Allie asked. It sounded like there was a tv on in the background.

"Hey Allie. It's Emily. How was your date the other night?" I asked, trying to keep my voice level and doing a very bad job of it. Allie wasn't buying that though. She could hear the pain in my voice.

"My date was just fine. But we can talk about that another time. What's going on Emily? Don't you have to be at school in the morning? It's like one in the morning."

"Yeah well, I called in sick for the next few days" I said, my voice starting to crack.

"Why? What's going on? Are you alright?"

"No Allie. I'm not." And with that, I started crying all over again as I relayed everything that had happened since I'd last spoken to her just two days earlier.

"Wow. Emily. I'm so sorry. Are you serious? Do you want me to come over? I can be there in like ten minutes." Allie said now, sounding genuinely concerned.

"No. That's okay. I just…I just needed to talk to someone, I guess. I'll be alright. Thanks for listening Allie."

"Are you sure?" Allie asked, sounding a little panicked. And why shouldn't she? I'd never reacted this badly by being dumped by any guy before. But this wasn't any guy. This was Alex. "I can't believe he just did that to you. It just seems so unreal. What an asshole!"

"Tell me about it" I said as my tears started to dry up again. "And yeah. I'm sure that I don't need you to come over. I'm going to try to go back to bed now."

"Okay well, I'll call you tomorrow to check on you and see how you're feeling."

"That sounds good. Thanks Allie."

"Anytime Emily. You know I mean that."

"Yeah, I know. Goodnight." With that I hung up the phone.

I sat there in my bed, looking at my phone at Alex's number which I'd pulled up once again. I don't know how long I stared at it, but eventually I started feeling antsy. Like I just couldn't *stay* here in this house a moment longer. I jumped up, grabbed my keys and ran out to my car. I got in and drove. I didn't know where I was going. I just drove.

Once I got on the highway, I turned on the saddest music I could find, turned it up really loud, and rolled down the windows. The night air was cool and crisp and belting out these sad songs with the wind blowing through my hair at a speed of 70 mph with almost no other cars around was just what the doctor ordered. Something about haunting music and city lights at night just made me feel like I was flying.

At some point the highway went down from two lanes in either direction to one and everything around me started becoming more and more rural. I had not seen any signs saying that the speed limit had dropped so I just kept going. I continued singing and now I realized I was crying at the same time. All of a sudden, out of nowhere, there was a four way stop in front of me. I realized that I didn't have time to slow down as I blew through the intersection. The last thing I remembered was big headlights bearing down on me.

Chapter Four

Allie was sitting in her living room thinking about her conversation with Emily. She had never heard Emily sound so upset before. It was very uncharacteristic of her. Emily was the strong one in their family. Emily was the one who had always taken care of her, even when they were children. Emily was the calm and rational one where Allie always wore her emotions on her sleeve. That's one thing everyone could always say about Allie. They always knew what she was thinking because whatever she was feeling, she let them know it and didn't hold anything back. So, for these reasons, Emily's call had shaken Allie, and she was worried about her sister.

It had been almost two hours since that phone call and now Allie couldn't sleep. She debated whether she should go over to Emily's and check on her. But no, she reasoned that she'd told Emily she would call her later in the day and plus, Emily was probably sleeping. It was 2:30 in the morning. It was just as Allie had reassured herself for the hundredth time that Emily would be just fine that her cell phone started ringing. The caller ID said that it was their father. Why would he be calling her at this time of night, she wondered. Then she answered the phone.

"Allie? It's your father. I'm calling to let you know that Emily has been in an accident. She's being rushed over to the hospital by an ambulance. I don't know any of the details, but your mother and me are getting into the car to head over there right now. Your mother is hysterical."

Fear suddenly spread through Allie. Emily had been in some sort of accident? What kind of accident? She was being rushed to the hospital...the only hospital in town...the hospital that Alex worked at. Alex! Allie suddenly felt an anger that she'd never felt before. This was all *his* fault! She was sure of it. If he hadn't pulled that disappearing stunt on her sister, she would be in bed right now, perfectly fine and sound asleep.

"I'm on my way" she told her father now as she jumped up out of bed. Allie quickly put on the first clean clothes she could find off the floor. She made a mental note to try to clean up later. It was ridiculous that she was in a crisis, and she had to dig through piles of clothes to find something to wear down to the hospital.

It was as she grabbed her keys to her beat up old car that barely ran, that fear grabbed her by the heart. What if Emily was really hurt? What if she died? Could she handle that with only her parents there for support? Her father was not known for being the type to be supportive of other's emotions. And he'd said her mother was hysterical, hadn't he? Which was understandable. But it wouldn't help Allie right now to be between them without a buffer. So, she pulled out her cell phone and made one more call.

Josh was Allie's date from Friday night. That night had gone wonderfully, starting with dinner at a nice restaurant, where surprise surprise, Allie had the best real conversation she'd had with a man in a long time. They talked about everything from Josh explaining what he did for a living, he was a banker, hired recently right out of college, to what they each liked to do for fun. They even got a little deeper into things by talking about how many brothers and sisters they each had. Josh had one older brother and one younger sister.

Dinner was followed by dancing out at a local night club. Josh was wonderful to dance with during the slow songs. After the date, Allie had invited Josh up into her apartment where they had spectacular sex. Josh had passed out in Allie's bed. Saturday morning, Allie woke up first and ran over to a bakery just a few blocks down the road for some doughnuts and coffee.

When she got back, Josh was sitting on the edge of her bed putting his clothes back on. He followed her into the kitchen and sat with her at her small table, enjoying the doughnuts. They talked a little about how much each of them had enjoyed the previous night, *all* of the previous night.

"I woke up and you weren't around" Josh said now, taking a bite of a doughnut. "I was going to find something to leave you a note on."

"Oh? And what would that note have said?" Allie raised her eyebrow and gave him an inquisitive smile.

"It would have said something like, I had a great time with you last night. The conversation at dinner was nice and you are a great dancer and, you know, the rest was great too." Josh's neck started turning a little red as he took a sip of his coffee. "I have to be honest, the last parts of our date I don't usually do too often."

"Well, that's great to hear. I enjoyed every part of our date as well." As she said this, Josh once again started going red.

"Well, I definitely want to see you again" Josh said as he got up from the table. Then he promised to call Allie sometime Sunday, gave her a hug and a kiss goodbye, thanked her for the donuts, and left.

By Sunday afternoon, Allie had started to feel a little anxious. Was he really going to call? Or would she just never hear from him again? But then, around five that afternoon he had called. He told her that he'd gone home and passed back out in his own bed when he'd left her place. Then today he'd had a family engagement and had just got home to call her. But he assured her, he'd been thinking about her the entire time.

During the date, Allie had found out that Josh had recently purchased a small house. Allie had almost been embarrassed by her little apartment by comparison. But Josh had reassured her that just a few months prior, he had lived in a similar small apartment. Only he also lived with a few other guys who never cleaned anything. He assured her that he had seen far worse and that her apartment wasn't dirty at all compared to what he'd been used to. It was just lived in.

By the time Josh called Allie on Sunday afternoon, she had been worried that maybe he had just said what he had about comparing her apartment to his old one to be nice. During their conversation, Josh assured Allie again that he'd had a wonderful time with her and would love to take her out again. So, they set up a date for the following weekend. Allie had been beaming with happiness the rest of the evening and into the night, until she had gotten that phone call from Emily.

Allie felt a little weird about calling Josh now and she was worried about how he would react. After all, they had only been on one date. But really, she didn't have anyone else to call she argued to herself as she dialed his number.

"Hmm...Hello?" Josh answered his phone.

"Hi. I'm sorry. I know it's really late. This is Allie."

"Allie? Wha...why are you calling me at..." Josh paused as he looked at his phone to see the time. "...at 2:30 in the morning?"

"Look, I know we barely know each other, and I normally wouldn't do this, but I didn't have anyone else to call. My sister Emily was in some kind of car accident. She's at the hospital and the only people there are my parents who are kind of hard to deal with under the *best* circumstances. I don't know how bad it is and I just really don't want to go up there alone. So, I guess I was wondering..." Allie let her sentence trail off, afraid that she'd already ruined this relationship before it had even started.

"Oh, yeah. Wow. Um, alright are you at home?" Josh asked.

"Yeah, I'm…I'm sitting in my car…"

"Okay. Just…give me ten minutes and I'll come pick you up."

Allie could hear the sound of frantic rustling in the background as she released a giant sigh of relief. "Thank you, Josh. I…just thank you. Again, I'm so sorry for waking you up."

"Don't be. Be there soon. Bye."

"Bye." With that, the line went dead, and Allie sat there in the silence of her car and realized that she was shaking. Her heart had been pounding as she'd made that call and she couldn't believe this man, whom she'd only been on one date with, was actually on his way over to her place to bring her to the hospital.

Fifteen minutes later Allie was in Josh's car as they raced to the hospital in total silence. Allie's mind was racing with worry and Josh knew enough not to try to break her concentration. They ran into the ER together as Allie frantically asked the nearest nurse about her sister. The nurse typed in Emily's name and told Allie that her sister was there in the ER but that she didn't have any other information.

Then the nurse directed Allie to the ER waiting room. Allie and Josh found it easily enough and as they walked in, Allie saw her parents sitting there, both completely stone faced and silent. They were sitting next to each other, but it seemed as if there were an invisible wall between them. There were only a handful of other people in the room, all focused on their own problems. Brenda Bartlett, Allie's mom, looked very haggard, and had her arms wrapped around herself while Allie's father, Bob Bartlett, had his arms crossed in front of his chest, a look of frustration etched on his face.

Allie's parents looked up at her as she entered the room with Josh. Brenda then burst into tears as Bob stood up and gave Allie a tight hug instead of trying to comfort his wife. They didn't even seem to notice Josh.

"Dad, what happened?" Allie asked her father as he let her go.

"Well, all we know is that she was in a car accident. She was hit by a dually when she ran a 4-way stop. We don't know how bad it is, but considering that she's in the ER, we can only assume the worst right now."

"What would she even have been doing driving anywhere at this time of night?" Brenda asked, looking directly at Allie, her wide eyes filled with tears. "Doesn't she have to be at school to teach in a few hours? It just doesn't make any sense! And what about the school? Someone needs to call them and tell them what's going on. It would be horrible for her to get in trouble for not showing up without notice!"

"I'm really not sure mom. But in a few hours when I'm sure someone will be there, I can call the school and let them know" was all Allie could respond with. She wasn't sure that Emily would want their parents to know about what had happened with Alex. Her parents treated Alex like the son they never had and the news that Emily had been hurt so badly by him right before her accident could only serve to devastate her parents even more. Allie felt a second burst of anger at Alex at this thought. She was angry at him for everything including the fact that she had to keep this secret to herself.

It was only then that Brenda's gaze drifted over to Josh who was standing in the corner of the room. "And who is this?" she asked and looked back at Allie.

"Oh, this is Josh. He's a friend of mine. He brought me here because I was so upset when you called that I didn't want to drive myself."

"Well, thank you Josh" Bob said as he walked over to Josh, shaking his hand.

"It was no problem, sir" Josh replied as Bob walked back to his seat.

Josh walked over to where Allie was standing now and gestured that they should take a seat. Allie obliged by sitting down on her mother's other side while Josh sat next to Allie. They all sat there in silence for what seemed like an hour but had actually only been twenty minutes. Josh had absentmindedly taken Allie's hand and was rubbing her knuckles in a circular motion with his thumb. No one seemed to know what to say to each other.

Then a man who looked like he must be a doctor walked in. He was wearing scrubs and a surgical cap. He had a look of concern on his face as he walked up to Allie's father.

"Are you Emily Bartlett's parents?" he asked.

"Yes, we are." Bob answered as everyone stood up.

"If you'll come out into the hall for privacy, I can relay to you what we're looking at" the doctor said. Everyone followed him out into the empty hallway.

"I'm afraid the dually hit pretty hard into Emily's driver side causing her head to hit her window. She was brought in with some severe brain swelling and bleeding. We were able to bring the swelling down and stop the bleeding, but your daughter is in a coma. Right now, it's too soon to tell whether or not she has a chance of recovery. We'll know more in the next 24-48 hours. I'm so sorry."

"Where is she?" Brenda asked the doctor causing him to look over at her with a very sad look on his face.

"Right now, we've got her in a room in the ICU. We want to keep a close eye on her vitals for the next few days and make sure that she continues to breathe on her own. She is allowed to have visitors, but only two people at a time."

Everyone thanked the doctor, who shook Bob's hand. Bob and Brenda decided to go first while Allie and Josh waited for them in the waiting room. Once Allie's parents were gone, Allie looked at Josh who seemed as if he wasn't sure what to do now. She thanked him again for bringing her and for being there at the hospital with her. Josh had a look of concern on his face as he told her that it was his pleasure. Then he asked her if she wanted him to stay. Allie was once again awestruck at how wonderful this man seemed to be.

"If it's not a big deal, would you go in to see her with me? I'm not sure I can handle what I might see in there. If you're ready to go home, I totally understand, and I can get my parents to bring me home." Allie looked down at the ground as she said this. She didn't want to make Josh feel any more uncomfortable than he must already be.

"No, sure that's no problem. I can stick around a little while longer. Just let me make a few calls and I'll be right back."

With that, Josh walked out of the waiting room and made a call to his secretary leaving her a message that as soon as she got into work in the morning, she would need to reschedule his morning appointments as he wouldn't be able to make it to them. Then he walked back to Allie and sat with her while they waited for Bob and Brenda to come back.

Ten minutes later, it was Allie's turn to go see Emily. Josh followed her into Emily's room, where Emily lay all bruised and broken. Her head had been wrapped in gauze and her eyes were closed. Her face was covered in bruises, and her lips were pale. Her arms were covered with horrendous giant bruises ranging from cranberry red to almost black. She had tubes hooked up to her everywhere it seemed, and Allie could hear the beeping of the heart monitor.

Suddenly it all felt too much for Allie and her legs buckled underneath her. Luckily, Josh had been standing right behind her and he was able to catch her under her arms and keep her from hitting the floor. Allie regained her composure as Josh helped her over to a chair next to Emily's bed.

Allie felt as though she wanted to cry, but the tears just wouldn't come. Josh put his arm around her as she stared at her bedridden sister. Anger for the third time that night, overtook Allie as she thought about the cause for Emily's current condition. She vowed to herself that she would make sure that Alex Coleman would never be able to hurt her sister again.

———————

My head was pounding, and my entire body hurt. I struggled to open my eyes and once I had, everything was a little blurry. As my vision started to clear, I realized that I was staring up at the sky, which was orange as if it were evening, but it was a solid orange. There were no streaks of pink or purple, and no clouds to be seen. I couldn't see the sun or moon at all either. Where was I?

I pulled myself up slowly and realized that I had been lying on a wooden bench. As I slid my legs to the ground, I realized that I was on the bench in front of the school. The school that I had attended kindergarten through twelfth grade in and had been a teacher at for a few years now. But something was wrong.

There was no street or sidewalk in front of the bench like there should be. In fact, there was nothing in front of the bench. No grass, no trees, no houses, and no people. There wasn't even any wind. The air was warm and completely still. Stretching out in front of me, all the way to the horizon was nothing but sand. As if I were in the middle of a desert.

I stood up slowly and turned around to take a better look at the school. It was the same school alright. Only now, it looked dark and abandoned. All of the windows looked black and blown out and the building itself was an ashen shade of grey instead of its normal dark red brick. Once again, there was nothing around the building. Only sand. A shudder ran through me at the sight of the tall, dark, imposing building.

I looked away from it. In that instant, I saw movement out of the corner of my eye. I looked back at the building, but it seemed that whatever I thought I'd seen was gone. As I looked around, it hit me that I was completely alone in this strange place. What had happened, and where was I?

There didn't seem to be anywhere else for me to go except this strange, extremely creepy version of the school. Although, I was afraid, I was even more afraid that wherever I was, I might be stuck unless I found answers. So, I started walking towards the school. I took a deep breath, pulled open the door, and took a step inside.

The inside of the building was no less creepy than the outside. There didn't seem to be any electricity. The lockers that lined the hallways looked rusted out as if they hadn't been touched in years. Some of them were missing their doors, creating small dark caverns along the wall. There were random pieces of paper strewn up and down the hall. I picked one up, but there was nothing on it. I picked up a few more, but they were all blank.

As I continued walking, I passed a few classrooms. Every door that I opened sported dark empty rooms filled with old wooden desks, more blank paper strewn all over, and graffiti sprayed all over the walls. What was going on? I came to the staircase that led to the second floor. As I looked up at the landing, once again I saw movement out of the corner of my eye. It had come from further back on the first floor. I looked towards the classroom door where I had seen it, but once again, there was nothing there.

I walked slowly towards that room instead of going up to the second floor and looked in. This one looked the same as all the rest, but with one major difference. Sitting there, behind the teacher's desk, was a dark hooded figure. It looked over at me as I stood in the doorway. All I saw where a face should be inside the hood, was nothing. Just a dark empty hole. The figure stood up silently and started slowly coming towards me. It seemed to be gliding instead of walking. It was then that I screamed.

Chapter Five

I tried to run but my body was frozen in fear. By the time I was able to get my legs to move, I turned to go, but it was too late. The figure was close enough to reach out and grab my arm. As I looked down, I saw that the hand that grabbed me didn't have any skin. It was just bones! I screamed again and tried to rip my arm away, but its grip was just too tight. Then it spoke to me.

"Do not try to run" it said in a deep booming voice. The sound seemed to come from everywhere except for under its hood. "It will do you no good. There is nowhere for you to run to."

I had to admit the figure was right. Where could I run to even if I had gotten away? From what I had seen, there was nothing around but this school. That's when panic really started to build up within me.

"Where am I?!" I practically screamed.

What if this thing, whatever it was wanted to kill me? I thought. There's no one else around to help me. Could I really die here? My fear and anxiety were starting to reach a boiling point as my heart pounded in my chest. I was having a panic attack. I'd never had one before, but I'd read about them and there was no doubt in my mind that this is what I was dealing with. I forced myself to close my eyes, as much as I was afraid to take my eyes off this thing and tried to focus on my breathing.

Then the creature boomed, "Come. Sit. I have many things to tell you."

Okay, I thought as my breathing started to regulate itself. So, this creature didn't want to kill me. At least not yet. But I still didn't know where I was. All I could do was follow this creature into the room as it let go of my arm, glided back to the desk, and sat back down. I wished so much for anyone, anyone at all to come walking through this door to help me. But no one did. After a moment of hoping fruitlessly for another answer, I decided that all I could do was what the creature had told me. I walked slowly up to one of the old wooden desks in the front row and took a seat. Now what, I thought.

"You are in your own head" the creature said. I must have looked confused, because the creature clarified its statement with, "You are in a coma. This is the inside of your mind. You are trapped inside of it."

"What? But how can I be in a coma? And why would the inside of my mind look like this?" I gestured around the room with my hand. "No, this can't be right. I must be dreaming. This is just a nightmare. Wake up Emily!" I yelled. I closed my eyes and tried to concentrate on pulling myself out of this, whatever this was. But it was no use.

"What do you remember of how you came to be here?" The creature asked.

"I don't remember anything" I said. "The last thing I remember was..." I trailed off trying to think. What *was* the last thing that I remembered?

I remembered being at home, in my bed. I remembered staring longingly at Alex's phone number on my phone. I remembered calling Allie and talking to her for a few minutes. I remembered feeling consumed with grief and getting into my car… That was all I could remember.

"The last thing I remember was getting into my car" I told the creature.

"You were driving too fast" The creature said. "You ran through an intersection and were hit by a large truck."

As the creature said this, the memory came at me hard and fast, just like that truck had. The memory hit me with such force that I closed my eyes and was instantly back in that last moment, when those large headlights were staring me in the face, and I had screamed. Then there was a loud crash and the sound of glass breaking. I gasped for air as my eyes opened and a shudder ran through me. It had happened. I remembered it. This is all so overwhelming, I thought as I wrapped my arms around myself and started to cry.

"Wha…what are you?" I asked the creature while blinking away tears.

"I am a manifestation of your mind. I represent all that is known to you consciously that you deny."

"That I deny? What do you mean? What do I deny?"

"That is for you to determine" The creature said. "I am merely the vessel that your mind created to guide you to that determination. It is this conscious denial that is keeping you trapped here."

"What do I need to do? How can I get out of here? I *need* to get out of here!" I started rocking back and forth slightly trying to calm down.

"You are trapped here by your own hand. You have unfinished business to attend to. Just as everyone else has a path to follow, you too have been following down a path. For a time, it was the correct path. But at some point, you diverged from it, and it has ultimately led you here. Until you can find a way to correct that mistake, you will be trapped. If you take too long to correct it, you will die."

"How did I diverge from my path? And what do you mean I'll die?"

"Your life is now being held in the hands of others. Once they decide to end it, your time will run out. As for the other question, only you know how you diverged from the correct path and your reasons for doing so. You must explore these reasons so that the truth will be revealed to you. Without the truth, you cannot hope to escape your situation alive."

"How can I explore anything?" I asked getting completely frustrated. "There's no one here but me and whatever you are" I gestured to the creature. "There's not even anywhere else that I can go from the looks of it, outside of this building anyway."

"You must start by looking at where this path began. You must follow it to its conclusion. Only then will you hope to be able to correct your course." The creature gestured around the room we were in. "Does this room hold any particular significance to you?"

This room? This specific room? I looked around not seeing anything that separated this room from all of the others. Except the door. As I looked at it, I saw the number on the door. All of the doors had different numbers of course. This one said 107. Room 107... I mentally backtracked how I had gotten to this room from the front doors of the school. Then I remembered.

"This was my fourth-grade classroom." I told the creature.

"Was there an event that stands out which occurred in this room?" the creature asked.

"The first time I'd ever met Alex was in this room. He'd come in on his first day and the teacher told him to take the empty seat next to me." I turned around in my seat and looked at the two empty seats surrounded by all of the rest. There was nothing distinguishing them from the others physically. Only my memory allowed me to know which ones they were.

I turned back around and looked at the creature. "Is that the event you were talking about?"

"That is for you to decide" The creature said. "You can start following a path from that event and if it is wrong, you will have to go back and start again."

"From what you're saying, I don't really have time to have to start again. But I can't think of any other major event in my life that happened in this room, so I guess I'll have to go with that. How do I do this? How do I follow this *path* as you call it?"

The creature raised its arm above its head and made some kind of swirling motion with it. That's when something appeared on the desk in front of it. It was a large crystal ball. "Here you can come to view the parts of your path from an outside perspective. You can only view the past in the order that it occurred. You can view the present at any time to see those who control your fate and what they are doing. To do so, you must ask to view a specific person and the crystal ball will follow that person in real time until you ask it to stop."

"Well okay then I guess let's get started" I said as I pulled my chair up closer to the desk.

Alex was trying to enjoy his drive up north. About as much as anyone could under the circumstances. He told himself that this was a good thing. He needed this new start. He could make some new friends any maybe even meet woman that would help him forget all about Emily. So why did he feel so anxious? The further he got from home, the more he wanted to turn around and the more he had to tell himself to keep going.

He was a little more than halfway through his drive now on the I-95 and he was making good time. With the help of his best friends back home, he had been able to get everything packed up and ready to go within just a few hours. He didn't own a whole lot, what with living on his own and all. He had been able to start his drive out of town on Sunday night around midnight and now the sun was starting to come up.

The directions he'd been given to get to his new apartment seemed easy enough and he just hoped the place wouldn't be horrible. He was being given this day along with Monday and Tuesday to get settled before starting his new job on Wednesday. That would be plenty of time for him to scope out the neighborhood as well. Maybe he could find a few quick places around to grab something to eat.

Speaking of food, he thought, he was starting to feel a little hungry. He pulled off the highway a few exits down the road and found a nice little diner open 24 hours. The place was clean, and he was seated right away by a nice older woman. The place was about half full at this time of the morning which was a good sign because it was so early. Everyone seemed to be enjoying what they ordered. When the waitress came back to his table, he ordered a cup of coffee and looked at the menu. He was starting to feel like this move would be good for him after all.

———

It had been a couple of weeks now since Emily had crashed. The doctor's tests were all coming back that she was not brain dead. She seemed to have some cognitive function, and as long as that continued to be the case, there was no reason, the family was told, that Emily had to be taken off of life support. She was still breathing on her own, but she needed a feeding tube to survive. While there was no way to know for sure if she would ever wake up, there was always a chance.

This was good news to Bob, Brenda, and Allie and for the time being, they made no plans. Allie came to visit Emily every chance she got, which was almost every day. Their parents came and visited once. Bob sat in a chair in the corner while Brenda held Emily's hand and cried. Inevitably, when they were ready to leave, Bob walked up to Emily's bedside and told her that he loved her, looking a little uncomfortable, and told her that he hoped she'd wake up soon.

Emily's room was pretty quickly filled with flowers and cards. They were from Emily's friends as well as her fellow teachers and her students. A prayer vigil was held outside the school the evening after the accident. Everyone in town it seemed, had shown up. Everyone that is, except Alex.

It was as Allie was sitting there visiting her sister, that Emily's best friend Samantha knocked lightly on the door. Allie had just been telling Emily how her new beau, Josh, had been calling her every day to ask how she was doing and how her sister was. She wished Emily could hear her although she wasn't so sure she couldn't. At the sound of the knock, she got up and answered the door.

"Hey" Samantha said to Allie pulling her into a hug. "I had some time, so I thought I'd just stop by to see Emily. The nurse told me you were already in here."

"Yeah, I was just talking to her you know... I don't know if she can hear me, but I like to think that maybe it's helping her get closer to waking up. Anyway, um... come on in." Allie said rubbing her eyes and moving out of the way for Samantha to enter.

"Thanks. Yeah, I know it's been a few weeks, and I feel guilty that I haven't been able to make it sooner."

"Don't be. Everyone knows you have a hectic life with a toddler running around. God knows I couldn't do it. And it looks like Emily won't be going anywhere anytime soon." Allie gestured towards Emily lying in her hospital bed.

"Yeah, I guess you're right" Samantha said as she walked over to Emily and took a good long and hard look at her.

Silence seemed to hang in the air for a moment. Allie decided to bring up the one subject that she knew Samantha was also privy to. She hadn't told anyone else, including Josh, about the phone call that she had received from Emily shortly before her accident. Now that Samantha was here, she suddenly felt the weight of that. She needed to talk about it with someone.

"So, can I ask you something?" Allie said now causing Samantha to break her concentration on Emily's face and look over at her.

"Of course." Samantha said pulling up a chair to sit down.

"I don't know quite where to start. Emily called me just before her accident. She told me about Alex. She was really upset but she told me she was going to bed right after she got off the phone with me. I guess she decided to get up and drive around instead."

"Yeah" Samantha said now. "Emily met me at the park Saturday around lunch time. She told me that Alex asked her out to dinner the evening before and that he told her that he was in love with her. I asked her how she felt about him, and she said she didn't feel that way towards him. Basically, I told her to let him down gentle. Last I heard from her was Sunday morning when she called to tell me that he was at her house waiting for an answer."

"So then, you don't know about what happened during that conversation?" Allie asked.

"No. She didn't call me back to tell me about it. I just assumed I'd hear about it later."

This was a shock. Allie had assumed that Samantha knew everything. She decided to go ahead and tell her because had Emily not had the accident, she felt sure that Samantha would've been the next person Emily would have called.

"Emily did let him down. But then, Alex apparently had another surprise to spring on her. He told her that he had been offered a job in Maryland and that he was going to take it. He told her that he couldn't be friends with her anymore and that he'd never see her again. Then he just walked out. As far as I know, he was gone the next day. I don't even know that he knows about her accident."

Samantha gasped. "Are you serious? Wow. I can't believe he would do something like that!"

"Believe it" Allie said now. "As far as I'm concerned, he's the one to blame for Emily being here and I have no intentions of trying to find him to let him know what's going on. In fact, if it were up to me, if he were to find out somehow from someone else, I would do everything in my power to stop him from coming here to see her. He doesn't deserve to see her."

Samantha could feel the anger pouring off of Allie. Should she be honest about how she felt about the situation and risk Allie exploding? She decided to take that chance. Allie was only seeing things from one perspective. It seemed as though she needed someone to blame. Unfortunately, Samantha was afraid it could possibly cause more harm than good.

"I agree that it was a lousy thing for Alex to do" Samantha said. "However, you know, he has been in love with her for a very long time. It seems like he just reacted with his emotions instead of his brain. I'm not saying that I would try to find him either. I'm just saying, as devastated as Emily was, and I can only imagine how devastated she was, she was still the one who made the choice to go driving in that state of devastation."

"How can you blame Emily?!" Allie asked raising her voice. "You know as well as I do that it is not like her to get that emotional about anything! Alex did a number on her for her to react that way. There's no other explanation."

"It's not that I'm blaming her" Samantha said carefully. "I guess I'm just trying to say that it was an accident, you know? It's not really anyone's fault. It's a horrible, *horrible* situation, but it was just an accident."

"Well, I still think he doesn't deserve to see her. I intend to be here in case he ever tries."

Alex pulled up outside a red, three-story brick building surrounded by other tall buildings on what looked like a busy city street. He looked down at the address printed on the paper in his hand. Then he looked back up at the building. This was it. This was where he was going to be calling his home for the short-term future. He parallel-parked his truck on the street and headed inside. According to the paper in his hand, his apartment was on the third floor, apartment 310.

As he looked around the lobby, he spotted an elevator to his right and a staircase to his left. The lobby itself was clean enough, but a little shabby. It sported a light colored, striped wallpaper pattern that had seen better days and an old, stained, thin, and worn carpet under his feet. Well, beggars couldn't be choosers.

It was just as he was thinking this and heading toward the elevator that the little light above it lit up and made a ding noise. The doors opened and out walked a gorgeous, exotic looking woman with long dark hair. She was wearing a black, long-sleeved blouse, dark washed skinny jeans, and black riding boots. She was carrying a black sequined clutch and had dark, smoky eyes. Her eyes themselves were a rich, warm brown. Upon seeing Alex, she smiled.

"Hi there" Alex said, clearing his throat. "I'm Alex. I just moved here. I was just on my way up to take a look at the place where I'll be staying."

The woman continued to smile as Alex stuck out his hand. "I'm Veronica" said the woman taking his hand. "What floor are you on Alex?"

"The third floor. Apartment 310."

"Well, it looks like you're my new neighbor. I'm in apartment 311. I was headed out to meet a couple of friends for a drink at the bar I work at since tomorrow is my day off. But I think I'll take a moment to show you around first. My friends won't mind waiting on me." Veronica said with a mischievous smile on her face.

Alex gulped and replied, "Um, sure that sounds nice."

"Step right this way and let's go have a look at your new place." Veronica stepped back onto the elevator followed by Alex as the doors closed and whisked them up to the third floor.

Chapter Six

I was sitting on the other side of the teacher's desk in room 107. I had just finished watching the first day that I had met Alex in the crystal ball, as if it were a movie. It was a little strange. I watched as Alex came into the classroom, with his freckles that had since faded and his crooked front baby teeth that hadn't fallen out yet. I watched as he handed the teacher, Mrs. Dinger, a note he was carrying.

Mrs. Dinger read the note and smiled down at Alex. Then she looked at the class and announced that we had a new student. She said his name was Alex Coleman and that he had just moved here from Virginia. Then she turned to Alex and told him he could have a seat in the empty desk next to me. He did as he was told, quietly, and I watched my young self turn in my chair and tell him hello.

Young Alex smiled at me with a look of shy, bashfulness, before saying hello back to me. I hadn't remembered him blushing like that in that first interaction. But as I watched, I now wondered, did he have a crush on me that very first day? I quickly pushed the thought away. We were only nine years old after all. Most boys didn't like girls yet at that age. At least, none of the ones that I had ever taught had.

Instead of me having to watch what we learned that day in class, the scene suddenly skipped to the lunchroom. Now I saw myself, sitting alone at a table, eating a hamburger that had been served to me in the lunch line. Why was I alone? I had friends after all. Samantha usually ate with me every day back then. Then I remembered. Samantha had been out sick that day. That's why I had been eating alone.

I watched as little Alex took his tray from the lunch lady and looked around the room. He seemed anxious. No one else in the room seemed to notice him, including me. Then I saw his eyes light up when he looked in my direction. Little me was focused on eating my hamburger and didn't even notice him walk up until he was standing right in front of me on the other side of the table.

"Hi" he said, turning a little red. "I was just wondering, since you're the only person I've talked to so far, if I could sit with you for lunch?" He seemed to be twisting his left foot back and forth on the linoleum floor slightly.

Little me just looked up at him and smiled. "Sure," I had said. "I'm Emily."

"I'm Alex" little Alex said as he sat down.

Little me giggled. "I know. Remember the teacher told us your name in class."

Little Alex turned bright red then. "Yeah, I know. I just didn't know what else to say."

"I'm sorry," Little me said. "I didn't mean to laugh. It was just a little funny."

"That's okay," little Alex said. "So, what is there to do for fun around here?"

The conversation continued with me telling him about the things our town had to offer us kids like the movie theater and bowling alley. Alex seemed to listen to little me intently as he ate his lunch, looking up at me between every bite. When the bell rang signaling the end of lunch, Alex didn't move right away. He nervously looked at me. I was getting up to go empty my tray. From what I could see of the scene, I hadn't even noticed Alex not making a move to get up from his seat. It was only when he spoke again that I had stopped what I was doing to look back at him.

"Emily? Um... do you think we could be... I don't know... friends? It's just, I don't really know anyone..." he said as he trailed off his sentence and looked down at his tray, which was still sitting on the table.

"Yeah, sure. See you in class." Little me said to him. And just like that, I had walked away from the table.

The scene hovered on Alex for a few seconds who was now looking immensely relieved at what I had said. Watching this, I realized now how hard it must have been for him that first day, being the new kid and all. I started to wonder, if Samantha hadn't been sick, would Alex still have asked to sit with me at lunch? I'd never thought about this before but, the truth was, now that I was seeing how hard it had been for him, in my heart I felt like I knew the answer. Things would have been completely different. Wow, what a coincidence that was, I thought. The scene suddenly ended in the crystal ball by going black.

"Are you ready to see more?" asked the creature.

"Yeah, I guess. I mean, this isn't so bad. It's like watching home movies almost. And I want to get through this as soon as possible because I don't want to die here. I want to wake up!" I sighed loudly.

Now the crystal lit up with a scene from fifth grade, a year later. Me and Alex were sitting under a tree at recess arguing in a good-natured way about video games. During this time, Samantha usually joined us as well. She was now friends with Alex too, but she was also popular with everyone else in our class. Anytime anyone asked her to come join them for something, like a game of kickball for instance, she would go. Prior to Alex coming to our school, when this would happen, I was happy enough just to read a book by myself.

The day I was viewing now must've been one of those days when Samantha was off with other kids. I didn't have a problem with that as I used to spend a lot of overnight weekends at Samantha's house.

We would hang out, eat junk food, paint our nails, etc. All the typical young girl stuff.

"Almost every day you come to school with a small bag of Oreos" little me was saying to Alex as he pulled a small Ziploc bag out of his backpack. "Don't you ever worry that you'll get fat?" I giggled a little as I said this and covered my mouth with my hand.

"No. I never thought of that." Said Alex opening the bag. "I'm just a kid. Why should I worry about that? Besides, I run around all the time. Want one?" he said as he held his hand out to me with an Oreo sitting on his palm.

"No thank you. I don't really like Oreo's." Little me answered and made a gross out face.

"Well, what do you like?" Alex asked me as he twisted the Oreo apart and licked the cream on the inside.

"If I had to choose my favorite, I would say my favorite is Fudge rounds."

"But Fudge rounds are like little cakes, not cookies." Alex said.

"I guess I don't really like cookies that much." Little me responded.

"Suit yourself." Alex said shrugging his shoulders as he ate the rest of the cookie and went to take another one out of the bag.

The scene went black again inside the crystal ball and came back up on another scene. We were sitting underneath the same tree, but we were wearing different clothes. I couldn't tell how much time had passed from the last scene, only that it was a different day. Samantha was with us this time as well. Pretty quickly, as the scene began though, Jenna Thompson ran up to us and asked us if we wanted to play foursquare with her. Me and Alex both said no, but Samantha got up and told Jenna that she would play. Then they ran off together.

A few minutes passed with me and Alex talking about the test that we had taken in class earlier that morning and how we thought we did on it. Then Alex opened his backpack to pull out his plastic bag of Oreos. But this time, after he put the bag on the grass in front of him, he reached into his bag and pulled something else out. It was a single, plastic wrapped Fudge Round.

"I brought this for you," Alex said as he handed it to me. "My mom bought a box of them. She asked me if I wanted another snack besides Oreos and said I could have one a day."

Watching this play out, I couldn't help but feel just a little misty eyed. If it were any other kids besides me and Alex I would have said, those two are going to grow up and get married! But it was me and Alex. It kind of made me feel bad that he had been so sweet as a little boy, and I hadn't even noticed because I was just a kid myself and really wasn't thinking about any boy in a romantic way just yet. I was little behind the rest of the girls in that department because at that time, my focus was completely on my concern for what me and Allie would walk into when we got home every day.

But if I had been thinking about boys in that way, would it have made a difference? Anything's possible, I thought to myself. It could be that if we had met just a few years later when I had started liking boys that I would've liked him because I wouldn't have already had that close history of friendship with him. I mean isn't that the biggest reason why I don't see him in a romantic way? Because we're such good friends and I don't want to ruin that? We *were* such good friends, I reminded myself. My heart started feeling like it was flooding with sadness all over again.

Back in the scene I was watching, little me responded to Alex's sweet gesture by taking the cake from him and telling him thank you and saying that he was so thoughtful. His cheeks burned red a little at that, but he didn't say anything else. Right then, some of the boys in our class came running up and singing Alex and Emily sitting in a tree... Alex turned an even brighter red and his whole neck seemed to burn red as well.

Then, one of the boys, Calvin, who was basically the leader of the group said, "It's so gross that you brought a snack for a girl. You're such a weirdo Alex. You're always spending all your time with Emily. What are you in love with her or something?" The other boys started laughing as Calvin said, "What a loser. Come on guys." Then they all ran off to terrorize someone else.

Little me turned to Alex once they were out of earshot and said, "You're not a loser Alex. You're just a lot nicer than they are and there's nothing wrong with being nice."

Alex stared off in the direction those boys had gone for what seemed like forever but was actually only about 30 seconds while the red in skin drained away. Finally, he turned to look at little me and said, "Thanks." Then he opened his bag of Oreos and pulled one out while I unwrapped the snack that he had brought me. We ate them in silence until the scene went black again.

At this point, I was holding back a few tears as I thought about what I had just watched. I looked up at the creature on the other side of the desk and said, "I'd like to stop for a little while. I need to take a break."

"As you wish." Said the creature. Then he swirled his arm and the crystal ball disappeared.

Suddenly I felt completely worn out by all of the emotions that were stirred up inside of me. I wanted to just go curl up in my bed and go to sleep so that I could put my thoughts to rest for a little while. But where was I going to sleep? There was nothing outside of this creepy version of the school. Was I supposed to just curl up on the floor?

But then I remembered the bench that I had woken up on. Well, not really woken up since I was technically in a coma. That bench seemed a lot more appealing to me right now compared to the floor in a dark, creepy building. Especially, if the sky was the same as it was when I woke up there.

As I stood up from the desk I asked, "Do I just come back here every time I'm ready to see more?"

"For now." Said the creature.

"O-kay then I guess I'll be back later."

The creature said nothing as I walked out of the room and out of the building. The sky was still the same solid orange that it had been before, and it was still comfortably warm outside. So, I made my way back to the bench in front of the school and laid down and closed my eyes.

When I opened them, I had no idea how much time had passed. I only knew that I felt a little better since everything wasn't so fresh in my mind anymore. I saw that the sky was still orange, and it didn't look as if anything had changed. I didn't feel hungry at all. I guess I must not need to eat here, I thought, which made sense, if my body was really in the hospital being fed through a tube. I sat up on the bench for a few minutes and took a few deep breaths.

"Well, might as well get back to it." I said out loud to no one.

I stood up and stretched. Then I turned around to head back into the school. What I saw then shocked me. It wasn't the building. It still looked exactly the same. But behind it, where the recess area was supposed to be, was one single tree. The same tree that me and Alex used to sit under in the exact same spot. It was just far enough to the left of the school that the building didn't block it from view. All around it was nothing but sand as far as the eye could see. Just as it had been before. But I knew that tree had not been there before.

And now as I looked back at the school, already feeling confused, I noticed the school did look a little different. There wasn't anything that I could really put my finger on though. It just did. I walked around the outside of the building now to that tree. I reached out and touched it, not sure what I would feel. It felt as real as any tree I had ever felt before. Weird. Then I walked back around the building and went inside the school.

When I got back to the classroom, the creature was sitting there as if it had never left, sitting silent and still as a statue. Maybe it hadn't ever left, I thought with a shudder. Maybe, since it's part of my subconscious, it just shuts off when I'm not around it.

As I walked back toward the desk that I had sat at previously, the creature said, "Are you ready to view more?"

"Yes." I said. "But actually, I'd like to view the present right now if I can. I'd like to check in on my family."

"Anyone in particular?" the creature asked.

"Yes. I'd like to see Allie."

With that, the crystal ball reappeared on the desk and lit up with a scene of Allie. It looked like she was sitting in a hospital room. I looked over at the bed. It was my hospital room! And oh my god did I look like a wreck. It shocked me to look at myself all banged and bruised up with my head wrapped in gauze and tubes coming out of me. It was almost too much. But I took a deep breath and concentrated on Allie. She seemed to be talking to me.

"Oh Emily. You have to wake up so that you can meet Josh. He was the guy that I had that date with the other night. It turns out, he really is a dream come true."

Allie teared up a little, wiped her eyes, and continued. "He brought me here to the hospital the other night you know. The night that dad called me and told me that you'd been in an accident. He sat in the waiting room with me Emily. He sat with me all night until we heard that you were stable. And then he brought me home. Now he's been calling me every day to ask about you and to see how I'm doing. No guy has ever done that for me before. You have to wake up so you can meet him. You hear me, Emily?"

"I'm trying!" I yelled at the crystal ball.

But of course, she didn't hear me. She sat there for about a minute in silence just looking at my body lying in the hospital bed. I wondered what she was thinking about now. Then there was a knock on the door. Allie answered it. It was Samantha.

I sat there and listened as Samantha told Allie that it was her first time visiting me. I sat there as Allie relayed the events that led up to my car crash. I gasped when Allie mentioned that Alex didn't know about the accident because he was already gone.

Then I cried out in anguish when Allie told Samantha that she blamed Alex for my accident. I started crying when Allie said if he did find out about it, she wasn't going to let him visit me. But then, God bless Samantha. She tried to get Allie to see reason when it came to Alex. But it seemed that Allie was having none of that. I felt so helpless. If it were up to me, I wouldn't want Alex to be prevented from coming to see me. The thought just broke my heart all over again.

The more time went on, the more Allie feared that Emily would never wake up. The more fear that Allie felt, the angrier she felt towards Alex. It finally reached a boiling point a month after Emily's accident. Allie was at her parent's house, eating dinner. Her mother had called and begged her to come. Brenda had been calling Allie a lot lately, and it was starting to make Allie feel a little suffocated. She realizes she's probably lost one daughter, Allie thought, so she's leaching onto the other one.

So, it was as Allie and her parents were eating dinner together, that Brenda brought up the subject of Alex. "You know who we haven't seen at all since Emily's accident?" said Brenda sounding so exhausted as if it hurt just to talk. She slowly cut a piece of meat with her knife and stuck it in her mouth. "We haven't seen Alex at all. Have you heard from Alex?" she turned to look at Allie as she asked this with half-opened blood shot eyes.

"No mom, I haven't." was all Allie said as she looked down at her plate to avoid eye contact with her mother.

"It's just so strange." Brenda said now. "They've been best friends forever. I wonder if we've just been missing him, and he's just been visiting Emily when we aren't there?"

Allie didn't know what to say. She didn't want to tell her parents what had happened, but she didn't want to outright lie to them either. So, she chose to say nothing and just let the subject drop. Only, Brenda wasn't ready to let it drop.

"Maybe I'll reach out to him at the hospital." Brenda said. "I'll just go try to find him in the physical therapy department and see how he's doing."

"You can't do that mom." Allie replied.

"Why not?"

"Because you just can't mom." Allie said a little louder than she wanted to.

"What are you getting all upset about Allie?" her father asked. "Your mother is just trying to do a good thing and I don't like you taking that tone with her!" Bob slammed his fists which were holding his knife and fork down onto the table.

Allie knew she had to say something now. She had no choice. "You can't do that mom, because Alex is gone. He moved away!"

Chapter Seven

"What do you mean he moved away?" Brenda asked, her eyes going wide.

Allie sighed loudly and rubbed her forehead by scrunching it together with her fingers. "It's a long story." When Allie heard only silence, she knew her parents were waiting for an explanation. "Basically, Alex decided that he was in love with Emily, or rather, that he's been in love with her for a long time and he sprung this revelation on her two days before the car crash. Then, the morning before the crash, he came to her house and demanded to know how Emily felt. He wanted to know if she would give him a chance at a relationship."

"That doesn't sound like Alex." Brenda said. "I've never seen him be demanding with anyone about anything."

"Well, I guess when you've had something like that bottled up for so long and then you finally let it out, you become impatient!" Allie snapped at her mom.

She took a moment to calm herself before continuing. "It gets worse. When Emily said no to him, he told her that he had a plan in case she answered that way. He told her that he'd found a job in another state that would pay him a lot more than he was making here and that he was going to move away. He told her that he couldn't be her friend anymore and that she'd never see him again!" Allie felt her voice breaking and took a few deep breaths.

"Oh my." Brenda said bringing her hand up to her mouth. She suddenly looked pale as she looked down at the table and then back up to Allie. When she did, her eyes looked glazed over.

Allie continued. "It devastated Emily. She called me really late that night and said she'd been in bed all day. She told me everything that happened. I asked her if she wanted me to come over and she no, that she'd be okay. I should have gone over there. Maybe if I had, she would have never gone out for that drive."

If Allie had expected her parents to make her feel better by telling her that it wasn't her fault, she would've been disappointed. Both of her parents sat in silence for a few minutes, presumably absorbing everything she had just told them. She could feel how tensed up her father was as he sat there vibrating his leg under the table. Then when Allie could take it no more and felt like maybe she should try to say something else, her father pushed his chair away from the table and stood up.

Bob threw his napkin down onto his plate and said, "I need to get out of here for a little while." He turned, grabbed his wallet and his keys from the side table by the door.

"Where are you going?!" Brenda wailed after Bob.

"I don't know. I can't stay here right now. Let me have some time, Brenda!" Bob yelled as he walked out, slamming the door behind him.

Brenda looked stunned for a long silent moment as she stared at the closed front door. Then she turned to look at Allie and burst into tears. Allie, wishing she hadn't said anything to them about Alex, got up and went around the table to comfort her mother. She stooped over and wrapped her arms around Brenda's neck and laid her cheek on top of Brenda's head. She stayed that way for a while until Brenda's tears slowed and eventually stopped. Then they both cleared the table and Allie helped her mother put up the food and wash the dishes in silence.

———————

After viewing my sister in my hospital room and seeing how upset she was with Alex, I wanted to scream. I wanted to pick up the desks in this room that I sat in and throw them. I had absolutely no control and I just couldn't handle it. I was tempted to ask to see Alex, to see how he was doing so far away. But I thought better of it. If he was happy, it would hurt all over again to see how easy it had been for him to leave. So instead, I decided it was time to get on with viewing the past. I told this to the creature and looked back at the crystal ball as the next scene began.

In this scene, me and Alex were sitting on the bench outside of school. The same bench that I had recently slept on. We looked a little older now, maybe around 12 or so. There were kids running, walking, and laughing with each other all around us. Judging from how bright it was outside, I guessed that this was after school instead of before.

"So hey, I was thinking," Alex said to me, "I don't have anything to do this afternoon and I've never seen your house. I'm kind of curious about where you live."

I saw the deer stuck in the headlights look that had come over my face. This was the day that I had told Alex about my family. I watched as our two younger selves sat in silence on the bench while Alex had waited for a reply, and I had been thinking about what to say. I remembered trying to decide whether I should lie and come up with an excuse or just let it all out.

In the end, I'd decided not to lie because I'd now been friends with Alex for about 4 years and he'd never lied to me about anything as far as I knew. Plus, he'd have to find out eventually, I thought. And how would he react if he found out that I had lied to him?

"The thing is," younger me said, "my house is not exactly the kind of place I want to take my friends. My parents don't really get along and when they're both home, there's usually a lot of yelling and screaming… I've never taken anyone to my house before except for Samantha."

Alex sat there for a minute presumably trying to figure out what to say. I watched his face as his brows furrowed in thought and he stared out into space. Then I saw my young self's expression drop into a frown and my shoulders round as I hunched a little on the bench in a defeated sort of way. I remember being so afraid in that moment that Alex would freak out at what I had just told him and take off and stop being my friend. But that's not what happened.

Alex suddenly lifted his arm and put it around my shoulders. I saw the look of surprise cross my young face and the look of determination on his. He didn't say anything, and my younger self quickly relaxed as I straightened my shoulders back up and leaned back against his arm. Neither one of us said anything for a few minutes.

Finally, he said, "Well, if you don't have to go home right away, we could just take a walk around my neighborhood."

That's where the scene faded out and the image went black. Wow, I thought. I couldn't believe that a 12-year-old boy had handled something as heavy as that so well. My eyes teared up a little as I thought about how good of a friend Alex had always been, right from the beginning. The more I watched of our time together, the more I saw just how special Alex really was, and the more I started to wonder if I'd made the right choice in turning him away.

Watching this scene made me think back over my childhood at home. Samantha was the only person outside of my family that I'd told about any of it both because she'd been my best friend since kindergarten and because her being female herself, I knew she would understand how it affected my life. She could give me insight from an outsiders perspective. Even as an adult, I never shared anything about my home life with Alex, and the subject just really never came up again.

One dark memory in particular creeped into my head now. I was ten at the time, making Allie about seven. For a few weeks, my father had been coming in late from work, without bothering to call. This was actually an upgrade from his usual behavior. Normally, he wouldn't come home every single day for weeks at a time like he had been doing during this time. Usually, he'd come home three or four nights in a row, my parents would fight, and he'd be gone who knows where for a few days before the cycle would start all over again.

This particular night, my father walked in late for the probably the twentieth time in a row. But this time, instead of keeping dinner warm for him, my mother decided when we were all done, she'd simply put it away if he couldn't make it home to eat with the family. So, when my father walked in, the first thing he did was to get angry that everything was cold. He screamed at my mother, the sound of which we'd started to get used to not hearing anymore.

"Brenda! Where is my dinner?!"

"I put it up Bob. You're never here to eat with us. I just decided that when you finally decided to walk in, you could reheat it yourself."

"You knew I was coming home though. Haven't I been coming home every night for the last few weeks? Why would you want to make me angry like that when you knew I was coming home?!" Bob screamed, grabbing a clean plate out of the dry rack on the counter and smashing it on the floor.

"Why should it be good enough for me that you come home late? You should want to be home with your family! Are you sleeping with someone else again?"

Me and Allie were listening behind my bedroom door at their exchange. We'd known that our father had cheated on our mother in the past, but it was a shock to hear the accusation being thrown around again. I just didn't understand how he could do that. We'd also seen our parents act completely in love with each other. It seemed they were constantly going back and forth between love and hate actually.

"I'm not going to dignify that with an answer" Bob said now. "And if you're not satisfied with how I've been coming home, then I can just leave until you do become satisfied with it!"

With that we heard the front door slam as our dad left the house. We heard the ignition to his car start and saw the headlights pass over my bedroom window as he backed out of the driveway. Our mother started screaming in an anguished sort of way. She ran to where she kept alcohol hidden behind cleaning products under the sink and started drinking straight out of the bottle. We knew to stay out of her way when this happened, until she passed out, usually in the living room on the couch. That was just one incident of many that went on while me and Allie were growing up.

I wiped away my tears and decided that I needed to take another break. I got up, went back outside to my bench and laid down. I felt so confused and overwhelmed. I closed my eyes and tried to wipe the thoughts from my mind. It was easier than I thought it would be and soon I was fast asleep again.

Alex loved his new job. It was always rewarding to help people who were hurting get back on their feet. He had just clocked out from work for the day and was headed home to his apartment. It had been about a month since he'd gotten to Maryland and already, he was well on his way to finding a nice place of his own to move to.

He had his eye on a condo that he'd visited a few days ago with the realtor who was helping him look. It was sleek and stylish in a masculine sort of way as the current owner had been a bachelor. He was selling the place to buy a small house in the suburbs for him and his soon to be wife in hopes of starting a family. Hopefully one day, Alex thought to himself, that would be him.

After Alex had met Veronica that first day in the lobby of the apartment building, he had taken her out on a few dates. She had seemed interested in him, so he thought, why not? Wasn't that the whole reason he had moved here? To start over in a new place. He and Veronica seemed to be hitting it off pretty well, and in more ways than one. There was an advantage to living right next door to the woman he was dating, as it turned out. The chemistry between them was like a wildfire. She was insatiable and he was happy to be the one to oblige her.

Just thinking about it made his pants tighten in an all too familiar and uncomfortable way. He just had to make it home, he told himself. He had to force himself to drive carefully, not allowing himself to go too fast out of excitement for the evening ahead. Veronica was off today and was waiting for him for dinner. She'd told him that she planned to cook and that he should come right over after work. Once he got home, he went straight up to the third floor without even bothering to stop to check his mail.

He knocked on Veronica's door and was met with the sight of her clad in a silky red negligee as she opened the door. The look on her face was one of a predator ready to pounce on her prey.

"I thought we'd start with dessert" she said. She grabbed him by the wrist and pulled him inside, causing Alex to hurriedly slam the door behind him.

———

I woke up, once again feeling more refreshed, the emotions that were so strong before felt more numbed out. I was ready for to go back into the school. I slid my feet to the ground and noticed that there was a patch of green grass in a circle surrounding the bench that I slept on. Everything else was still sand that seemed to go on forever, but right here, below my feet, was green!

I stood up and turned around to look at the school. The building was changing I could see now. Where it had looked gray and drab and dare I say it, condemned, now, the bottom half of the building looked the way it was really supposed to look. The bricks on half of the building were now a deep red and the color seemed to fade away back to grey right below the second-floor windows. What was going on?

I went back inside the school. It was still dark as there didn't seem to be any electricity. However now, the floors were clean from the paper debris that had been littered all over it before and the lockers were free of graffiti. I went back to room 107 which now just looked like a clean, empty room. But the creature wasn't there. Where did it go?

I panicked for a moment before deciding that the best thing for me to do was to look everywhere I could. I opened every door on the first floor and looked in every room. I walked around the cafeteria and went into the kitchen. I walked into the gym and checked out the locker rooms. Nothing. The creature was not there.

All that was left was the second floor. I walked slowly up the stairs and stopped to look around. The second floor looked like the first floor had before with blank papers strewn all over the floors and graffiti all over the walls and lockers. Once again, I started opening doors and looking in classrooms. I finally found the creature sitting in room 223. I knew that this room was one that I had definitely had a class in during high school, but I couldn't think of anything significant that had happened here.

"Why did you move?" I asked the creature as I walked in.

"You are now ready to move on to another phase of your past." The creature said.

I wasn't sure what it meant by phase, but I decided it was probably a good thing. I pulled up a chair to the new desk that the creature was sitting behind. This room had been an art classroom. Instead of desks there were long tables with chairs pushed under them. Cabinets lined the far wall that had contained all our supplies.

Although I was ready to see another past event from my life, I wanted to start out by checking in to the present. I wanted to see my friend Samantha. So, I asked the creature if I could see her. The creature obliged, and Samantha came into view inside the crystal ball. She was sitting at her kitchen table, and she seemed to be alone. I could tell something was bothering her because she was chewing on her thumbnail and staring out into space. That had always been her tell.

Samantha took a deep breath and picked up her cell phone which had been sitting on the table in front of her. I watched as she scrolled through her contacts and clicked on a name. Then I could hear the line ringing on the other end as she put the phone up to her ear.

"Hey it's Samantha. I need to talk to you."

I looked up at the creature sitting on the other side of the desk and asked, "Is there any way that I can listen to whoever she's talking to? I mean it might be kind of hard to understand what she's talking about if I can't hear the other end of the conversation."

The creature snapped his fingers and suddenly it was as if Samantha was talking on speaker mode.

"Hey, how are you doing?" I heard Allie say.

Samantha took a deep breath and let out a big sigh. "I'm doing well considering. How are you doing?"

"Well, that's a tough one. I went to dinner at my parent's house the other night and I told them about what happened between Emily and Alex."

Oh my God! I thought. That was one of things that I had dreaded as I laid in bed after Alex left. My stomach had turned at the thought of telling them that they would never see Alex again and having to explain to them why. As it turned out, I didn't have to tell them. That didn't mean I wanted to find out how they'd reacted to Allie telling them. My stomach started churning again just thinking about it.

"Yikes." Samantha said. "How did they take it?"

"About as well as you'd expect," Allie said. "Dad got up and walked out of the house and mom broke down crying. I helped her clean up dinner and then I got the hell out of there."

"Wow. Well, I'm sorry to hear that. But I guess they would've had to find out sometime, right?"

"Well not necessarily. I mean, it's been a month since the crash and the more time goes on the more I start to worry that Emily may never wake up..."

"A month?!" I shouted out loud to the creature in front of me. "But this is only my third time coming into the school. How can it have been a whole month? It feels like it's only been a few days!"

"Because your body is so damaged, when you go to sleep, you sleep for several days at a time. It cannot be helped. The sleep has been helping you physically. Coming here and viewing your past has been helping you mentally."

"How long could I possibly have left if it's already been a month? I'm sure they won't leave me on life support forever."

"That is not for you to worry about just yet. As long as you continue coming here to try and get back on the right path, you have a chance."

Honestly, that didn't really reassure me much. But what could I do? I was doing the best I could already. So, I sighed and turned back to the scene playing out in front of me.

"Yeah." Samantha said back to Allie. "Speaking of how long it's been. Allie, I really think one of us should try to contact Alex and tell him about Emily. I know you're angry with him, but just hear me out. What if she dies? I mean, I hate to say that, but what if? I wouldn't be able to live with the guilt of letting her pass away without Alex even knowing to come to her funeral. It just feels so wrong."

"Well, I for one still believe he doesn't have a place in Emily's life anymore. He left. He left here without ever planning to see Emily again. If she hadn't gotten into that accident, we wouldn't be having this conversation. I don't understand why her getting into a potentially fatal car crash should change anything. If he really cared about her, then he'd call someone here and check up on things. If he even called just one of his other friends, I'm sure they'd mention it to him. But either he hasn't called anyone or he knows about it and he doesn't care. Either way is fine with me."

Samantha sighed loudly and ran her fingers through her hair. "Well, I guess there's just no convincing you is there?"

"No, there's not. I mean, I appreciate where you're coming from, but I just can't deal with it. I don't want to deal with it. Alex coming back would be too much for me right now. I don't know what I would do. I'm still so angry at him for hurting my sister that I'm afraid I would probably punch him on sight."

"I understand." Samantha replied. "Alright, well I've got to go. I just thought maybe I could convince you."

I listened as Allie's end of the line was silent for a moment. Then she just said, "Bye Samantha" and hung up the phone.

I was in complete agony. Now I felt, more than ever, that I wished Alex knew what was going on. But at the same time, I was terrified that if he was told, then he would still choose not to return. The thought of that ate me up inside. Was it possible that he really wouldn't care?

Samantha paced her kitchen floor holding her cell phone tightly in her hand. What was she about to do? I was excited and terrified at the same time as I watched her pace. My eyes were glued to the scene in front of me. I felt my heart beating a hundred miles an hour as she pulled her contacts back up on her phone and scrolled through them again.

I heard the faint ringing again coming from her phone as she held it back up to her ear. All I had to do was look at the creature. It snapped its fingers again as the ringing suddenly became much louder, sounding as if it were back on speaker mode. Then the ringing stopped mid-ring, and a voice I knew all too well answered Samantha's call.

"Hello?" said Alex.

Chapter Eight

"Hi Alex. This is Samantha."

"I know who it is" Alex replied in a tense voice.

All was silent and awkward on both sides of the phone before Samantha continued. "This is kind of hard to say. Do you have a few minutes?"

I listened as I heard the sound of Alex blowing out a big puff of air. Then he said, "Yeah, I guess I do. Just give me a second."

As he said this, a woman's voice in the background said, "Babe who is that? Is something wrong?"

I don't know why but hearing the sound of a strange woman calling Alex 'babe' just made me feel weird. It had only been a month since he'd told me that he was in love with me, and he'd already moved on with another woman? I guess he wasn't as in love with me as he thought.

If I had been in love with someone the way he had claimed to be in love with me, I wouldn't have been able to just move on from that so quickly. I recognized the feelings that I was having. I felt hurt by this. But why should I feel hurt, I thought. It's not like I wanted to be with Alex. This was confusing. Part of it, I knew though, was that to me it felt like it had only been a few days since he left and not a whole month.

Alex responded to the woman in the background by saying, "No, everything's fine. It's just a friend from back home. I'll be right back."

"Already got a new girlfriend?" Samantha asked raising one eyebrow.

"Yes, as a matter of fact I do. Is there something wrong with that? That *is* why I moved up here, to move on with my life."

"Hey, no judgement here" Samantha replied. "It just seems a bit quick is all. But look, that's not why I called."

"No? You mean you didn't call to give me your opinion about me moving on? That's a shock. I've actually been kind of waiting for you or Allie or someone to call me and tell me how wrong I was for leaving."

"That's really not my place Alex. The only person who has a right to do that is Emily in my opinion. Which brings me to why I called. Like I said, this is kind of tough. You may want to sit down."

I listened to the sound of Alex scraping a chair across the floor. He sighed as he said "Okay. I'm sitting."

"Alex... Emily was in a car accident. It was pretty bad, and her car was completely totaled. Emily's in the hospital."

"What?! Well... is she alright?" Alex asked. He actually sounded concerned. It tugged on my heart strings to hear it.

"We don't really know. I mean she's alive, technically. But Alex, Emily's in a coma. It's been a month and she hasn't woken up. I just thought you should know."

Everything was silent for a few moments before Alex said, "So let me get this straight. Emily's been in a coma for a *month*? And you're only just calling me now? Samantha this is serious."

"I know it's serious Alex. Believe me, I wanted to tell you before now. It's just, Allie is very angry with you. She's blaming you for the accident and she didn't want you to know about it at all. I only called you now because I just felt like it was wrong for it to be kept from you. Especially since we really don't know if Emily's ever going to wake up."

"Well why is it Allie's decision whether or not I should be told about this?" Alex asked angrily.

"Because their parents didn't know until the other night why Emily had been out driving at one in the morning. They didn't know why she was driving too fast, or why she ran a stop sign. Alex, this accident happened the night after you told her you were leaving. And look, I'm not saying I blame you for this the way Allie does. I'm just saying the reason Emily was out that night at all was because of how badly she was hurting over you leaving."

"Huh. Um wow, okay... I guess I did need to be sitting down for this. Thanks for letting me know."

"You're welcome. Are you going to come see her? I'd hate the thought of her dying and you never getting to see her while you had the chance. That's really why I called."

"I uh... I don't know. I just, I guess I just really need to think about this." Alex let out a deep sigh.

"Alright, just don't wait too long, okay?"

Samantha told Alex goodbye and hung up the phone. Tears welled up in my eyes. Please God, let Alex come back, I thought.

Alex stared at his phone for a minute until the screen went black. What should he do? Should he go back to visit Emily in the hospital when he was never supposed to see her again? Or should he just forget the call he had just received and continue to try to forget about her? Could he really just decide not to act on this new information? Or would his conscience eat him up until he regretted it for the rest of his life? God why did this have to happen, he thought. Things were not supposed to be this way.

Alex went back and forth weighing his options for several hours. He had still been in Veronica's apartment when Samantha called, and they had just finished letting off a little steam. Once he felt the shock of the call start to wear off, he went back into Veronica's bedroom where she was sitting up in her bed waiting for him. He told her he had to go and started getting dressed. He apologized for leaving her and told her he'd make it up to her. Veronica said it was fine and so he left and went home, right next door, to his own apartment.

He spent the rest of the afternoon debating with his heart about what he should do. He tossed and turned all night thinking about it. What if she really died? His heart was telling him that he should go. That he knew for certain. But what about what Samantha had said about Allie? Did he really want to take the risk of having to fight with her just to see Emily?

When he went to work the next day, he was still thinking about it. He was tired and distracted, and at the end of his shift, his new boss called him into his office and asked if something was wrong. Although Alex had only been there a month, his boss had already come to judge Alex's work ethic as good which made it all the more obvious that something was wrong.

Sitting in his boss's office, Alex broke down. He explained the situation in detail and when he was finished, his boss sat there for a minute, thinking. After a few moments, his boss sat back in his chair and told Alex that he thought he should go back. He was off on weekends anyway, so as long as he was back for Monday, it wouldn't hurt his work.

Running home, Alex called Veronica who didn't answer and left her a voicemail. He told her that an emergency came up back home and that he had to go back for a few days. He made sure to tell her that everything would be fine and that he'd see her next week. Then he grabbed a bag out of his closet and threw a few pairs of clothes in it. Quickly, he ran out of his apartment and jumped in his truck.

Once he was on the road, Alex called his friend Brendan who was still trying to sell his house.

"Brendan Bailey" he answered distractedly.

"Brendan hey it's Alex. Look I'm on my way back home for a few days and I just wanted to let you know that I'll be staying at my house."

"Yeah, hey buddy, that's totally fine. I've had a few people look at it, but no definitive bites and I haven't scheduled anyone else to take a look at it yet. But thanks for letting me know. Can I ask why you're coming back though? I mean, I know how bad you were hurt by Emily and when you told me you weren't planning to come back, I definitely didn't blame you."

"Yeah um, so I don't know if you've heard but Emily was in a real bad accident and she's in the hospital in a coma. No one is sure if she's going to wake up from it. I just, I couldn't live with myself if I didn't at least come see her one last time. Especially if..." Alex swallowed hard trying to hold back his emotions.

"Wow, no I hadn't heard about that. That sucks buddy. If it were me, I don't know that I'd be able to go visit someone who broke my heart the way she did to you. You're a better man than I am."

After the phone call with Brendan was through, Alex made it to the highway and started the long drive home. The further he drove, the more anxious he felt. How was it going to feel seeing Emily hurt like that? Would he be able to handle it? And how would her family react if they were there when he showed up? His stomach churned just thinking about it. But he couldn't let fear stop him. He had to keep going.

When Alex finally made it back to town, it was late, and he was exhausted. He drove straight to his house, and it was only when he walked in that he realized that he had no bed to sleep in. Thank God he had left his second couch behind. He'd only moved with the bare essentials that he needed and had planned to take the rest once someone bought his house. Then he'd have to put it all in storage until he could find a permanent place to live. Alex collapsed on the couch that he had left behind and fell into a deep sleep.

Unfortunately, he didn't sleep for more than a few hours because he'd set an alarm for early the next morning. He wanted to try to get to the hospital before anyone else would be there to visit Emily or to see him visiting Emily. Maybe he could slip in and out without anyone else knowing.

At 6 am the next morning, Alex woke up with a start. He'd forgotten where he was for a moment and had to get his bearings. It was Friday and he had to be back in Maryland by Sunday evening. No time to waste, he thought, as he got up, took a shower, and got dressed. Within half an hour he was out the door and on his way to the hospital.

He walked in and went straight to the nearest nurse's station to ask about Emily. The nurse behind the desk knew him so Alex asked how she was doing and made a little small talk with her as she looked up Emily's room number. Once he got the information he needed, he was off again. He went up a few floors and took a few turns until he was in the hallway that went directly to her room.

He stopped cold when he saw Allie walk out of a room that must be Emily's and into the hallway. What is she doing here so early, he thought? Allie never got up before noon unless she had to. What should he do? Should he turn around and wait till she was gone? But what if she wasn't actually leaving and was only going to get a drink of water or something? Well, it was too late now. Allie turned in the direction that Alex was standing. Even from this distance, Alex could see the frown that suddenly crossed her face.

Allie marched up to Alex stiffly with her hands balled into fists. "What are you doing here?" she demanded to know.

Alex wasn't sure how to respond. He understood Allie was upset but she didn't have to be so angry towards him. He decided not to give into his urge to be angry back at her as he knew that it wouldn't help anything. He just decided to tell her the truth. "I heard about Emily, and I came to see her."

"Why? Why do you care to see her now? You didn't care to see her the day you tore her whole life apart!" Allie practically screamed at him.

"I didn't tear her whole life apart Allie." Alex sighed. "She's the one who chose to turn me away."

"So, you chose to just run and desert her with barely a warning. And for what? To get back at her for saying she didn't want to be in a relationship with you?"

"Allie, how long have you known me? You know it wasn't like that."

"I thought I knew you to be someone who would never run out on a friend. It turns out I didn't know you very well at all." Allie held firm with the look of anger on her face. "I don't know who told you about her condition, but I don't want you here. Do you hear me? I don't want you anywhere near my sister!"

"How are you going to stop me Allie? Are you in control of who comes and goes from her room?"

"As a matter of fact, I am. My parents sure couldn't handle that responsibility and somebody had to do it. So yeah, the nurses and doctors here know not to let anyone in Emily's room that I say is not allowed to see her. All I have to do is turn around walk right over to that nurse's station and tell them to put you on the list."

"There's a list?" Alex asked trying to keep the incredulous sound out of his voice. "Who else is not allowed to see her?"

This took Allie off guard a little. "Well... technically there's not a list. But that's beside the point."

"Allie, I put my heart on the line when I told her how I felt." Alex said now, letting some of his emotion show. He took a deep breath as he brought his hand up over his eyes as if he had a headache and then dropped it heavily. "Look, I came to see her because I still care about her. Hell Allie... I was in love with her."

His voice cracked a little at that last statement. Allie didn't know what to say. Seeing Alex seem so torn up about the whole thing made her anger start to subside. She still hated him after how he'd hurt her sister, but she'd have to be made of ice not to feel his words. No, she thought to herself, don't let him get to you with his sob story. His side of it does not matter. It's what he did that matters. Stay strong.

"Well, if you were so in love with her, then you shouldn't have taken off on her the way you did. You destroyed her! She called me that night before she got in that car. Did you know that? She called me crying. I've never heard her sound like that before Alex. *Ever.*"

"I'm sorry I hurt her the way I did. I had just been in love with her for *so long*. I couldn't stay after she turned me down like that without even a thought as to how I felt. It's no excuse, I know. I was hurting pretty bad too Allie. I just... I shouldn't have let my emotions control my actions I guess."

"No, you shouldn't have. And you may be sorry now about how you hurt her, but it doesn't bring her back to us. It is your fault she is in that hospital room. Yours. She may not ever wake up. She may die without any of us ever being able to say goodbye. I will never forgive you for that. So no, I do not want you here and I do not want you visiting my sister. Please leave and don't make me call security."

"Fine" Alex said. "I'll leave."

As he turned and walked away, he was already trying to come up with a way to find out when Allie would not be there, so that he could come back and see Emily. He left the hospital and drove around town for a while, trying to let his anger at the situation gel. But it wasn't working. After a while, he decided to go back to his house. Still riled up with angry energy, he went into the workout room that he still had set up in his spare bedroom and started beating on his punching bag. He punched out his anger until he was physically exhausted.

Chapter Nine

As soon as Samantha had ended her call with Alex, I had to see him. It was like I couldn't control myself. I had to see his face to see for myself how he had taken the news. I asked the creature to switch views to Alex and in an instant, there he was. The face of my best friend who I used to think I knew better than I knew myself filled the crystal ball.

He was sitting in a chair at a small kitchen table still holding his phone in his hands. Was this his new place? I didn't have to wonder long. After a minute or so, I watched as Alex got up and walked into another room. It was a bedroom. It was a woman's bedroom from the look of it including a bedside lamp with a maroon shade and pictures on the walls of things like maroon high heeled shoes surrounded by blocky or swirly patterns in various shades of brown. The comforter on the bed was maroon, dark brown, and gold. It even had gold fringes surrounding the edges.

What was in the bed shocked me even more, although it really shouldn't have. There was a woman in the bed, sitting up with the comforter pulled up over her lap. She was beautiful with long, dark brown hair, and dark eyes, and she was wearing a cherry red negligee. No wonder he moved on so quickly, I thought. She had the look of a maneater.

"Are you coming back to bed?" the woman asked him in a coy manner as he walked into the room.

"Actually, I'm sorry Veronica. I think I'm going to have to take a rain check on that dinner. Something came up back home that kind of took me off guard and I really need to be alone this evening to think about it. I'm sorry. Please, don't take it the wrong way. Everything's fine. I promise."

"Oh… okay." This woman named Veronica said. Although the look on her face clearly said she wasn't so sure everything was fine. But she didn't press the issue. Instead, she simply said, "Well, if there's anything you need to talk about, I'm right next door."

"Thank you." Alex said. "I appreciate that. But I have to go for now. I'll make it up to you. I promise. I'll talk to you tomorrow." With that, Alex started to walk out of the room, but then, as an afterthought, turned around and walked back to the side of the bed, leaned down, and gave Veronica a kiss before leaving.

I watched as Alex went next door to what I gathered was his own apartment. Wow, I thought. So, this woman is his neighbor as well. How convenient. I felt a stab of jealousy and it annoyed me. What did I really have to be jealous over? I reminded myself, that I didn't want Alex. There was no reason really why he shouldn't be someone else. It was the woman I didn't like. She's completely the wrong type for him, I told myself.

I watched as Alex paced his living room for a few minutes. I watched as he decided to go into his bedroom and change for bed. I watched as he took his shirt off. Something made me feel compelled to look. It felt weird to be thinking about how Alex was more built than I'd ever really noticed before. Then he threw on an old t-shirt and climbed into bed. I watched as he turned on his television and surfed through the channels in a frustrated manner. Eventually he gave up and went to bed.

I had yet to view any more past memories since I found the creature in this new room upstairs, so I decided to go ahead and switch gears while Alex slept. The creature pulled up the next scene for me to view. It was in this very room that I was in now. In the scene, the classroom only had a few students sitting around talking to each other. But neither Alex nor I were there. Then, Alex walked in and went to his table. He set his backpack down on it and started pulling things out. He looked to be about 14 or 15 which would've been about right for the time that we had a class in this room.

Suddenly, younger me came running in looking very excited. I watched as my younger self ran straight up to Alex. "There you are Alex. Guess what?" I said to him as he turned to look at me.

"What?" he asked calmly as a smile started to spread across his face.

"Robbie Monroe just asked me to Homecoming!"

The look on Alex's face seemed to waver just slightly before he forced it back into place. I hadn't noticed it at the time, of course, because I had been so excited about a guy asking me to a dance. But now, as an adult, I saw Alex's face and it broke my heart a little. Here I was, just so happy to be asked to my first dance by anyone at all, and Alex had been standing there trying not to show how much it hurt him. I could see the sadness in his eyes.

Now the scene faded out and when it faded back in, my younger self was sitting alone under that same tree from when we were nine. By the time we were in high school, we didn't sit there as much as we used to. Only every now and again when we had time to sit together at lunch. Most of the time though, we were separated elsewhere at lunch, either with other friends or trying to catch up on homework in the library.

I knew immediately that this was the following Monday after the dance both because of the depressed look on my face as I sat there alone as well as the clothes I was wearing. The memory of Robbie finding me in the library that morning and telling me that he was going to go out with Sherry was forever seared into my brain as it was the first time I'd ever been hurt by a boy.

I had gone through my morning classes feeling like crap without anyone to talk to besides Samantha who I shared one of those classes with. I didn't have a class with Alex until after lunch. Samantha had written me a note asking why I looked so upset and passed it to me when the teacher wasn't looking. I wrote back what had happened to which Samantha responded that Robbie was a jerk. When lunch came, I went straight to the tree and sat there alone. This was where the scene had started.

Alex came walking up. He shouldered off his backpack and sat down next to me without a word. Then he handed me one of those party cups of ice cream that they sold in our cafeteria and a spoon.

"Samantha told me what happened." He said. "I know in movies girls like to cry over a pint of ice cream, but this was the best that I could do."

Smiling a little at that, I said, "Thanks." I opened the ice cream and took a small bite. "It was just so horrible. How could he do that to me after we had such a nice time the other night? Or at least, I thought we had had a good time…"

"I agree with Samantha. Robbie's a jerk. Don't lose any sleep over him Emily. He's not worth it. You'll get asked out again by someone better."

"Thank you, Alex." I said as I gave him a weak smile and ate the rest of the ice cream.

"No problem." He said as he pulled out his lunch and started eating. Then the scene faded again.

Wow, I thought. I had been so oblivious for so long. Now that I knew what Alex had felt and could go back and see all the times that he had tried to show it to me, it felt more real. It was like, I realized that I didn't really feel anything about what he had said to me that night at the restaurant because I had never consciously experienced it. Now that I had, I started to wonder if my feelings were changing, or if I was just feeling sorry for him?

I felt like I just wanted so badly to reach into that scene and wrap my arms around Alex. Even though he was younger in that scene, I had known him most of my life, so it wasn't really weird to me. I had a lot to think about. I decided to take a break for a few hours. I didn't want to sleep because who knew how much time would pass? What if Alex decided to come back and I missed it?

I went back out to my bench, laid down on my back and stared up at the orange sky. I had so many emotions running through me, and I felt very confused by all of it. After a few hours of thinking about everything and not feeling any closer to an answer, I decided to go back in and check back up on Alex in the present.

During the time that I had been watching the past and taking a break outside, Alex had apparently drove home and was now sleeping in the living room of his house on his couch. "Thank you, God!" I cried. I couldn't tear my eyes away now. Soon after I started watching, Alex woke up, got dressed, and went to the hospital.

When Alex ran into Allie in the hallway, I gasped. What was going to happen. "Please Allie! Please let him see me!" I cried out to the scene in front of me. But it was no use. Of course, she couldn't hear me no matter how much I really wished it to be.

———

It was now about noon and Alex realized how hungry he was as his stomach grumbled angrily. He'd left his house that morning without having eaten anything before he went to the hospital. He decided to call Brendan again and see if he had time to take a lunch break with him. Once it was established that Brendan was free for the next few hours, they decided to meet at the local burger joint to catch up.

Alex made his way there and got a booth for him and Brendan while he waited for his friend. One of the waitresses was a girl they'd all gone to high school with, Amy, and she stopped at his table to shoot the breeze and flirt with him a little. Alex politely asked how she was doing and told her about his new job before she had to run off to one of her other tables.

Brendan walked in then and Alex flagged him over. He sat down across from Alex with a goofy grin on his face. "You always had a way with women" he said glancing over towards Amy and back at Alex. "I saw the way she was smiling and batting her eyelashes at you from outside the window as I walked up."

"Yeah, maybe she was flirting with me but really, I don't have any interest in her and plus, I live in Maryland now. That's too far away for a relationship with anyone here."

"Maybe so, but you got to get back on the horse sometime" Brendan said gesturing in a way that made it obvious he was talking about more than dating.

Alex rolled his eyes at his friend. "Well, I have started dating someone actually up in Maryland. She's my next-door neighbor."

"I'll bet she takes real good care of you" Brendan responded moving his eyebrows up and down. "What's her name?"

"Her name is Veronica" Alex responded. "We've had a few dates and you know how I'm not the type to share all the gritty details. But this time I guess I will because, yeah, she is phenomenal in bed."

"Alright Alex. Finally moving on from Emily then."

"Yeah. But I don't want to talk about her right now."

"That's perfectly fine by me" Brendan said holding up his hands in a mock surrender kind of way.

The waitress stopped by their table then and took their drink order. Alex was happy for the small interruption as he needed a moment to refocus his thoughts on catching up with Brendan and asking about the progress with his house. He knew how Brendan felt about the Emily situation, so he didn't feel that there was any point in talking about Allie refusing to let him see her.

Once Alex got back home after his lunch with Brendan, the silence around him was deafening. There was nothing to do now but think. How was he going to get around Allie to see Emily? Maybe he could just call the nurse's station for the floor that she was on and ask when the quietest time for Emily's room usually was. He could always use the excuse that he was a friend who just wanted to be able to grieve at her bedside alone.

Alex pulled his phone out of his pocket and called the number for the hospital which he still had saved in his contacts list. He asked the operator for the floor that Emily was on and talked to the nurse. The nurse indicated that no one usually visited Emily's room at night after 10 pm until around 5 in the morning. Alex thanked the nurse for the information and ended the call. Now he had to set up a plan.

Wiling away the rest of the afternoon, Alex tried to watch some television. He had a hard time focusing on what he was watching because he was anxious about getting in and out of the hospital undetected. Somehow, he managed to pass the next several hours without going out of his mind. When it was finally after 10 pm, he got ready to set out and go see Emily.

He got cleaned up, and quickly stopped at a sandwich shop for a small bite to eat on his way to the hospital. Once there, he drove around the parking lot looking for either Allie or her parent's cars. By the time he'd finished a full lap around the lot, he was satisfied that he hadn't seen any recognizable vehicles. So, he parked and made his way back to Emily's room. Sure enough, Emily was alone.

No amount of preparation could really prepare Alex for what he saw. The sight of Emily with her skin and lips pale and lifeless and dark circles under both her eyes made Alex's breath catch in his throat. She looked as if she were already dead and the sudden thought of that caught Alex off guard making his throat seize up and a tear run down his cheek.

Alex walked over to Emily's bed and sat in the chair that was next to it. "Why Emily?" he asked her. When she didn't respond he kept going. "Why did you get into your car that night and drive like that? Maybe I shouldn't have left you the way I did. I'm sorry you were so upset. I'm sorry. What can I do? What can I do to help you wake up? Please wake up."

Still there was no response. All at once, Alex's exhaustion coupled with everything that he felt sitting there seeing Emily like that overwhelmed him and he started to weep openly. He hadn't cried like that since he was a small child and he'd forgotten how it felt. He didn't even cry like that when his parents passed. Oh, he'd felt just as bad as he did now, and maybe he did shed a tear or two. But he didn't cry.

Alex took Emily's hand in his. It didn't feel cold, but it didn't feel warm either. Please don't die, he thought to himself as his tears continued to fall. Alex rubbed the top of her hand with his thumb as he laid his head down on her leg. He stayed that way, continuing to rub circles with his thumb while he closed his eyes, a million memories of the two of them running through his head. As he laid there, time seemed to slip away and soon, his exhaustion got the better of him. He fell asleep still holding her hand.

Even after Allie refused to let Alex see me, I continued to watch him. I watched him all day. I watched as he let out his anger on that punching bag and I watched as he ate lunch with Brendan and talked about Veronica. I was starting to lose hope until Alex called the nurses station on the floor that I was lying on. I felt a wave of relief when she told him when I'd be alone. I watched Alex suffer through the rest of the afternoon as he waited for night to fall. And I watched as he walked into my hospital room.

Then I watched as Alex talked to me. I started crying as I watched him cry. I couldn't help it. I hated to see him that way, no matter what had happened before. I watched as he took my hand and I wished so much that I could feel it. I watched as he fell asleep laying on my leg, his tears streaked and drying on his face.

Alex opened his eyes slowly. He seemed to be laying in the grass. How had he gotten outside? And why had he been sleeping there? He sat up and looked around. It seemed to be that the patch of grass that he had been laying in was very small and there was nothing but sand in front of him as far as the eye could see.

Chapter Ten

I felt so emotionally drained now after witnessing Alex cry. I wanted so badly to be able to talk to him again and there was nothing I could do. I wanted to scream out, punch the wall, something! But I knew it wouldn't do any good. Also, I was a little afraid of what the creature would do if I lashed out that way. So, I took a deep breath, told the creature I needed another break, and went back outside.

My plan was to get out to the bench and let out the loudest scream of my life. There would be no one around to hear it. But as I walked out the door of the school, there seemed to be someone standing out in the distance. Standing out by the bench to be exact. How was that possible, I thought? Curious, I started to make my way over. It was a man for sure. He had his back turned to me and he was looking out at the vast, open horizon. As I got closer, my heart sped up. I knew who it was before he even turned around. It was Alex!

He turned around taking in everything, from the bench to the school, and then finally, me. The look that crossed his face when he saw me was one of total shock and confusion. I was afraid my face didn't look much different. I started running. I ran straight up to him and threw my arms around his neck before he ever had a chance to respond.

"Alex!" I breathed his name as I squeezed him as hard as I could.

He was solid. I could touch him. He could touch me. My brain was trying to work out how he was even here, in my head. Was he really here? Could this be just my imagination going overboard because I had wished to see him so much? But if this really was him, shouldn't my arms go through him or vice versa like a ghost? It was only when he pushed me off of him, that I realized he hadn't been hugging me back.

"Where am I? Are you real? Am I dreaming? What is going on?!" he asked frantically as he started pacing and looking around wildly at everything.

"I was wondering the same thing. I'm real so I guess this must be really happening. You really are here!" I practically screamed with joy. "But how are you here is the question. You didn't get hurt like I did. I just watched you fall asleep..."

At that, Alex stopped suddenly and turned towards me. "Where is here? And what do you mean you just watched me fall asleep?" he eyed me warily.

"Well, here is kind of hard to explain. Here, from what I was told, is my subconscious. I'm trapped here Alex. I'm trapped inside my own head. How I watched you fall asleep is also kind of hard to explain." I said looking as him sheepishly.

"Try." He said. His eyes were boring into mine.

"Okay. Here goes." I said taking a deep breath. "Inside the school there, behind me, is a crystal ball. I can use it kind of like a tv screen. I've been watching you. But not just you!" I hurried on as the look on his face changed to anger. "I've also been watching Allie and Samantha."

Alex crossed his arms in front of his chest. "What all did you see?"

Why was he angry? I didn't deserve that from him. Not now. I had been so happy to see him, and he was acting like this? My anger surged back as if it had never left. Only now, it was directed at Alex as it dawned on me what it was he probably didn't want me to see.

"I didn't see you and your new girlfriend sleeping together if that's what you want to know!"

Alex looked shocked for a moment as he dropped his arms and then crossed them back over his chest. "Good, that's none of your business anyway! Neither is anything else going on in my life!"

"I wasn't watching you because of that. I was watching you because, I was watching Samantha when she called you. I was able to listen to both sides of the conversation and after that, I just had to know what you were going to do..." I said feeling so emotionally overwhelmed and tearful.

Alex didn't seem to understand how I was feeling as he said, "Well I'm glad you don't care about Veronica. Because I moved on. I told you. I was tired of waiting around for you. Now, I'm here in this horrible place! And I just want to get out!" He threw his hands up and looked up at the orange sky.

"Welcome to the club." I responded.

"How did I get here?!" he screamed.

"I really don't know Alex. Like I said, you fell asleep in my hospital room and that's when I got up and came back outside and saw you standing here."

"Great. That's just great. So not only did you watch me after Samantha called me, but you watched me in your hospital room." He said incredulously. "I guess I just have no privacy anymore."

"Look Alex," I sighed, "I didn't mean to invade your private moment of grief, okay? Honestly, I was just relieved you cared enough to have one."

"Well, you did intrude!" He said, cutting me off. "That's not fair. It's not fair that I've had all these feelings built up since I found out about you yesterday and when I really let them spill over, because I thought I was alone, you were watching every second of it. And then, somehow, I end up here immediately after, face to face with you." He started pacing again.

"I don't believe this." He said stopping suddenly and looking back up at me. "I'm dreaming. I have to be. This is crazy!"

Alex went back to pacing as I said, "I'm sorry. I don't know what to do. All I can say is that you're not dreaming. Or really…" A thought started creeping into my head. "Maybe you are. In a sense. You fell asleep. Maybe your subconscious somehow conjoined with mine. Maybe you'll only be here until you wake up."

"God, I hope so." He said as he started pacing at a slower speed. "But until then, I want you to stay over there." He stopped and pointed at the bench. "Stay far away from me. I was never supposed to see you again. I moved on. I won't let you get under my skin again." This he said as if I were some nasty bug on the bottom of his shoe.

This was not the Alex that I knew. I felt overwhelmed with grief of my own now. What if that Alex was gone for good? Was there really anything that I could say now to make the man that loved me come back? It didn't seem likely. Alex was done.

He only came to see me in my hospital room because of how long he'd known me. The history that we had pulled him back for just a temporary moment. But he was done. He thought he had severed that history when he left. But now, I could tell that he really meant to make it permanent. He wasn't happy to see me, even after knowing that my body was lying lifeless in a hospital bed. If it didn't make him happy to see me walking and talking right now in front of him, I knew nothing would.

I could feel my heart shatter all over again. Just like the morning he told me he was leaving. I started walking towards the bench because I really wasn't sure I could stand much longer anyway. There was nothing left to be said.

Suddenly Alex gasped. I turned around to look at him and he was looking down at his hands. His whole body started to fade slowly. "Alex!" I screamed as he disappeared. Where did he go? I ran back into the school and up to the room where the crystal ball and the creature now were. I had to see if he had woken up.

Alex's eyes shot open, and he nearly jumped out of his skin when he felt a hand grasp his shoulder and shake him. He looked around wildly and realized that he was back in Emily's hospital room. Sunlight streamed through the window into the room. It was Saturday morning. It was Emily's father, Bob, who had grasped him on the shoulder. Alex looked quickly at Emily who was still lying there silently with her eyes closed. Had he really just been in her subconscious? He didn't even have a moment to think about it because he was now being barked at by Bob.

"What are you doing here?" Bob asked angrily. "Don't you think you've caused enough trouble?"

"Now Bob," Emily's mother Brenda was saying, "It wasn't really his fault."

"The hell it wasn't!" he yelled at his wife. Then he turned back to Alex. "I don't want to ever see you here again. Do you understand me? I may not be able to see you prosecuted for your role in my daughter's accident, and believe me I would, but I can sure as hell make sure that you can't cause any more harm."

"I...I'm sorry you feel that way." Alex said looking up at Bob's hulking angry figure.

It wasn't that he was afraid to get into a fight with Bob. He just knew this wasn't the best time or place for it. Plus, he wasn't sure at the moment whether he was even planning to come back anyway. He needed to go home and thoroughly dissect what had just happened to him. Without another word, he slipped out of Emily's room, looking quickly at Brenda's stricken face as he left.

Quickly, Alex left the hospital and drove back to his house. It was only once he pulled up in the driveway and shut off his engine that he let the memories of what he experienced flood back into his brain. His hands started shaking on the steering wheel however, so he decided it would best to get inside his house where he wouldn't be bothered by passersby who might see him sitting there and think something might be wrong.

Once inside, Alex collapsed on his back on the couch he'd slept on the night before and started to sort out what he'd experienced. He mentally retraced the dream he'd had from the moment he opened his eyes in that place which was little more than a wasteland to the moment when he felt his body start to tingle all over and he looked down to see himself fading out.

He'd felt so embarrassed that Emily had watched him cry over her like that. He'd yelled at her and acted angry to cover his humiliation. He could admit to himself that that was what he had done. But had he really? He wasn't totally sure that it wasn't just a regular dream after all. And anyway, even if it was real, what did it really matter? It wasn't like he could do anything to help Emily.

What was the point of even thinking about it if it wasn't real? Because if it was real, then he kind of felt bad for the way he had treated her. She had seemed so happy to see him. Well of course she'd be happy to see you Alex, he told himself. She was there all alone and hasn't talked to anyone in a month. Her joy wasn't personal. And if it was, it was only in a friendly kind of way, he reminded himself.

He hated that he had to remind himself of that. He was supposed to be over her. He had a beautiful woman back in Maryland that wanted him and who was waiting for him to come back. Something told him that he should go ahead and stay till Sunday morning like he'd originally planned though. Instead of making plans to see Emily again, he'd just catch up with his other friends while he was here. He was only staying till the next morning in case something happened with Emily. Or at least, that's what he told himself.

Running as quickly as I could to that art room on the second floor, I dashed in, my heart racing, only to find that once again, the creature was not there, and neither was the crystal ball. As quickly as I could, I opened every other door on the second floor and found nothing. Then I ran downstairs, again opening every classroom door. Nothing. Then I went directly into the cafeteria where there was still nothing, followed by the gym. The creature was now sitting on the top row of the bleachers on the left side of the entrance.

"You moved again" I said climbing the bleachers and sounding out of breath.

"You are ready to move on to the next phase of your past" the creature said.

The next past scene that I would watch would more than likely have something to do with the gym although at the moment, I really couldn't imagine what it would be. I told the creature that I wanted to see what was going on inside my hospital room to which the creature obliged. I took a seat on the same top bleacher as the creature sat, with the crystal ball sitting between us.

I watched as Alex had been awoken by my father. At least he woke up safely, I thought. I watched as my father yelled at him. I wanted to scream at my father to stop and was once again left frustrated that I had no control of the situation. I watched as Alex didn't even try to defend his decision to come. Then he just left.

Well of course he did, I thought to myself. Why would he bother to argue with my father when he doesn't care? It's not like he's ever planning to come back to see me again. At that thought, I felt completely defeated. Did I even really want to wake up now? After all that? I knew it was stupid to let myself feel that way because of just one person when I had others who were still hoping and praying for me. But at this moment, it was hard to focus on any of them.

Suddenly, the ground started shaking violently. I was suddenly very afraid of the bleachers collapsing out from underneath me. What was going on? I looked at the creature who just continued to sit there silently as if everything was fine.

Pretty quickly the shaking subsided, and everything suddenly went deathly silent once again. "What was that about?" I asked the creature.

"Current events have caused you to stumble away from your journey. The more you get set back, the more time you will lose to get to its final conclusion and the worse things will get. This world you have created here will eventually be ripped apart, and then you will be no more."

The thought of what the creature was saying terrified me. I couldn't even imagine what it would look like, let alone feel like, to have this world ripped apart while I was still stuck in it. I guess I wasn't quite ready to give up after all. There was nothing I could do except continue to do what I needed to do.

I turned back to the crystal ball, which was black, and looked back in on my hospital room. I was shocked to see that the scene was one of complete chaos. There was a doctor and a nurse crowded over my body which seemed to be spasming violently. I couldn't see exactly what the doctor and nurse were doing, but after a few seconds, my body seemed to relax and the alarms that had been blaring loudly, slowed back down to steady beeps.

I didn't have to wait long to find out what I had just witnessed. The doctor took his gloves off and threw them in the nearby trash can. Then he turned to my parents with a heavy look of worry on his face. The nurse left the room making sure to close the door behind her.

"I'm sorry to tell you this," the doctor said to my parents. "But your daughter just had a small seizure. Usually, with a patient in Emily's situation, a seizure means that they are getting worse instead of better. There's nothing we can really do but wait and see if she continues to have them, and if she does, whether they get stronger and start lasting longer."

"But there's hope that it was just a one-time occurrence, right? I mean you said that her brain function is still good." My mother said now.

"Yes, it is still good. Her brain waves have been starting to slow down, but at a very miniscule rate. Which is why, I'm still recommending that we wait and see what happens. However, it may be to start really getting prepared to have to make that tough decision. I'm really very sorry."

I gasped and threw my hand up to my mouth upon hearing this. No! I was working so hard to wake up. They couldn't pull the plug now. I needed more time!

Chapter Eleven

At work, Allie was having a hard time focusing at work. She wasn't so sure she'd made the right choice telling Alex he couldn't see Emily. But every time she tried to think about it, someone else came up to her to ask her a question about sizes and colors of an item they pulled off one of the racks. The first chance she got, she yelled to her co-worker that she was taking a quick break and ran outside.

Once there, she pulled out her cell phone. Time to find out if Samantha told Alex about Emily after all. She'd been so pissed off when she saw Alex, that she hadn't thought to ask him who he heard about her from. The phone rang a few times before Samantha answered.

"Allie. What's going on?"

Allie decided to cut right to the chase. It's not like she had a lot of time to talk. "Did you tell Alex about Emily after I explicitly asked you not to?"

Silence followed this question for a moment before Samantha sighed and answered, "Yes. I called him and told him what was going on. I know you didn't want me to but honestly, I just thought it was the right thing to do. Why? Did he show up at the hospital?"

"Yes, he showed up! Right as I was leaving to come to work this morning in fact. Had he got there just a minute later I wouldn't have even seen him."

"Well, what happened? Did you say anything to him?"

"Yes, as a matter of fact I did. I told him that I didn't want him to see Emily."

"Allie please think about this. What would it really hurt to let Alex see her? It's not like she would even know he was there."

Just then Allie's call waiting beeped in her ear. She looked at the screen and saw that it was her mother. She asked Samantha to hold on a minute while she flipped over to the other call.

"Hey mom, what's going on?"

"Your sister had a seizure is what's going on! We were right there in the room when it happened. Oh, it was the most horrible thing I've ever seen!"

"What? Is Emily alright?!" Allie asked frantically.

"For now. The doctor was able to make it stop. But it's not looking good. The doctor told us that she may start having them stronger than the one we saw today and on a more regular basis. He told us that it's not a good sign. I think we may lose her. And then to top it off, Alex was here last night, and your father and I caught him sleeping in Emily's room. Bob woke him up and yelled at him and then kicked him out." With that Brenda started crying into the phone.

That rat! Allie was angry now. It looked like she'd actually have to have Alex banned from Emily's room after all. "Alright well, look mom, I'm at work right now. If you want, I can come over afterwards for a little while." She said to her mother.

"Yes. That sounds like a good idea" Brenda managed to squeeze out.

Allie got off the phone with her mother and switched back to Samantha. She told her what her mother had just said. She also told her about her parents catching Alex in Emily's room. But she didn't mention that she was about to call the hospital and make sure it didn't happen again. She wouldn't make the mistake of telling Samantha her plans just so she could tip off Alex. Next, she called the hospital and told the nurses station on Emily's floor that under no circumstances was Alex Coleman allowed inside Emily's hospital room.

Then Allie quickly called Josh and gave him an update. He'd been so attentive these past weeks and had brought her out on a few more dates, never getting disgruntled when she'd space out worrying about Emily. He really seemed to care about her and what was going on with her family. She hadn't realized how much she really needed that until now. With Allie's voicemail left for Josh, she got off the phone and went back to work.

———

Alex decided to drive around town a little as he wasn't ready to go back to his house just yet. As he was driving, his phone started ringing. Thankful for Bluetooth, the caller's name came up on the screen of his radio console. It was Samantha. He didn't feel like talking to her, so he let the call go to voicemail.

A few minutes later though, she was calling again as he passed by the front of the school. He stopped to look at it as if to reassure himself that it looked the way it was supposed to and not like what he saw in that dream. A shudder ran through him as he thought about how dark and decrepit it had appeared. Annoyed that Samantha seemed intent to get ahold of him as this was now her third time calling, he accepted her call.

"Hey Samantha" was all he said.

"Hey, so I heard you're back."

"Yeah. I guess I decided I wouldn't be able to live with myself if something happened to Emily and I didn't at least come see her once. I went by there last night and fell asleep. But I'm guessing you already know that."

"Yeah. Allie just called me pissed off that I told you what was going on."

"We argued in the hallway, and she basically started yelling at me about how I ruined her sister's life. She made me so angry that I actually had a hard time keeping myself in check if you can believe that. I had to remind myself that I'm not that kind of guy. I kept my cool and tried to make her see reason. But it didn't work."

"Well, I'm glad you kept from getting angry back at her because that would have only made the situation worse."

"Right. I have no doubts that she would've used that as an opportunity to have me hauled off to prison or something. Anyway, so I left, and I went back to visit Emily late last night when no one else was there." Alex blew out a breath now. "I guess I just wasn't prepared for how bad she was going to look you know? Then her parents showed up this morning and her dad went crazy on me, and I left. I guess in a way I'm glad I went to see her, but I don't want to deal with that headache again."

"Well, you may want to rethink that" Samantha replied. "Emily had a seizure after you left. Well, I assume it was after you left because you didn't bring it up just now. Apparently, it's a bad sign from what the doctor is saying. He told Emily's parents that they may want to start getting prepared to stop the feeding tube."

At that Alex slammed on his breaks causing the car behind him to yell curses loudly at him and lay on his horn. Alex started moving again just enough to move off the road and park causing the guy behind him to flip him off as he passed.

"Alex? Are you there?" Samantha said as there was nothing but silence. She had heard the sound his truck made when he slammed on his brakes and heard some man yelling.

"Y... Yeah I'm here" Alex replied. "No... I hadn't heard about that. What am I supposed to do Samantha?" he said now clearly starting to sound frustrated. "I can't help her. I wish I could help her. But I can't. There's nothing I can do!"

"You can be here Alex. I know you want to move on but pretty soon that choice may be taken out of your hands anyway. The way I see it, you should be here for now."

With that, Samantha let him go. All was silence as Alex sat in his truck wishing he knew what to do. He wished that he had someone that he trusted enough to talk to about his experience that morning. But he didn't. If Emily were here, she would've been the one he could tell about it. That thought made him feel sad and suddenly very weary. He knew for sure that he no longer wanted to be around other people. Alex slowly pulled back onto the street and drove back to his house.

After what I saw happen to my body in the crystal ball and after listening to what the doctor told my parents, I was frantic. The possibility that I might not make it out of here started suddenly started to feel very real. I turned to the creature and asked him to show me the next scene from the past.

The crystal ball lit up with me and Samantha at our senior prom. We were standing in the gym in our prom dresses which had been transformed into a wonderland of paper Mache, tulle, and twinkle lights. The two of us were laughing at one of the guys we knew who was dancing in a crazy fashion out on the dance floor. Samantha's date walked up handing her a cup of punch. Then he took her hand and brought her out to the dance floor as the loud pop song that had been playing ended and was now transitioning to a nice slow song. My date, Cory Ballast, had been in the restroom and had been gone a little while. But now he also walked up and took me out to the dance floor.

Everything was fine, more than fine as we danced slowly, Cory with his arms around my waist, and me with my arms around his neck. As we turned slowly, I caught Samantha's eye and we grinned at each other, happy that we had both found dates for the prom. Then something happened to make the smile on my face drain away. Cory was moving his hands down to my butt and squeezing while pushing up very tightly against me. I could feel him, semi-hard, poking me. I was totally freaked out by it. I'd never done more than kiss a guy at this point in my life and I wasn't about to do anything more than that. I pushed Cory away from me causing him to stumble a little with a look of confusion on his face.

"What?" he asked loudly, turning his hands outwards at his sides in a questioning way. "Can't a guy get a little action here?"

He was completely serious. He was also drunk. He must've been hiding alcohol on him and downed it in the bathroom, because he hadn't seemed like he'd been drinking at all prior to that. He'd gone from being confident in a positive way by opening the passenger door for me when he picked me up, making reservations for dinner before the dance, and taking the lead when escorting me into the dance, to being confident in a negative way. It was like he was a completely different person.

When he'd asked me to prom, I remember feeling a little wary as he was a football player, and I was nowhere near his usual type. But ultimately, I was happy to be asked and so I took the chance. He'd been a good date up to that point, so I had been completely floored by his actions. Thinking back on it now though, I realized that his positive confidence hadn't been all positive. At the restaurant, he had made a show of ordering for me instead of allowing me to choose what I wanted, citing that it was no good to stick with the same things all the time and that a person had to try new things once in a while.

What a mistake that was, I thought now as I watched myself standing back from him on the dance floor looking completely shocked. "I hate to break it you," I had told Cory, "But I'm not that kind of girl."

Some people had stopped dancing and had started to pay attention to what was going on. Cory, realizing he had an audience, had decided to keep talking. The slow song was still playing, allowing for more people to hear him. He raised his arms in a defensive pose. "You're just a little tease!" he practically yelled, slightly slurring his words and looking at me with a look of disgust on his face.

I could see now how red my face had started to turn standing there in that moment. My fists had started to ball up unconsciously as well. I remembered that I had been thinking that I was so embarrassed that people were watching this and that I didn't know how to respond. A feeling of panic had started to envelop me. Cory then spat in my direction and turned and stalked off out of the gym, pushing people out of the way as he went.

All the while, the slow song had never stopped playing and was now transitioning into a more upbeat rap song. People started turning back to their dates then and dancing as if the drama they had just witnessed were already forgotten. Samantha ran up to me now, throwing her arms around my neck and rubbing her palm down my back. "It's alright" she'd said in my ear. "It's going to be alright."

What she didn't realize was that her saying that was making my embarrassment start to transition to something I didn't altogether recognize. I had been trying very hard not to cry in front of all those people. The next thing I knew, Alex was walking up to me, all spiffed up in a black tuxedo, asking what had happened because he could tell I was upset. He had just walked in with his own date and had missed the whole incident.

Samantha filled him in but also made sure to add that everything was fine now. Alex squared his jaw and looked like he was ready to kill someone. Both Samantha and Alex's date tried to calm him down and told him that Cory wasn't worth it. But Alex was seeing red and wasn't hearing anything anyone was saying. He walked quickly outside with his date half running behind him trying to catch up.

Me and Samantha had followed behind as well allowing the scene in the crystal ball to follow so that I could continue watching what had happened next. Cory was halfway across the parking lot when Alex yelled his name, causing Cory to turn around and start heading back our way. I remembered my heart jumping into my throat as Alex and Cory strode toward each other.

Once they were right up on each other, Cory didn't even hesitate. He threw a punch at Alex. Alex was able to duck out of the way pretty easily seeing as Cory was drunk. Then he threw his own punch, landing his fist squarely in Cory's eye socket, giving him a black eye.

Cory stumbled backward holding a hand over his eye and yelled, "Of course it's Alex to the rescue, isn't it? Figures." He said to Alex in a nasty tone.

"Just get out of here and sleep it off!" Alex yelled back at Cory as Cory turned and stumbled back across the parking lot.

"You better watch your back!" Cory yelled as he turned his head around for a moment in Alex's direction. "This isn't over!"

Once he was out of earshot, Alex's date, turned towards him putting her hands on her hips. She started yelling at him about how he'd ruined her night. Then she ripped her corsage off her wrist and threw it on the ground. She pulled out her cell phone and called one of her friends who presumably didn't make it to the prom to come pick her up. Then she stormed off to the entrance to the parking lot to wait.

Alex sighed and threw his hands up a little, letting them fall and make a slapping noise against his thighs. "Well," he said now and sighed, "the best laid plans." Then he turned to me, Samantha, and Samantha's date, and said, "No reason to ruin the rest of the night. Let's go back in I guess."

"Are you sure you don't want to try to go after your date?" I asked Alex as Samantha and her date headed back inside.

"No. I don't think there's any salvaging that. If it's alright with you, we can just dance with each other." He said this so nonchalantly that even now, watching this scene as an adult, if I hadn't known any better, I wouldn't have known that this was what he had wanted all along.

But I did know. And so did Samantha. I realized now that this was why she had no problem walking back into the prom with her date leaving me alone with Alex outside. Now I understood why Alex did not seem to care about making amends with his own date. And of course, I'd ruined his hopes once again by telling him that I just felt like going home after everything that had just happened.

Watching now, I saw his face fall as he said, "Oh. Okay I understand. I can bring you home. That's no problem."

And so, I let him drive me home. I watched the scene as I followed him to the first car he'd ever had, an old Honda. I got in and called Samantha's cell from Alex's cell because I didn't have one of my own. I let her know that I had left so she wouldn't be looking for me. The mile or so back to my house was filled with nothing but silence after that from both me and Alex. I'd been reeling over what had happened and Alex apparently had been feeling wounded that I'd rather go home than stay at the prom with him. Watching this scene now, I actually felt bad for Alex and the choice that I'd made that night.

———

Alex spent the rest of the afternoon trying to tell himself that he had done what he had come back to do, and that the rest was out of his hands. But it wasn't working. Finally, that evening, he resigned himself to the fact that he couldn't just leave things the way they were. He had to know if what had happened to him last night in Emily's hospital room had been just a dream. And if it was real, he didn't want the last conversation he ever had with her to be in anger.

That meant he would have to go back and re-create the conditions under which he'd had the experience. The plan was to go back to Emily's room, set an alarm for around 4 am, and fall asleep in the exact same way that he had the night before. If a nurse came in during that time and woke him up thinking that he'd accidentally fallen asleep, he couldn't control for that. But otherwise, he wanted to make sure that he was out of there before Allie or Emily's parents showed up in the morning to check on her. Then he'd go home, get a few more hours of sleep, and head back to Maryland with an answer one way or another.

But first, he decided to go ahead and call Veronica. He hadn't talked to her since before he left that voicemail on her phone saying that he was leaving town. He realized for the first time that she hadn't tried to call him back either. He wondered if that was a bad sign. Well, no time like the present to find out.

Veronica answered her phone pretty quickly; after only one and a half rings. "Hello?" she said in a quick, terse tone.

"Hey it's me. Listen, I'm sorry I had to leave town so quickly Thursday afternoon without getting a chance to do more than leave you a voicemail. I got a call that a friend back home had been involved in a really bad accident and may not make it." Alex decided it might be better under the circumstances not to tell Veronica that his friend was a female.

The tone of Veronica's voice changed as she said, "Oh wow, no I totally understand. I'm so sorry to hear that."

"Yeah, and unfortunately it is as bad as I was told. My friend is in a coma and the doctors don't know if they'll wake up. But I mean, there isn't really anything I can do to help so I'll be leaving here tomorrow morning to come back. I should be back later in the afternoon sometime if you want me to come by."

"Yeah, actually I'll be working tomorrow night. But I'll be up by the time you get back if you want to stop by. You can come by and tell me all about it and I can be there to make you feel better."

"Sounds good." Alex said. "Thanks for understanding. I'll see you tomorrow."

Once he was off the phone, Alex realized that he still had about 4 hours to wait before he could head out to the hospital. So, he decided to test his dream theory even further by going ahead and taking a nap. He set an alarm to make sure he didn't sleep more than an hour and drifted off quickly. Unfortunately, he woke to the sound of his alarm feeling disappointed because he had not dreamt about Emily or that place that he had seen her.

Alex got himself ready later that evening and headed back to the hospital. This time, as soon as he started walking past the nurse's station, he was stopped by the nurse who was sitting there. She asked him who he was there to see. When he told her he was there for Emily, the nurse asked him for his I.D. Alex handed it over, curious, but not otherwise alarmed. Then the nurse handed it back to him and told him that she was sorry, but he had been banned by Emily's family from visiting her again.

Chapter Twelve

Alex was stunned. Banned? Really? It was Allie. No doubt about it. It had to have been Allie. Didn't she say she would do that? Her parents must have told her about finding him there. Anger welled up inside him. What was he supposed to do now? He took a deep breath. It wasn't the nurse's fault. Better not to take it out on her, he thought.

"Thanks anyway" he said to the nurse who was looking at him with an apologetic look. He turned and walked away.

After everything that had happened including watching Alex's tearful moment in my hospital room, his somehow showing up here in ,y head and being angry with me, my finding out that my family might be starting to think about letting me go, and my visual re-visiting of my prom, I felt absolutely exhausted. I wanted so badly just to take a break now and go lie down on the bench outside. At the same time though, I was afraid to waste more time trying to get through everything that I needed to see in order to fix my problem.

I was feeling so incredibly overwhelmed because I still wasn't sure exactly where I had deviated from the correct path. The most obvious answer was that I deviated when I got into my car that night and got into that accident. But the obvious answer could not be the correct one. If it were, my acknowledgement of it would be all that was needed for me to wake up. But I was still here. If I took that thought and went with what had caused me to decide to jump in my car that night, it would be that I had been hurting so badly over Alex's leaving.

But Alex made the choice to leave. According to him, he was making the choice based off my choice. Which meant that my choice had indirectly led to me getting into my car that night. Bing bang boom. There was only one problem with that thought though. It would mean that I diverged off the correct path when I turned down Alex's declaration of love.

Surely that couldn't be it. I still didn't feel as though I could ever be in love with Alex the way he was with me. Sure, after watching how he cared for me over the years and got his heart broken over and over again, I felt a lot more empathy for what he went through, but that wasn't the same thing as feeling romantic love for him.

Could there have been an event not related to my relationship with Alex that made it to where I was destined to get into some accident on that night anyway? I mean, it didn't necessarily even have to be that I got into my car that night that caused me to be here in this situation. It could be that some event at some past point in time made it so that on that date and time, whatever I happened to be doing at that moment, would have ended in me getting hurt and being in a coma. Just thinking about all this made my head spin.

There was only one thing that I could say that I knew for sure. That I would not be able to even take a guess or make any kind of real determination at this point. I sighed loudly at this thought. I leaned forward, placing my elbows on the desk in front of me and rubbing my eyes.

Now that I'd finished watching the events of my prom night, I felt even more like I'd been a complete failure of a friend to Alex for all these years. But even if I had known back then how he felt, what could I have done? The only thing I really could have done is to break off our friendship back when we were still kids.

Maybe that would have been for the best. Maybe if we'd stopped being friends, he wouldn't have stayed hung up on me all this time. Maybe it was our friendship that allowed him to hang onto the hope that we would be more one day. But I hadn't known. So why did I feel so bad? Because I should have known. It was right there in front of me. I was just too self-absorbed to see it.

I couldn't go back and change the past, but at least now he really could move on. I didn't expect to ever see him again. Unless I watched him through the crystal ball. But was there even a point? No, there really wasn't. He was too angry with me when he left. I wouldn't even have been surprised if he was already all the way back up in Maryland.

I thought about when the last time I took a sleep break was. It was before Alex even found out what had happened to me. No wonder I felt so tired. I really needed a break I decided. To hell with trying to get through everything I needed to see for now. I was feeling reckless after this latest emotional upset. So, I went back outside and went back to sleep.

Driving back to Maryland Sunday morning, Alex tried to tell himself that he had done everything that he could do. He had to go back to work. He had no choice. He couldn't lose his new job when he'd only just started. The further away he got from Emily, the more anxious he became. He found himself with little patience, going around the types of drivers on the road who he normally had no problem staying comfortably behind.

How could Allie really ban him from Emily's hospital room. The thought made him so angry that for the first time in his life, he contemplated violence. No matter how hard he tried, he just couldn't seem to rid himself with the overwhelming desire to knock some sense into her. Too bad he was raised right and would never be able to carry out anything like that, he thought.

Allie had always made spur of the moment decisions that were based more on her emotions than on any logical thought process. If she weren't Emily's sister, she wouldn't be someone that Alex could ever see himself even talking to let alone being any kind of friends with. He was always nice to her for Emily's sake while on the inside he wished she'd just grow up and take responsibility for herself.

By the time he made it back to Maryland, Alex was so wound up that he didn't know what to do with himself. He'd never be able to explain it to Veronica though. He went upstairs to his apartment, quickly changed his clothes, and decided to run a few miles. He played music privately through his earbuds that reflected the angry mood he was in. He wanted to drown out his thoughts about the situation.

Once he made it back to his apartment he was physically spent, and this made it possible to drown his anger for now because he was too tired to feel it. He went upstairs and took a nice long shower. Shortly after dressing in some soft and comfortable clean cotton sweats, he heard a knock at his door. He went to let Veronica in.

She smiled when he answered the door. She was dressed in her work attire looking as hot as ever. If he hadn't been so tired, he might've wanted to give her a little present to celebrate being back. There was plenty of time for that another day though, he thought.

"Aw look at you, you're back. I'm so sorry about your friend. How are you feeling?" Veronica asked as she walked through the door.

"I've been better" Alex readily admitted.

"How is your friend?"

"Unfortunately, it doesn't look good. I honestly wish I could have stayed a little longer because I'm not sure how much longer my friend will hang on to life. But I had to come back. I can only hold onto hope that my friend will wake up, but they may not. If they end up passing, I don't want to miss the funeral." Alex thought about everything he'd just said and felt a wave of sadness wash over him. "Have I mentioned that I'm glad I have you to come back to?" he said, realizing that Veronica had been silent about his feelings on the situation.

"Well, I'm happy to be here for you to come back to" she replied. "Is there anything I can do for you right now?"

"Specifically? No. In fact, I'd really rather not talk about it anymore tonight."

"Want to just find something on television to numb our minds with and cuddle on the couch?"

"That sounds perfect. Pick anything you want. I'm up for watching anything right now." Alex followed Veronica to the couch and sat down next to her. It was going to be a long week.

Alex spent, the next few days constantly finding himself thinking about Emily. He focused on keeping it together at work, but at home, it seemed that it just wasn't possible. He was distracted by thoughts of worry and wondering. It was obvious to Alex that Veronica could see that he wasn't fully there with her. But she seemed to be keeping her thoughts on the matter to herself for now.

She must think that I'm just going through grief over "my friend", he thought. He hoped that's what she was thinking anyway. The less details she knows about the situation, the better he thought. He didn't want to scare her away by having her think that he was still hung up over another woman. But he wasn't hung up over Emily, he thought. He just didn't want her to die. Especially if there was anything he could've done to prevent it.

By Thursday, he just couldn't handle his anxiousness anymore. What was he going to do with his weekend? Was he going to try to go back to South Carolina after work Friday? If he did, he'd get in really late, he thought. So late that maybe he could find a way into Emily's room. He'd certainly be tired enough to go to sleep by then. But if he was really going to try and pull it off, he was going to need help.

As soon as he was off work, he called Samantha. "Hey Samantha" he said when she answered the phone. "So, I'm back in Maryland. Do you have a few minutes to talk?"

"I figured you were when I hadn't heard anything from you or Allie" she responded. "Yeah, I have a few minutes. I'm just taking a break from doing laundry before I start cooking dinner."

"How *is* James by the way? And Tyler?"

"James is doing just fine. Nothing much to tell on that front. He's still at work right now but will be home in about an hour. Tyler is currently finishing up his nap. So, what's up?"

Alex didn't even know where to start, so he just plunged right in from the beginning. He told Samantha everything from what he experienced when he visited Emily and fell asleep to being banned from Emily's room when he tried to go back. When he was done, silence followed from Samantha's end.

"You think I'm crazy, don't you?" he asked.

"Honestly, that is a fantastical story, and I really don't know what to think" Samantha responded.

"I swear I'm not making it up."

"I never said I thought you were. I have no doubt that you really experienced what you say you did. I guess I'm just wondering, could it have been a dream? Could it have been brought on by intense feelings of wanting to talk to her again or of wanting her to be okay?"

"See, that's what I need to find out. That's why I tried to go back again. But I couldn't even get in the room to try. I have spent all week trying to let this go and I just can't. I don't know what to do."

"I think you need to get back in that room and try again. At least then you can resolve this one way or another."

"I agree. But to do that, I need some sort of a plan. I can't just walk back in there and Allie will never change her mind. Believe me, I tried to reason with her. It did me no good. She didn't even let me know she had banned me from Emily's room. I'm sure she took great pleasure in finding out from the night nurse that she'd sent me away."

"You're right. I tried to talk to her about letting you visit Emily, but she just wouldn't hear it. She didn't tell me that she had decided to ban you either. She just told me about her parents finding you in Emily's room. And I haven't talked to her since then."

"I need your help, Samantha."

"I'm not sure what help I can be but if you've got any kind of idea, please lay it on me."

"Well, I was thinking. Maybe you could, if you have time that is, maybe you could meet me at the hospital tomorrow night. I won't be able to get there till around 11 because I'd be driving straight from work tomorrow afternoon."

"That's kind of late. But for this kind of situation, I guess I could swing it. I can get James to take care of Tyler if he wakes up for any reason and I'm not there. What would you want me to do though once I meet you?"

"Well, I was thinking we could meet up in the parking lot. I'm not banned from the whole hospital. Just Emily's room. I thought maybe you could go into Emily's room, you know under the pretense that you're just there to visit, and you could watch out for when the nurse leaves her station, I don't know, to go to the restroom or something. Then you could just call me where I'll be waiting out of sight but pretty close by and I'll sneak in."

"But if the nurse comes in to check on Emily while you're sleeping, you'll be caught, and I won't be able to help you."

"Well in that case, maybe you could just pretend we're together and that I'm your husband or something. Then we'll just say that we weren't aware IDs were being checked for male visitors and that I don't have mine on me. We can make up a different name for me and everything."

"Seriously Alex? That is crazy. But I don't see why it wouldn't work. Maybe I can find out from the nurse if they have set times to check on the patients. That way we can ensure you have the most time possible to visit Emily. It also would allow me to wake you up before the nurse walks in. It would look kind of weird for my husband to be asleep laying on Emily and holding her hand."

"You're right. I didn't even think about that. Thank you in advance for all your help."

"You're completely welcome. Heck, I'm honestly just kind of excited about pulling off something like this. It almost makes me feel like we're all back in high school. You know, sneaking around and pulling pranks. Those were good days."

———————

I woke up feeling a lot better. I must be still alive I thought as I sat up and stretched my arms. I noticed as I sat up on the bench, now there was a road in front of it extending to my right. It started in front of the bench and extended up over a small hill which I couldn't see past. There was nothing else along the road at all as far as houses or businesses or anything, at least not before it got to that small hill.

Just to be sure I was supposed to follow this road, I decided to go back into the gym first. What the heck, I thought as I turned towards the school. The rather large parking lot that expanded out to the right from behind the gym was now visible as well. Why were these things appearing, I wondered as I walked towards it? I took a tentative step onto the cement surface and sure enough, it was solid. I walked out to the center of the lot and looked around. It didn't seem that anything else had changed since I went to sleep. But this was a pretty big change. I stood there for another minute in awe before going into the school.

Sure enough, the creature was gone again when I got into the gym. I guess it's time for me to start walking, I thought. It was as I was about to make my way back out of the gym that I heard something. It sounded like footsteps. I could hear them in the empty hallway leading up to the gym doors. Was I so tired that I was now imagining things? I listened intently for a moment to the sound. The footsteps seemed to be getting closer.

Suddenly the sound stopped as the double doors to the gym burst open. Alex stood there on the threshold looking around in the dark. Then his eyes roamed up to where I was standing on the top of the bleachers.

Chapter Thirteen

I started to take a step down the bleachers as Alex came walking into the room. He gestured for me to sit down as he started to climb the bleachers, keeping his eyes on me the whole time. When he got to the top, he quietly took a seat next to me. Then he leaned forward, and, putting his elbows on his knees, he rested his head in his hands, looking out over the gym.

"So," he said now. "I guess it really is real."

"Yeah" was all I said. I didn't know what else *to* say. Him being back here was not something had I expected at all. I realized I felt anxious and nervous about how this was going to go.

Alex took a deep breath now and let it out. He sat up and ran his hand through his hair. "I heard about your seizure" he said.

I waited for him to say more. When he didn't, I figured he must be waiting for a confirmation that I knew what was going on in the outside world regarding my health. "It was like an earthquake in here" I said. "When it happened, I didn't know what was going on." With reluctance I added, "I looked in on my hospital room and saw myself having the seizure. The chaos of the doctor and nurses getting it to stop was a little bit traumatizing to say the least."

"That must've been terrifying."

"Yeah…it was."

"So, then you also know about what the doctor told your parents about it." Alex said this as a statement still looking out over the gym.

"Yeah" I said letting the silence fill the room once again.

After a moment, Alex sighed and said, "I don't know how I'm supposed to feel."

"I wish I could give you the answer" I said turning towards him now. "But I can't."

"It's not fair. I tried to get away. I tried to get away from you. And I just keep being dragged back in. I didn't want to *want* to find out if this was real or just a dream. But it's like, I feel like something is pulling at me beyond my control and I just had to come back. I couldn't help it. I don't know what I'm supposed to do…"

"I'm sorry for that. I didn't want to hurt you. I wish I could take away your pain. I hate that you're having to feel so torn" I said in response. "You've always taken care of me and taken up for me and for that I will always be grateful. But Alex, you can't fix my problem this time. This is something that I have to figure out on my own."

"What do you mean you have to figure it out on your own? Figure what out?" he said as he swiveled in his seat towards me now.

"Oh. Well, I guess I didn't really get to tell you about that part before. Remember the crystal ball I told you about? Well, it's not just to look in on what's going on with everyone in the current time. It's also to look back on past events in my life."

"Like?" Alex prodded.

"Like the day we met in the third grade. And some of the time we spent under that tree behind the school. And the time on the bench outside when I told you about my family. The time when Robbie Monroe asked me to homecoming and then dumped me two days after the dance. And most recently, my bad prom experience."

Alex sat silently for a few moments as if trying to mentally go through all of the events I had just listed. Finally, he asked, "Are you choosing those past events yourself?"

"No, they're being chosen for me."

"By whom?"

"By this creature that I guess is a manifestation of my imagination. It chooses what I see from my past."

"There's a creature?"

"Yes. And Alex, don't freak out or take this as a sign or anything, but the creature? It looks like the grim reaper."

Alex's eyes widened in alarm. "How am I not supposed to be freaked out over that Emily?"

"I told you. It's just a manifestation of my imagination. It doesn't necessarily mean anything. It just waits for me with its crystal ball to show me things."

"Why?"

"Why what?"

"Why do you need to look back on the past?"

"Basically, it told me that I had been following the correct path for my life, but that at some point, I deviated from that path, and it resulted in me getting into the accident. I was told that if I can figure out where I went off my path, and can acknowledge that I made a wrong choice, I would wake up."

"So, if you don't figure out where you went off your correct path..." Alex trailed off letting his thoughts finish the sentence for him.

"Yes. So, you see, that's why I have to figure it out. And that's why you can't help me this time."

"Where is this creature now?"

"I don't know. It moves around from time to time making me have to find it again. It's probably down that road somewhere that appeared just before you showed up."

"Yeah, that's another thing. What's up with that road?"

"Well see it's kind of like the creature chooses to be in places where the next scene from my past that I will watch was at. For instance, the creature was last here in the gym and I watched what happened at our prom. Then I went to sleep for a little while and when I woke up, now there's the parking lot by the gym and this road. I think the next scene that I'm going to watch won't be something that happened at the school, so the road appeared to take me to the next place."

Alex sat silently for a moment. Then he asked, "Are you scared?"

"Yes, I'm terrified. But fear isn't going to get me anywhere. I have to try and put that aside and not let it swallow me whole."

"You were always the most even-tempered person I know."

"Apparently except when it comes to you" I said.

"Yeah, I shouldn't have gone off on you like that before. I just didn't like that you witnessed probably the most vulnerable moment of my life. I felt violated. I still do, a little. It makes me feel like I can't do anything without wondering if you're watching."

"I get that. For what it's worth, I haven't watched you except for right after you disappeared before. And I only did that because I wanted to make sure that you woke up alright."

"Well, thanks, I guess."

"I feel like I have to tell you something."

"What's that?" he asked.

"It's just, in nearly every past event that I've watched, you were always there. And I don't just mean just physically. I mean, every time I watched something bad happen to me, like with Robbie, and with Cory at prom, you were there for me emotionally."

"Well, that's what friends are for" Alex replied.

"Yes, but it was more than that. I don't want to dig up old wounds, but I watched the time when I told you that Robbie had asked me to homecoming. I saw the pain on your face that I hadn't noticed in that moment when it actually happened."

Alex seemed to be trying very hard to keep a look of composure on his face. He was putting a wall up I could see now as he grew tense. I didn't want to upset him or make him angry again, but I felt like I had to get this off my chest. I mentally crossed my fingers and hoped for the best.

"It was the same on prom night, after Cory left. You asked me if I wanted to go back in to the prom with you and I told you that I just wanted to go home. I saw that same pain in your eyes. I just want to tell you, that I'm sorry. I'm sorry you felt that way all that time. I hated seeing that pain and knowing that I am the one that caused it." I saw something flicker over Alex's face for just a moment then. But just as quickly as I'd seen it, it was gone.

"It is what it is" he replied. "I couldn't make you feel things that you didn't, no matter how hard I wished I could. I'm starting to come to terms with that now."

"Like I said. I've been seeing certain events in my life through a fresh perspective. I really was just completely blind to everything you felt for me. It's made me start to rethink some things... maybe... but I'm not completely sure just yet about anything. I need more time."

"Well, I hope for the sake of your life anyway, that you figure it all out. I really do. But I can't sit around and wait for you any longer Emily. That's why I had to move on. I've got a new girlfriend now who really is great. I'm going to have to go back to my life tomorrow you know. I can't afford to mess it up."

I knew what Alex was saying was true. But even still, it hurt me to hear it. It was like reliving that day he told me he was leaving all over again. I didn't know why it hurt so much or what I expected from him really. But he was right. I couldn't keep him here waiting for me. It wasn't right.

"I understand" was all I managed to say.

Alex leaned forward and wrapped his arms around me then, giving me what I knew could possibly be the last embrace we would ever have.

"Can I ask you a question?" I asked as we released our hold on each other.

"I guess," Alex said.

"I just want to know what day it is. How long has it been since you came here the first time?"

"Don't you know?" Alex asked looking surprised.

"No, I don't. See, I have to sleep too while I'm in here. I just woke up in fact, before you showed up. I've only slept three times so far. But each time I do, it's for days at a time. I wish I didn't have to sleep because it takes away time that I could be getting closer to waking up. But I guess I don't have any choice. I get too drained if I don't."

Alex looked a little disturbed by this. "It's been a week since I was here before. It was Friday night when I came and now it's Friday night again. I actually went all the way to Maryland and came back just to find out if what I'd experienced was real. Looks like I got my answer."

"Looks like you did." I replied. I couldn't think of anything else to say.

"But the question is, why? Why have I been able to come here like this and experience where you are? And why does it only work when I sleep in your hospital room?"

"I don't really know. It could be that anyone could do it if they fall asleep there. But I guess no one else has tried."

"Well, the only person I've told about it is Samantha."

"Then maybe Samantha could give it a try."

"Maybe." Alex looked at his wristwatch. "And it looks like it's almost time for the alarm I set to go off. I'm sorry we didn't have more time, Emily. But I have to go." Then just like that, as I watched, Alex started fading away again to nothing.

Alex woke up to the darkness around him and turned off his alarm. Although Samantha was there watching for the nurse through the little window on the door, he had set the alarm just in case she had fallen asleep as well. He stared hard for a few moments at Emily who looked as if she were only sleeping. Then he leaned forward, laid a kiss on her cheek. Just as he was walking towards the door where Samantha was standing, now watching him, there was a small knock on the door followed by the door handle being turned.

They both jumped at the sound of the knock and Samantha quickly walked to Alex's side and grabbed his hand. The nurse on duty came in and at the sight of them, a look of confusion crossed her face. "I'm sorry but I thought you were alone visiting this patient" the nurse said to Samantha.

She was a young nurse. Not the same one who had told Alex that he was banned the week before, Alex observed. It was a good thing because otherwise his cover would have been blown before they even had a chance to use their made-up story.

"Well, I was" Samantha replied, "But my husband here showed up to be with me."

"I didn't see him walk by the nurse's station on his way to this room." The nurse continued.

"Well, I did walk by it" Alex said now. "There was no one there though."

"Oh, I must've been checking on another patient" The nurse said. "It's just that, for this particular patient, there is a man that is banned from her room. We were instructed to check any man's ID that comes to visit her."

"Oh well I'm sorry. We didn't know about that." Samantha said.

"Yeah, so I'll need to check his ID now" the nurse said looking at Alex.

Alex patted his pockets and looked back at the nurse with an apologetic smile. "I'm sorry but I don't have it on me. I must've accidentally left it at home" he said as looked over at Samantha with a sheepish look on his face.

"He's always losing things" Samantha said now, rolling her eyes. "He'd lose his head if it wasn't attached to his body."

"Oh okay" the young nurse said looking unsure. "Well, I guess I can overlook it this time. But if you could just give me your name, I'll write it down at the desk. Just in case anyone asks."

"His name is James. James Gables" Samantha said smiling at Alex. "We'll just be going now and getting out of your hair. Have a good night."

With that, they walked out of the room, trying not to move so quickly as to look suspicious, but at the same time, wanting to get out of there before the nurse could ask any more questions. Once they got to the parking lot, they both let out the breath they hadn't realized they'd been holding and laughed.

"That was kind of fun" Samantha said.

"Yeah well, I hate that I had to drag you into it that way. Thanks again Samantha."

"Oh, it's no problem. But now that we're out of there, tell me what happened. Did it work?"

As they climbed into Samantha's SUV to keep from being seen standing in the parking lot, Alex told her all about it. He told her everything Emily had said about why she was stuck and what she had to do to wake up. He told her about the creature, at which point, Samantha's eyes widened appropriately. She was glued to his every word.

Finally, Alex told her about the idea that maybe it wasn't just Alex that could visit Emily where she was at inside her subconscious. Samantha suggested that although she'd love to try, it might be better if he tried to talk to Allie again and get her to do it. That way, she could talk to Emily and hear straight from her that she didn't want Alex to be banned from visiting her.

"But what if it doesn't work for Allie?"

"Well why wouldn't it? I think that's a risk you may have to take. But if I think of something else, I'll let you know." Then Samantha told Alex goodbye as he climbed out of her SUV and into his truck.

Making his way back to his house, Alex thought over everything that he had experienced. It was a lot to process to say the least. He knew he should feel better knowing that he'd made peace with Emily as best he could, but he didn't. That same pull that brought him back to this place to begin with was still there. It made him feel anxious about the thought of leaving again.

A few hours went by with Alex laying on his couch staring at his ceiling, trying to understand why he was having these nagging feelings. He just couldn't seem to put his finger on it. Finally, Alex dozed off to sleep. He had put his phone on silent before even getting into Emily's room earlier the night before so that if anyone called, only the alarm that he had set would go off. He'd forgotten to turn the ringer back on once he had left the hospital.

It was 5 am on Saturday morning. Allie made her way up to Emily's floor with a fresh flower arrangement. She had been replacing the one in her room each week. She had been getting up early every day, much earlier than she was used to. She did this in order to visit Emily before having to go to work or in the case of the weekends, in order to visit Emily before spending time with Josh.

As she walked up to the nurse's station, the young nurse, Jennifer, who worked nights every other weekend smiled back at her. "Good morning, Allie. How are you doing?"

"Just fine thanks. It's time to replace my sister's flowers again" Allie said holding up the arrangement so that Jennifer could see.

"Oh, that's pretty" Jennifer said with delight.

"So, Jennifer, did anyone come to visit Emily since yesterday morning when I was here last?" Allie had taken to asking the nurse on duty each time she visited just to be sure Alex had not shown back up.

"Your parents were here for a little bit. They came before I clocked on and left shortly after I got here. Then around 11 last night, Samantha Gables showed up to visit her as well."

"Well, that's odd that she would come so late."

"I don't know anything about that, but I will say that her husband showed up at some point while I was checking on another patient. I didn't know he was here until I went to check on Emily. He was there with her in the room. I asked for his ID, but he didn't have it on him. Samantha said that they weren't aware of anyone's ID's needing to be checked."

"That is true. I didn't tell Samantha about that. But just out of curiosity, can you describe to me what her husband looked like?"

As Jennifer rattled off the details about the man's looks, Allie knew it wasn't James. James had dark, almost black hair, and brown eyes. He was about as opposite to Alex in the looks department as any two men could get. The way the nurse described the man, she knew it was Alex.

Seething on the inside, but keeping her emotions in check, she told Jennifer that Samantha's husband didn't look anything like what she had described and that it sounded like the man who was there was actually Alex. Jennifer went pale and wide eyed in fear. Seeing this, Allie assured her that she wouldn't complain about the mistake this time, but she could not promise the same if it happened again.

With that, Allie walked away, into Emily's room to replace the flowers. Once in the silence of the hospital room, she pulled her phone out of her pocket and made a call to Alex's phone. He didn't answer. He wouldn't, the coward. That was the thought that went through her head as the call went to voicemail.

At the sound of the beep, she said, "It's Allie. I know you were in Emily's room last night. Hear me when I say that it will *not* happen again. If I have to move into that room and watch it myself, you will not get in there again. That is a promise!" With that, Allie ended the call and started pacing the floor to calm down.

Chapter Fourteen

By the time Alex woke up it was after one in the afternoon. As he sat up on his couch, he picked up his phone and checked the screen. It showed that he had a missed call from Allie and a voicemail. Curious, he unlocked his phone and listened to it. Wow, he thought. His brows knitted together in anger. Was she serious with this message? He jumped up off the couch and started pacing around. It was a good thing she wasn't here right now, he thought. He wasn't sure he'd be able to restrain himself. That thought scared him a little as he took a few deep breaths to calm down.

Next, he called Samantha who was busy cleaning up Tyler who had just finished his lunch. He closed his eyes, gritted his teeth, and calmly told her about the voicemail Allie had left him. She told Alex that she would call Allie and try to talk to her. Meanwhile, she also told Alex that he should come to her house because James was at work, and she had no one else to watch Tyler, and she wanted to talk to him in person.

Allie was back home now, cleaning up her apartment. She had a lot of angry energy at Alex for managing to slip under the radar. She was making headway with scrubbing her kitchen countertops and cabinets and she found it ironic that this is what it took for her apartment to get cleaner than it had ever been before. Then her phone began to ring. It was Samantha. She must know that she's caught in helping Alex last night, Allie thought.

"Hello!" Allie practically yelled into the phone in an agitated manner.

"Allie, it's Samantha, we need to talk."

"Oh? Talk about what? Talk about how you helped the enemy sneak into Emily's hospital room?"

"Alex is not the enemy here, okay? He was wrong for leaving Emily the way he did. He has readily admitted that to you. But you want to talk about right and wrong? Alex cares deeply about Emily and you know that. He should not be banned from seeing her."

"You know what? I don't want to talk about this anymore. Ever. I'm hanging up now."

"Wait!"

"Why should I?"

"What's going to happen if Emily wakes up and finds out you banned Alex from seeing her? Did you ever think about that? I think you and I both know she would be pretty angry at you." Samantha paused while Allie sat silent on the other end. "Now that I've got your attention, Alex is on his way here to my house. I think you need to listen to what he has to say."

"I don't have anything to say to him."

"Oh, I think after the way you banned him without telling either of us, you do. You both need to talk."

Allie sighed loudly. "Fine. I'll be there. But I'm not promising anything." Allie hung up the phone, put away her cleaning supplies, grabbed her keys, and headed out the door.

Alex parked on the curb in front Samantha's house and made his way up to the door. He rang the doorbell which was opened by Tyler. "Awex!" Tyler yelled in his little kid excited voice as he smiled up at him and moved out of the way so that Alex could enter.

"How are you doing kiddo?" Alex asked ruffling Tyler's white, blonde hair.

Alex made his way through Samantha's house looking for her. She was in her laundry room, moving clothes from the washer to the dryer.

"Hey Alex" Samantha said without even turning around.

"Hey" Alex responded as Samantha closed the dryer and turned it on. "You always let Tyler answer the door alone like that?"

She turned around then and looked up at him. "No but I knew you were coming, and I'm swamped here so... here's the thing. I called Allie and she's on her way over."

"What? No. I don't want to deal with her right now. I'm not sure I'll be able to hold back my anger."

"Oh, you'll be able to hold back in front of my son. Besides, I'll be right here. You should know that the reason I was able to get her to come is because I told her that if Emily were to wake up and find out that you were banned from seeing her, she would not be happy about it. I think she really thought about that when I said it. I also think, you need to tell her about your experiences visiting Emily."

"Why? So, she can call me crazy and have a valid excuse for banning me?"

"Apparently, she didn't need *any* excuse to have you banned. So, it really won't make much of a difference, will it?"

Allie made it Samantha's house in record time. She parked on the street in front of Alex's truck for a quick getaway and marched up to the door ringing the doorbell with a hard jab for emphasis. She crossed her arms over her chest and tapped her foot getting more aggravated by the second. What was taking so long? Finally, after ringing the doorbell a second time, Samantha opened the door.

"Allie" Samantha said in greeting in a completely neutral tone. She allowed Allie to pass and walk into the living room where Alex was sitting in an armchair watching Tyler color with crayons in a coloring book on the floor.

Allie walked over to the nearby couch and sat down, crossing one leg over the other and shaking her foot in an agitated way while crossing her arms over her chest. "Alright, I'm here." She said as Samantha stood off to the side. "What is it you wanted to say Alex?"

Alex looked over at Samantha with a look that said, 'is she serious right now?' before standing up out of the armchair. "Here goes" he said. "You're going to think I'm crazy, but I promise you I'm not making any of this up."

"What? What is it you're not making up? Please just spit it out."

"Well I could get there if you'd give me a chance! Now, I've visited Emily twice as you already know. The first time I went, you know I fell asleep and was woken up by your father."

"Yes, I definitely remember" Allie said with an angry growl.

"Well, what you don't know is that while I was asleep, I saw Emily. What I mean to say is… it was like my subconscious joined with hers. I dreamed that I was in this weird version of our town, and not even really our town, but just the school. Emily was there and she told me that she was stuck inside her own head. She said she had been watching me and you and everyone."

"Well, that is definitely crazy" Allie responded. "Is that what you got me here to tell me? That you have some weird otherworldly connection to my sister?" Allie scoffed while quickly getting back up off the couch. "I can't believe I wasted my time with this."

"Wait" Samantha said now. "Let him finish."

"Yeah, I thought it was crazy too" Alex continued. "But ever since then I haven't been able to stop thinking about it. What if it wasn't a dream? What if I really did visit Emily inside her head? What if it was real? So, I went back last night and re-created how it happened before. I was going to try last week, but I couldn't." he said giving Allie a very pointed look. "Last night, I laid down the exact same way and held her hand just like I did before and went to sleep again."

Alex went silent for a minute causing Allie to respond, "And? What happened?" She asked impatiently.

"Allie, it happened again. I went back inside her head and talked to her again. It wasn't a dream."

"That's the craziest thing I've ever heard" Allie laughed now. "Do you really expect me to believe that?"

"Why would I lie?" Alex raised his arms to the sides and let them drop. He knew she wouldn't believe him.

"I don't know. So maybe I'll un-ban you?"

"Okay. I'll admit that is the reason I'm telling you about this, but I'm not making it up. You can believe me or not. I don't really care. But if you don't believe me, why don't you try it yourself?"

"You seriously want me to sleep in Emily's hospital room just to prove you're crazy? Why should I? Why should I believe a single word you say?"

"What do you have to lose?" Alex responded. "Just make sure that you hold her hand while you do it. I don't know if it's important but that's what I did both times."

Allie left Samantha's house feeling completely confused. Not that she let Alex know that. In fact, she refused let him know whether or not she was even going to partake in his crazy experiment. Which she wasn't. But maybe she should, she thought. What could it hurt? Well, if it didn't work, she'd look completely stupid for believing him as well as being completely disappointed for getting her hopes up. She needed someone to talk to about it.

That evening, she met Josh for dinner out. She wasn't sure she should talk to him about what Alex had told her. She was distracted thinking about it. Josh noticed how quiet she was being along with her lack of appetite.

"Everything all right?"

"Oh. Yes, everything is great. Thank you, Josh, for taking me out tonight. I'm just tired and I kind of have a lot on my mind."

"Anything I can help you with? You know I'm a great listener."

"Yes, you are. You really are. And I really appreciate that. It's just, Alex told me something completely crazy today and I just can't stop thinking about it."

"Alex…" Josh said now. "You mean the guy that broke your sister's heart?"

"Yeah, that's the one. I told you how her friend Samantha called him and told him about Emily's accident. Well, he came back last week to visit her."

"Wow. Well, at least he cared enough about her to come see her."

"See and I'm not so sure. I think he just feels guilty about causing her to get into her car that night."

"Well, I don't know the guy so I don't really know what he would do."

"I've known him practically my whole life. He'd been friends with Emily since they were nine. And I never expected him to hurt her the way he did. So, knowing someone doesn't always guarantee you'll know what they'd do."

"That's true I guess."

"The thing is, he told me today that he fell asleep in Emily's room and visited her inside her subconscious or whatever you want to call it. He said, he thought it was a dream, so he went back last night and tried again, and it worked again. He said he talked to her and everything. I mean it sounds totally insane."

"And you're wondering what if it's not."

"Yeah, I guess. But that's crazy right? I mean, that can't be possible. Still… he said I should try it myself."

"You know, I believe there are all kinds of things in this world that we can't explain. I'm not saying what Alex said is true. I'm just saying that maybe you should try it. I mean worst case scenario nothing happens right? If you want, I'll come with you and watch you sleep. You are cute when you're asleep."

Allie blushed as a smile crept across her face. This guy really was just too perfect. How could she have gotten so lucky with him? He seemed to be completely understanding about everything. And he was right. What did she have to lose? She decided to go ahead and try what Alex had done. She and Josh made a plan to run to Allie's place so that she could change into something a little more comfortable before heading over to the hospital. He would set an alarm and be there to keep watch in case Allie seemed to be having some sort of difficulty in her sleep.

After Alex left me in the gym, I decided to start walking down the road that had appeared outside. I followed it up over the small hill and down to a field of grass on the left-hand side of the road. The field seemed to be just a few acres and as I made my way across it, I could see a house on the far end of the field. It was Jenna Thompson's house. The house where I'd gone to that one college house party. The party where Alex said he'd first told me that he loved me.

I felt dread spreading through me. Was that the next scene that I was going to be watching? I wasn't sure I was ready for that. Near the center of the field, I found the creature sitting in the grass. I sat down across from it and decided to put off watching the next scene hoping that by watching the present first, I could mentally prepare myself for that college party scene. I asked to pull up Allie.

I was watching Allie's date with Josh through the crystal ball as they talked about Alex's revelation. I couldn't believe Alex told Allie about his visits with me. But I was excited. Allie was going to come visit me! I watched Allie all the way up to the point where she laid down in my hospital room, took my hand and closed her eyes. Josh sat in the corner in another chair with a tablet on his lap. He was going to use it to pass the time and to keep himself awake while Allie slept.

Once Allie closed her eyes, I let the creature know that I was done watching for the moment and then ran back up the road to wait. I walked around a little bit keeping my eyes on the park bench. Time passed. I couldn't tell how much, but it seemed like a good half hour. Nothing was happening. I wanted to go check the crystal ball again to see if Allie was asleep, but I didn't want to miss her either. Finally, I couldn't wait anymore, and I went back to the field.

I asked for Allie to be pulled back up in the crystal ball again. She was asleep in my hospital room. I wondered why it wasn't working for her the way it did for Alex. It made no sense to me. I just hoped that this wouldn't make her feel more discouraged about the odds of me eventually waking up.

Chapter Fifteen

Now I looked at Allie's new beau sitting in the corner. He seemed to be reading something on a tablet, his brows furrowed in concentration. He wasn't bad looking; I could give him that. He was kind of tall and slightly lanky, but he had dark hair that was neatly combed to one side and green eyes. He had just enough stubble to be handsome in a good masculine way and he was wearing a nice button down, pressed pants, and penny loafers. He looked ten times more adult than any of the men I'd ever seen Allie with before. Way to go Allie.

There was nothing left for me to do for now but to try and continue on, looking at things from my past. So, I took a deep breath, and told the creature that I was ready to look at the next scene. What unfolded was me and Samantha in the apartment we had shared in college. We were in our bedroom (because together we could only afford to rent an apartment with one bedroom) and we were laughing and pulling things out of the closet. We were holding up outfits for each other's inspection. There was music playing on a radio that we used to have sitting on top of Samantha's dresser.

We'd had many nights like this in college. This was our ritual when we'd been getting ready to go out to a party. While I watched, Samantha had settled on a light pink tank top with some white short shorts that had wide one-inch-long hems around the bottoms and some wedge sandals with hot pink straps. I on the other hand, seemed to have settled on a bright yellow halter top sundress with an A-line skirt and some suede gladiator sandals with short heels.

This was the night we'd gone to Jenna Thompson's house party our freshman year. This was the night that I'd gotten far drunker than I'd ever been before or since. And this was the night that Alex said that he'd told me he loved me. My stomach turned as I realized what I was going to see in the crystal ball. But there was nothing I could do. I had to continue watching.

I watched as me and Samantha had posed in the mirror and danced to the radio as we put on makeup and fixed our hair. I watched as we rode in Samantha's car down to the Jenna Thompson's house talking the whole way about who may or may not be there. And then I watched as we got out of her car and walked up to the house together.

We'd made our way to the kitchen and grabbed one of the many bottles of hard liquor lining the counter and each made a drink in a solo cup with soda added to it. Then we walked around for about an hour making small talk with people we'd known all our lives. We were also introduced to some new faces during this time. Some were cute I'd remembered thinking. There were also some others we both quickly wanted to move away from.

After we finished our first drink, we went back and made another and then made our way out to the front porch of Jenna's house which wrapped all the way around it. We found a quiet spot near the front corner and sat on the porch railing talking amongst ourselves about what we thought of the turnout and some of the new people that we'd met. Then after a few more minutes, Alex showed up to the party.

Alex had ridden with a few of his roommates, and we watched as they all piled out of his friend Brendan's rather large truck. Alex was looking sharp in a nice light colored dress shirt with his sleeves rolled up over his forearms. His shirt tails hung loose over slightly loose-fitting jeans and shoes that kind of looked like bowling shoes. I laughed when I thought about how embarrassed he'd be now to recall wearing those shoes.

As he and his friends made their way toward the house, Alex had his hands in his pockets and his head slightly bent down in an aw-shucks kind of manner. The rest of the guys were hooting and hollering and high fiving each other as they walked on both sides of him. When they reached us, his friends told him that they'd see him inside and kept going while Alex stayed behind.

"Hey guys" Alex said nonchalantly as he approached us still sitting on the porch rail. "How's the party?"

"Not bad" Samantha said. "Pretty much everyone is here. We've been here for about an hour and caught up with a lot of them already. Now we're just kind of chillin' out here, taking a break from the crowd."

"I hear ya" Alex responded. "Well, I guess I'll go get a drink and mingle a little bit. You guys gonna be out here for a while?"

"Yeah" I said now. "It's such a nice night out so we're enjoying the weather."

Alex nodded. "Do you guys need anything? Another drink?"

"No thank you" we both replied to him.

"Have fun" I said to Alex as he started walking into the house. He spun around and saluted us awkwardly before turning back on his heel and going through the front door.

"Well, Alex is looking pretty cute tonight, isn't he?" Samantha said to me now that he was out of earshot.

"Yeah, I guess. But what about James Gables? I thought you had a crush on him."

"I do really like him" Samantha said. "I was just making an observation is all. Can't a girl think another guy looks good without it meaning anything more than that?"

"Well yeah of course they can. How is everything going with James by the way?"

I laughed at my younger self in this moment. James was Samantha's husband now. They had met our freshman year in college in an intro class. It had been love at first sight for Samantha. She had not spared any of the details about anything having to do with James from what he looked like to every word that he had spoken to her. Samantha over analyzed every single detail of their encounters becoming more and more frustrated as time went on that he hadn't asked her out.

It turned out, that James liked Samantha too. The problem was that he wasn't from around here and he had a girlfriend back home that he was still trying to make things work with. Samantha hadn't known this because they'd never spent any real time getting to know each other outside of the classroom.

Finally, one day, near the end of the semester, Samantha decided to throw caution to the wind and ask James out on a date. According to Samantha, he was taken aback by her proposition. But then he explained to Samantha his position with his long-distance relationship and apologized for not being able to take her up on her offer.

The Christmas break went by and when the spring semester had started, Samantha and James once again had a class together. Over the break, James and his girlfriend had broken up and now he was free to date Samantha. They've been together ever since. But at the time of this party that I was now watching, Samantha had not yet tried to ask James out. It was still early in the first fall semester.

Samantha proceeded to tell younger me all about her frustration with James not having asked her out while younger me listened intently. Current me though, was now thinking about what Samantha had said about Alex that night. She knew he was in love with me even then. At the time, I had taken her word at face value that she'd just been making an observation that he'd looked nice for the party. Now I saw that what she'd really been doing was casually trying and get me to observe Alex in a different way.

Another half hour went by slowly of me watching myself talking to Samantha and trying to brainstorm with her why James had not yet asked her out. Finally, I told her to remember that it was James's loss if he didn't see what a wonderful person she was. It was just as I was saying this that Alex came back outside, with three drinks in his hands.

"I figured you guys were about ready for another one" he said now as he set the new ones down on the porch railing.

"None for me thanks" Samantha said. "I haven't even really been drinking the one I already had."

Sure enough, Samantha's second drink looked like it had been barely touched. She poured it out into the grass in front of us before hopping down off the railing. "I think I'm actually about ready to go home. I'm getting kind of tired."

I knew Samantha was just upset about James but there was nothing more I could do to help her. "Do you want me to come home with you?" I asked her.

"No. There's no need for the rest of your night to be ruined. Alex, can you make sure she gets home, okay?"

"I didn't drive here but yeah we can definitely call a cab and share it if that's okay with you Emily."

"Sure" I said.

I told Samantha to feel better and that I'd talk to her later. Samantha said goodbye as we watched her walk to her car and leave. Then I looked down at the second drink I'd already had in my hand and saw that it was almost empty. I finished it off as Alex finished his first drink. Then I took the one he'd brought out for me while he took the one that he'd brought out for Samantha. We clinked our glasses together and toasted to a good party.

We downed those drinks pretty quickly and Alex went back inside to get us some refills. I remembered at this point that I could feel myself feeling a bit tipsy. I watched myself lean back on the porch rail, holding on tight with both hands, before pulling myself back up and doing it over again. I looked totally silly, I thought to myself. But it didn't look like anyone else outside was really paying any attention to me anyway.

Alex came back out of the house with new drinks and asked if I'd like to take a walk with him. He seemed a little tipsy himself as he took my hands to help me down from the porch railing. I hopped off with a little too much force causing me to land almost on top of him, putting my hands on his shoulders. We were chest to chest, silent for just a moment. And then I started giggling.

My stomach flipped at seeing how we'd been so physically close. A sudden fleeting thought passed through me that the girl in the image should kiss that boy. Then I realized the thought I'd just had and was shocked. What was going on with me? Then I saw the look of desire in younger Alex's eyes and felt guilty once again that I had caused him such suffering.

I watched younger me take a step back and almost back up right into the railing as a look of disappointment crossed Alex's face. Then it quickly turned into a grimace that was not quite a smile but not a frown either. Alex handed me my new drink and asked me if I was okay before we started walking away from the party.

Jenna Thompson's house had sat on a few acres of land without any neighbors nearby so there was plenty of open area to walk around. As we got further from the house, it got darker with only the moon and stars to give us light. We walked up and over this small rolling hill which completely blocked off our view of the house behind us. Then we collapsed on the ground, laughing, and proceeded to sip on our new drinks. Watching this from the outside, I realized just how little I actually remembered of that night. I'd barely remembered jumping off the porch rail, let alone walking away from the rest of the party.

I watched as we sat side by side with our backs against the bottom of the hill leaning back against it. We looked up at the stars and talked about how beautiful they were. At one point, I shivered a little and Alex responded by putting his arm around my shoulders. I watched myself let my head fall sideways and leaning into him. Something deep inside me stirred at the sight of it. Something that also made my heart race. I knew what was coming and I felt like I could barely contain myself waiting in anticipation. Something is definitely wrong with me, I thought.

A minute or so of silence went by before Alex spoke. Still looking up at the sky he said, "Emily, I have something I need to tell you. I'm just going to say it before I lose my nerve. This is hard. It's just…damn it. Emily, I love you. And I don't mean how friends love each other. I mean I really *love* you. This is coming out badly. Emily? Emily?"

Alex looked down at me with my head still leaned against him. I had passed out. My eyes were closed, and I held a loose grip on the drink in my hand that was almost empty. Alex let out a deep sigh. He stared down at the ground in front of him for a minute. I guess he was deciding what to do. I felt a strong sense of sadness watching this now.

Then I watched as Alex slipped his arm back from around my shoulders and propped me against the hill. He slowly stood, taking care not to disturb me and pulled his phone out of his pocket. I watched as he called for a cab. Then he shook me awake at my shoulder. It was enough to rouse me so that he could help me stand and walk to the end of the driveway of the property.

Within a few minutes a cab showed up and he helped me inside before climbing in himself and giving the driver my address. He made small talk with the driver until we had arrived at me and Samantha's apartment. He paid the driver and said he'd be right back. I watched as he climbed out of the cab and shook me awake again to help me out. Then he picked me up with both arms underneath me and carried me inside.

I watched as he painstakingly made it down the hall to our first-floor apartment and maneuvered himself to be able to knock on the door. Samantha answered and quietly moved to allow Alex inside. Then she followed him to our shared room and watched as he slowly lowered me into my bed.

"She'll be alright" he said as he maneuvered my legs to pull my blanket up over me. "She just drank a little too much." He didn't say anything else. He simply looked down at my sleeping form for a minute before bending down and giving me a kiss on the cheek. My heart jumped at the sight, and I felt all choked up.

Then I watched as Alex told Samantha goodbye and left. The scene in the crystal ball ended leaving me with a feeling of want. But what was it that I wanted? All I could say for sure was that my heart felt stuck in my throat and in that moment, I wished more than I had at any other time in my life, that Alex was here with me.

———————

Alex slept fitfully that night. He was due to go back to Maryland in the morning, but could he really leave now? It would be one thing if he hadn't experienced what he experienced, he told himself. The plan had been just to come and pay his respects to Emily and go back to his new life guilt free.

But now, he kept replaying what Emily had said to him over and over again about how she had to figure out where she went wrong in order to wake up. She'd said he couldn't help her at all. So why did he feel so strongly that he needed to do something? Why did he feel like a heavy weight was sitting on his chest? Why did he feel like there was something that he was missing?

He was awoken the next morning by someone pounding on his door. He looked at the time on his phone. It was almost 11. He'd forgotten to set an alarm and had overslept! Now he'd never make it back to Maryland in time for any kind of decent dinner with Veronica.

Alex jumped up off the couch just in time to hear the pounding on his front door again followed by Allie's voice screaming "Hey open up! I know you're in there!" He quickly checked that was decently dressed and then ran quickly to the door and opened it before Allie could bang on it again.

When he opened the door, Allie had her fist raised up in the air. Clearly, she had been about to knock again. She had an angry look on her face as she started to lower her arm and put her hands on her hips. Alex was guessing that his experiment hadn't worked for her.

"To what do I owe the pleasure?" he asked.

"I'll tell you what you owe it to!" Allie said crossing the threshold and walking into his living room. "I went to the hospital last night and did exactly what you told me to, and it didn't work! I can't believe I fell for that bunch of garbage. But then again, what did I expect coming from *you*." She said this last statement with a look of disgust on her face.

"Now look here" Alex said getting angry. "Just because it didn't work for you does not mean I made it up. Why would I make something up that sounds so crazy and put my own reputation on the line?"

"What reputation? That went out the window when you hurt my sister causing her to be nearly killed! And the jury is still out on the nearly!"

"I didn't cause her to do anything. She did that to herself. If she hadn't been driving that night, hell, if she'd just been paying attention to her driving that night, she'd be just fine right now."

"No, she wouldn't. Because even if she hadn't been driving that night, her heart would still be broken."

"She broke my heart when she turned me down for nothing more than a real chance to be with her."

"You just don't get it do you? But of course, how could you? You didn't grow up in our house."

"What does growing up in your house have to do with anything?"

"Have you never noticed that Emily has never been serious with anyone? Have you never noticed how she's broken up with perfectly nice guys and made excuses over the years? It has *everything* to do with growing up in our house!"

With that, Alex's temper simmered down as he thought about what Allie had just said. He had noticed how Emily had never gotten really serious with anyone, but he'd never really asked about it. He had just chosen to take her excuses at face value. Why shouldn't he have done that? Emily talked to him about everything. If there was more to the story of her breakups, surely, she would've told him about it, right? Suddenly he wasn't so sure.

What if he was wrong, he thought now? What if there were some things too hard for her to talk about, even with him? That thought sobered Alex as he blew a large breath out and turned to walk over to the couch. "Explain it to me. Please" was all he said as he collapsed down onto it.

That was all it took. Allie calmly explained how things were in their family. She detailed specific occurrences that Emily had never mentioned to him before. Occurrences that made him turn pale and feel like a complete ass for how he handled things with her. Allie explained how their father was never there for their mother and how their mother, completely broke down every time he walked out. She explained how Emily took care of her like a surrogate mother, despite only being a few years older, and the impact it had on her sense of security in relationships.

By the end of it, Alex was having a hard time keeping his composure. He had only known what he remembered Emily telling him that day when they were in middle school, and he had wanted to see where she lived. She had told him that her parents yelled at each other sometimes. But that was all she had said. Why hadn't he ever asked her more about it?

He'd met their parents a few times. But never at their house. He'd never gone to Emily's house or seen her room or anything like that. He'd met Brenda in town when he'd run into her with Emily or Allie. He'd met Bob when he and his wife were together for some of the school events that they'd attended such as their high school graduation. Neither of them seemed like they were very close to each other, but they also didn't seem like the type to yell and fight and walk out the way Allie was describing.

Alex could feel tears forming behind his eyes and he forced himself to hold them back. "Thank you for telling me all of this" he managed to squeeze out.

"You're welcome" Allie said. "So now maybe you see that her not giving you a chance is more complicated than you thought. She's not just afraid of losing a good friend Alex. She's afraid of letting her heart get involved only to have it hurt the way our father has always done to our mother."

"I don't even know what to say Allie. I feel like what you're saying makes sense. But, as far as me and Emily are concerned, it doesn't matter anymore. I'm just here as a friend" Alex sighed. "I swear I didn't make up what happened to me when I visited Emily. I wouldn't do that."

Allie sighed. "I guess I don't know what to believe anymore" she said.

"I understand. Just whatever you do, don't give up on her just yet. Okay? I believe she's fighting to wake up right now and she *will* win. She just needs time." Isn't that what Emily had said to him before he woke up the second time, he thought to himself.

"We're not giving up just yet. But I'm not sure how long we can hold out hope. Anyway, I'll leave now. I said everything I came to say."

With that, Allie left, leaving Alex alone to think about everything she had told him. How was it that he had never known anything specific about the things Emily went through at home? They were supposed to be best friends that could tell each other anything. He realized now that he had never pushed Emily to tell him anything at all about her home life. It wasn't that he didn't want to know. It was just that he felt like she was just embarrassed by her parent's dysfunctionality.

He'd never really thought about it much. But now he was. What was he supposed to do? He had to go back to Maryland today. He had to report back into work first thing in the morning. And what about Veronica? She was at work right now, but she knew he was coming back today. Surely, she's anticipating my arrival, he thought.

If he'd known about how Emily's life had affected her trust in relationships, would he have done things differently? Would he have told her how he felt the way he did and left the way he did? He would like to think he wouldn't have, but there was really no way to know, was there?

And really, there was nothing he could do about it now. He couldn't change the past. Even if he explained to Emily that he hadn't understood her point of view, she would still hold that memory of how he'd ambushed her forever. He told himself that over and over again as he packed up the clothes that he'd brought with him and tidied up the house. He continued to tell himself that as he pulled out of his driveway and headed for the highway. In his heart though, he felt an ache that came from feeling guilty about the way he'd handled the entire situation.

Chapter Sixteen

Allie was completely confused. She pulled out of Alex's driveway and made her way back home. How could Alex really visit Emily inside her head? Was it really possible? And if it was, what did that mean that she, Emily's own sister, could not do the same? I must be losing it, Allie thought.

But what if Alex was being truly genuine? Was she going soft for even entertaining such a thought? Maybe Alex really could visit Emily inside her head. But why? Allie pondered this as she walked inside her apartment. As she was slipping her shoes off, her phone started ringing. It was Josh.

"Hey, what are you doing right now?"

"I just got home. I went and talked to Alex about his little experiment not working for me."

"I hope you were gentle at least. You seemed pretty angry when we left the hospital."

"Who me? I was an angel."

"Come on Allie. Were you really?"

"Okay fine. I laid into him. But I think some good may have come from it."

"Really? Well let's have a late lunch and you can tell me all about it. Want to meet me downtown?"

"Sounds good" Allie said slipping her shoes back on.

Once they decided on a place to eat and were seated, Allie told Josh the rest of the story. "So, the thing is, Alex didn't know anything about our home life growing up. That was a shock, let me tell you. I mean, Alex and Emily have been friends for so long that just a few years longer and you could use the word *decades*. Plural. And she never told him anything about it."

"Well, I can understand why she wouldn't want to. But you're right. Knowing someone for that long, you just assume at some point she would've confided the feelings she had about the situation to the person closest to her."

"Exactly!" Allie said.

"I mean, I know I haven't known you very long, but personally I feel I should let you know that I feel honored that you would share such deeply personal things like that with me."

"Aw. Well thank you for that." Allie said with big gushing smile.

"Anytime" replied Josh who then stood up and leaned over the table where he met Allie halfway to give her a kiss.

"So anyway," Allie said sitting back down, "I told him all about it, which took a little bit of time. He seemed upset when I told him. Whether he was upset that she had never told him or upset about the experiences themselves, I'm not totally sure."

"I'm guessing it was probably a little bit of both. His pride might've been hurt that she'd never said anything about it, but if he really cares about her, he'd be more upset that the things you told him about happened at all."

"That makes sense. See? This is why you're good to talk to. You can give me the male perspective on things."

"Plus, you like me" Josh said smiling in a silly way.

"Yes, I really do" Allie said back. "You've been wonderful. Where have you been all my life?"

"Well, let's see, I grew up in Colombia, then I went to college..." Josh started to say. He was cut off by Allie reaching across the table to pinch him, making them both laugh. "Okay okay, but seriously, I'm glad to have met you Allie."

"I'm glad to have met you too."

Once Allie got back home, she started to really think about what Josh had said. He made it sound like he thought Alex really did still care for Emily. She spent the next few hours thinking back over every memory she had of Alex and Emily together. There were so many instances where she'd seen that look of love on Alex's face when they were together. She couldn't imagine that feelings like that just went away instantaneously because the other person wasn't interested.

But that still didn't answer the question of if his story about being able to visit Emily was real, why would that be? She no longer thought he'd just make something like that up. Maybe they were soulmates if such a thing really existed. The thought of that warmed Allie's heart and made her think of Josh. She was really falling in love with him and for once, it seemed, the feeling was pretty mutual.

Maybe she needed to call off the ban on Alex at the hospital. Samantha was right. What did it really hurt to let him see her? So, she called the hospital and told them to allow anyone to visit Emily that showed up there. Then she called Alex and told him he was free to see her anytime. Alex was thankful it seemed, as she hung up the phone. Allie felt the anger and bitterness she'd been carrying now start to slip away.

Sitting in Emily's room later, Allie just looked at her sister's face. It seemed to be almost completely healed now from all the bruising. It almost seemed as if Emily were just sleeping. Allie stared at her, still wondering why she couldn't visit Emily the same way Alex said he had. She tried again a few days later, but still nothing had happened.

Alex had said that Emily was able to watch all of them in real time and see what they were doing. She'd gotten the idea that maybe Emily was blocking her from visiting because she was mad at her for banning Alex from her room. So, she figured now that she had changed her mind, maybe Emily had seen and would let her inside. But it didn't work. What else could she do?

Maybe, she thought now, still staring at her sister's face, she could get someone else to try. She would feel better if it wasn't just her that it didn't work for. But who to ask? She didn't want to drag her parents into it so that only left one person. Allie pulled out her cell phone and put in a call to Samantha.

"Hello?" Samantha said after answering on the fifth ring. She sounded a little distracted.

"Hey it's Allie. Are you busy?"

"Kind of. I was in the middle of washing dishes. But I can stop for a minute."

"Okay, the thing is, after Alex told me about his experiences there at your house, I decided to try to visit Emily myself."

"Really? Well, what happened?"

Allie sighed. "It didn't work. I woke up feeling like a complete idiot. Then I got mad."

"Oh no Allie. What did you do?"

"Why does everyone automatically assume I did something?"

"Well, did you?"

"Yeah, I did."

"Then that's why. So, Allie, once again I ask, what did you do?"

"I went to Alex's house and chewed him out."

"That sounds about right. How did he react?"

"Well first he got defensive and angry, which I guess I should've expected."

"Of course." Samantha responded.

"But then, the conversation shifted and let's just say that I found out that not even Alex knew everything about Emily. I had to explain some things to him and in the end, I actually felt bad about banning him from seeing Emily."

"Wow. It must've been something big that he didn't know. I mean there are some things that Emily has never talked about with me, but I assumed Alex knew everything."

"Me too. That's why it was such a surprise. Suffice it to say I ended up calling the hospital and having him unbanned."

"Well that's good to hear."

"Thanks. Anyway, so a few days later, I decided to go try to get inside Emily's head again and it still didn't work. So, I guess I'm wondering if it's just me that can't visit her, or if it's only Alex that can?"

"And you're wanting to find out by having me try to do it. Am I right?"

"Yes exactly. Do you think that's something that I could convince you to try?"

"I guess at this point I don't see why not. When did you have in mind?"

"How about tonight?"

"Let me clear it with James and get back to you."

Later that evening, Allie met Samantha up at the hospital. They made a plan that Samantha would take a few Benadryl once they were in Emily's room, and then talk or watch tv or whatever until Samantha started to feel drowsy enough to fall asleep. That way there was no danger in Samantha driving to the hospital feeling drowsy. Allie mentioned that she could've picked Samantha up at her house, but Samantha was content to drive her own vehicle and was prepared to stay all night. Her husband James would be home to take care of Tyler.

They talked a little bit about whether or not Samantha was nervous to which Samantha replied that she was not. If anything, she was excited by the idea but at the same time, she would not feel totally let down if it didn't work. At this point, she had a 50/50 shot, she thought. Within 30 minutes, she was feeling drowsy and within 45, she had laid her head down on Emily's leg, taken Emily's hand, closed her eyes, and fallen asleep.

Allie watched Samantha sleep for a while, feeling nervous about the result. She tried to watch tv, but she couldn't concentrate on it.

She was too anxious. She paced the room a few times and even tried to take a walk around the hospital to pass the time. It just seemed like time was barely moving to Allie as she struggled to take her mind off of the waiting.

At some point, Allie fell asleep in another chair in Emily's room. Samantha awoke to the sight of Allie, slumped in the chair, her head straight back laying on the back of it, her mouth wide open, with a small snoring sound escaping from it. Samantha got up, stretched a little, then walked over to Allie and shook her shoulder to wake her up. Once Allie opened her eyes and realized where she was, she jumped up out of the chair startling Samantha.

"You're awake!" Allie nearly screamed. "How did it go?"

"Unfortunately, not well" Samantha responded, her lips forming a straight line for a moment. "I didn't experience anything either. I don't think I even dreamed at all."

"Damn" Allie said in a muttered tone. "Well, you gave it a shot. At least it's not just me I guess."

"Yeah. At least now you can say for sure that it wasn't personal."

Another week went by, and Alex spent every day feeling like he was in a fog. He was now free to come and go as he pleased from Emily's bedside. But did he really want to? It seemed to him that they'd pretty much said everything they needed to say to each other. She'd described her predicament and made it clear there was nothing he could do.

They'd made up with each other which should have given Alex a sense of peace about the situation. Sure, he didn't want Emily to die, but continuing to worry about it really didn't help anything. So why couldn't he shake the feeling that he was missing something?

Maybe it had to with the scenes that she mentioned that she'd had to relive. Every one of them had something to do with him. In fact, a few of them were about times when he'd been hurt by Emily going out with someone else. Both times that she mentioned, the guy in question turned out to be the loser of the year and hurting her. He wondered if she'd had to watch how he was there for her afterwards? She hadn't mentioned that.

On the one hand, Alex felt annoyed with himself for not being able to let Emily go. On the other hand, he reasoned with himself, there must be some reason why he was able to visit her in her head when seemingly no one else could. Granted, the only other person who had tried was Allie. But still... why wouldn't it work for Allie?

If he could bring himself into Emily's head, maybe he could bring in other objects. The idea had just popped into his own head quite suddenly and now he felt like he had to try it. But what should he try to bring? He decided that he had the entire drive back to decide as he once again packed some clothes back up and started making that drive.

Brendan had told Alex just the other day that if he *did* decide to come back again, it may be his last time being able to stay in his house. He now had an interested buyer and if the sale went through, Alex would no longer have any physical ties to what he considered to be his hometown. In a way, it was a sad thought but wasn't that what he wanted?

He had Veronica now and she had been such a trooper with him leaving every weekend to go see Emily. Sure, she didn't know what Emily's name was or even that Emily was female, but that wasn't the point. Veronica had been great about him leaving to go see a dying friend that she knew nothing about and wasn't that worth something? He decided it was and he could only hope that Veronica would continue to be so understanding.

Stopping off at his house just long enough to drop off his clothes, Alex made his way back to the hospital. Once he got into Emily's room, he sat there looking at how much she was healing physically from the crash. He still hadn't decided what he should try to bring into her head with him so he tried to think about things she might need.

He remembered that she had told him that she had to sleep sometimes. He realized now that she hadn't told him where she slept. If all she really had around her was the school, then she couldn't have anywhere comfortable to lay down. He looked at the mattress her body was lying on. Maybe he could bring that, he thought.

But how would he do it? If falling asleep holding Emily's hand is what sent him into her head, maybe holding the object in his other hand would allow him to bring it with him in some way. It was worth a shot. Alex took Emily's hand in his own, then grasped the corner of the mattress down by her feet with his other hand as he laid his head down and went to sleep.

———

After watching his first declaration of love several days ago, I felt an overwhelming sense of sadness that I couldn't control. What bothered me even more was that I didn't know why I was feeling that way. But it was so pervasive that I just felt like I needed to go back to sleep to get away from it. I didn't walk back to the bench to sleep. I just found a nice spot in the grassy field that I was already in faraway enough from the creature that I didn't feel like it was hovering over me.

When I woke up, a few days had passed but I wasn't sure how many. And yet, the sleep hadn't eased the hollow feeling in my chest in the slightest. I reluctantly sat up and looked around. The creature was gone from the spot it had been sitting in the field. I looked out towards the road. I could see something in the distance. From where I was sitting, it just looked like a large dark blob. So, I got up and walked back toward the road.

Once I made it back onto the road, I could see that it was a small square building, just a few feet farther up on the right. It was a bar. And not just any bar, but the bar that me and my friends had spent a lot of nights at in college, just hanging out. It was called The Spot. It was so named because it was literally the college hang out for anyone that was anyone here in this small town. I had so many memories of playing pool, singing karaoke with Samantha, and watching guys play beer pong.

I walked up to the building which looked dark inside. I pulled on the glass door, which surprisingly opened right up. Inside, I had to let my eyes adjust before I saw the creature. It was sitting at a table near the stage. I had so many memories in this place that I really wasn't sure which one I would be revisiting here.

Before I delved into that though, I decided to check up on Alex. When he appeared, he was in my hospital room. I watched him as he took my hand and took the mattress in his other hand. I watched as he laid his head down and closed his eyes. What was Alex doing, I thought to myself as I watched him fall asleep. I felt guilty about watching him again. Especially since I'd basically implied that I had only done so the one time and wouldn't do so again.

But I couldn't help myself. After watching him tell me that he loved me at that college party, I just felt like I had to watch him. Call it loneliness, call it longing even. I was really confused about what it was that I was feeling for Alex now. Was he coming back to see me again? My heart jumped in my chest. I felt like my emotions were all over the place and I wasn't sure how I felt about him coming back. But I was about to find out.

Chapter Seventeen

Figuring Alex would know to walk down the road to find me, I left the old bar and started back towards the school. I hoped a few minutes of walking would be enough to help me know what to say. I replayed his declaration of love from that college party through my head as I walked in silence. Picturing him sitting there, saying the words that he said made my heart do little flips in my chest. What was wrong with me? Surely, I couldn't really be starting to have feelings for Alex?

The thought made me feel uncomfortable. I felt so confused. Why did he come back, I wondered? The last time I'd talked to him, he had basically told me that he had to move on. I looked up from the road as I'd been staring blankly at my feet while I walked and saw Alex coming towards me from the opposite direction. We continued walking till we met on the road.

He hadn't made it yet to the hill that obscured the view of Jenna's house and the field that surrounded it. I was kind of glad about that because although I wanted to have a conversation about it, I wanted to make sure everything was calm between us first. We stopped in front of each other and stared in awkward silence for a moment before he broke it by saying, "I'm back."

"Yeah, I see that" I responded.

Awkward silence followed my response for a few moments as I contemplated what to say. I was about to bite the bullet and ask him *why* he was back when he said, "I have something to show you back this way."

"Oh… okay" was my response as he turned around to walk back from where he had come from.

We walked in silence side by side for a minute. Then out of nowhere Alex's ankle slipped a little as he stepped on the edge of a rock, causing his hand to bump mine. I felt a surge of energy shoot through my hand at the contact making me gasp. I pulled my hand away in a lightning quick motion as I looked at Alex and felt my cheeks flood with heat. What was that, I thought, as I cleared my throat and turned my head back towards the road in front of us.

Alex didn't show any signs that he'd noticed anything. Why should he, I thought to myself. He had a woman out there now waiting for him. So why was he back here? I felt like I just had to know. I was already so confused about my feelings for Alex, maybe his answer would help.

After another minute passed and I could feel that the heat in my face had subsided, I tried to ask him again. "Why did you come back?" I didn't look at him, just continued to look straight forward.

I could feel him looking at me now as he said, "I'm not really sure." He was silent for a few seconds before continuing. "I *do* know though that I need to apologize to you."

"Apologize? For what?" I turned to look at him now.

"I had a conversation with Allie."

"I know you told her about how you came to visit me. And I know she tried to do the same and that it didn't work for her."

"Okay. But there's a little bit more to it" he said as I looked at him quizzically.

"She came and told me how it didn't work for her, and then the conversation shifted..."

"Shifted how?"

"She asked me if I had ever wondered why you had never been in a lasting relationship with anyone else before."

"What did you say?"

"Honestly, I'd never really thought about it. That's what I told her. How could I have never thought about it? It amazes me how much I didn't pay attention to all those years of knowing you."

"What did she say?"

"She told me it was because of the things the two of you experienced growing up. Naturally, I had no idea what she was talking about..."

"So, she told you all about it" I finished for him.

"Yeah. She did. I'm still reeling over how I never knew about any of it. I was supposed to be your friend."

"You *were* my friend. You didn't know because I didn't share it with you. I didn't share it with you because I didn't want to scare you away. And besides, telling you wouldn't have changed anything. You were just a kid yourself."

"Yeah, but in all that time, I could have asked. I mean, I remember that day on the bench in front of the school when you basically hinted at it. Why didn't I ever press you for more details?"

I didn't have an answer to that. I didn't know what to say. Thankfully, I didn't have to say anything. It seemed he had the answer to his own question.

"I've been thinking about it a lot. I think I never pressed you about it because I was too preoccupied with my feelings for you. I was so preoccupied that I wasn't really being the friend to you that I was supposed to be. Well, that's over now. So, I guess I'm here to make amends and be that friend the way I should've always been."

"What do you mean?" I asked.

Alex looked away from me now to look back in the direction we were walking. Then he came to a stop and said, "Look." Then he pointed straight out in front of us.

I turned to look at what he was pointing at. We were just a few feet away from the school and the bench now. Sitting on the ground behind the bench, was a mattress.

"I wanted to try and bring an object with me" Alex said when I looked at him. "I decided to try the mattress because I figured you didn't have anything comfortable to lay on when you go to sleep."

I was stunned. I didn't know what to say. "Thank you" I managed to choke out as I started to tear up. "That was very nice of you."

"Emily, it's no problem. This is the kind of thing that a friend should do. And seeing as I'm the only one that seems to be able to come here on my own, it's the least I could do."

"What do you mean, on your own?"

"Well, see I figured that if I could bring in an object just by holding it in my other hand when I came to see you, maybe I can bring in another person the same way. This experiment seems to have worked so now I'm thinking maybe tomorrow night I can try to bring in Allie."

Hearing this, I actually felt deflated. I realized now that I kind of liked the idea of Alex being the only one who could visit me. But why? I should be happy that maybe Allie could come and visit me. I was happy about it before, wasn't I? The answer was that yes, I had been. But that was before I'd watched Alex profess his love to me at that college party...

Then I thought of something else. "What does Veronica have to say about all this?" I asked now.

"Well... truthfully right now all she knows is that I'm visiting a sick friend. She doesn't know anything about our history or even that you're a female."

"Gee thanks" I snapped at him. Where had that come from, I instantly thought to myself?

"Is something wrong?" he asked me with a look of confusion crossing his face.

I could feel that my mixed-up emotions were starting to spill out, but I felt completely helpless to stop them. "Why wouldn't you just tell her?" I asked. "I mean, you said you've moved on. That you cared about her. Starting a relationship with secrets is not the best way to express that to her you know."

"Yeah, I know." Alex responded defensively. "I guess I just don't want to risk her getting jealous over me coming to see you. Don't get me wrong, there's nothing to be jealous of. If you weren't literally dying right now, I wouldn't be here. I feel bad for how I put you on the spot before and then handled the situation badly by picking up and moving away. This is just my way of making up for that."

"So maybe you shouldn't" I said while simultaneously screaming at myself inside my head to stop talking.

"Seriously?" Alex said looking angry. "What the hell is going on with you Emily? Just a minute ago you were thankful that I brought you something better to sleep on. Now you're telling me to leave? You are seriously cracked."

"And once again I say, gee thanks!" I started walking away from him quickly as I felt tears forming behind my eyes. What was wrong with me?

Alex caught up to me quickly and grabbed my arm, spinning me around. "This is *not* news to you. I already told you before that I'd moved on. Why are you acting this way? Don't tell me you have feelings for me now?"

"No," I said, gulping back the panicky feeling rising in my chest. "I don't."

"Then what is it?" he asked angrily.

"I don't know" I almost yelled at him. "Maybe I just have a lot going on here with this whole possibly dying thing!"

"Fine" he said stoically, setting his jaw. Then he let go of my arm. "I'll try to be back tomorrow night with Allie." With that he started fading out again, and in just a few seconds, he was gone.

———————

Alex woke up still clutching the mattress. What the hell just happened? He looked at Emily who still appeared to just be sleeping. Looks can be deceiving, he thought. He felt so angry he wanted to punch the wall. But he held himself back. If Emily wasn't appreciative of his trying to do something nice for her, why was he even trying? Maybe he shouldn't try to bring Allie in or do anything else for that matter.

His anger was quickly replaced by fear however, when Emily started seizing once again. He watched in horror at her flailing limbs as nurses rushed in, pushing him out of the way. He felt completely helpless while he watched the scene in front of him. After a few minutes, the nurses had been able to calm the situation down and Emily's body returned to normal. He had never actually seen someone seize before, let alone someone he cared about. He knew then that no matter how much she aggravated him, he had to keep trying to help Emily.

He left quickly after that, running home to get a few more hours of sleep before the sun came up. He also needed to think, and he needed somewhere quiet to do it. Once he was alone, sitting on his couch, he replayed the conversation he'd had with Emily through his head. He still didn't understand why she had gotten so upset. Yes, he needed to tell Veronica everything. He knew that.

Maybe she felt like he really was still holding on to her by not telling Veronica. Maybe that's what it was. In that case, if he was able to bring Allie in with him later, he would just have to tell Emily that he would tell Veronica everything once he got back to Maryland. He was able to pass out quickly after that and slept until dawn.

The first thing he did once he got up was to put in a call to Allie. She was surprisingly awake. It turned out that the hospital had put in a call to her soon after Emily's seizure had subsided, and she'd been up there with her sister ever since. He told Allie all about his having experimented by bringing in the mattress for her to sleep on and how it had worked. Then he told her how he wanted to next experiment by trying to bring in her. Allie seemed very excited about that. They made a plan to meet at the hospital that evening around ten.

Next Alex called around to the few local storage facilities in town to compare rates and accommodations for the rest of the things in his house. Once he decided on the place he wanted to go with, he borrowed Brendan's trailer and spent the day loading it up with the rest of the things from his house. The only thing he left behind was the couch so that after his experiment that night, he'd have something to sleep on for the last few hours before he had to leave again. He'd drop the couch off with the rest of his stuff on the way out of town.

By the time Alex had finished moving everything to the storage unit, he was exhausted. He was able to make it till ten however, when he met up with Allie. When he walked into the hospital room, she was already there waiting for him. Her boyfriend, Josh, was also there. She introduced the two of them as they shook hands heartily and assessed each other.

Alex thought he seemed a little more mature than the type that Allie usually went out with. And from the way he looked at her, Alex could tell he really cared for her. Maybe Allie had finally found someone she could settle down with. He wondered what she had told Josh about him, if anything at all. Not that it mattered much. Josh seemed as though he had no problem with Alex, not like Allie had only the week before.

Josh sat back and watched as Alex and Allie pulled up two chairs on either side of Emily's bed. He was only there just in case something happened that required someone to call for help. He wanted to make sure nothing happened to Allie. Once they were all situated and comfortable, Alex took Emily's hand in one of his. Then took Allie's hand in the other. They both laid their heads down on Emily's legs and soon fell asleep.

———————

After Alex had left the way he had, I was stood in the silence for a moment, realizing that he was gone. The emptiness that I felt was so strong that I suddenly felt as if I couldn't take it. I let out the longest, loudest scream that I had probably ever screamed in my life. It wasn't as if there was anyone around to hear it anyway. So, although no one came running and everything around me continued to be still in the silence, I screamed again.

This time though, as my scream died down, I began to sob, loudly. As I sobbed and screamed at the same time, purging my emotions, the world around me began once again to shake violently. I watched as leaves fell off of the tree that me and Alex used to sit under and a few small pieces of the school building, which was almost fully colored back to normal by the way, broke off from the top of the building and crumbled down to the ground.

Now I started running. I ran all the way back to that bar, tears now stained on my cheeks, trying not to fall down as the world continued to quake. By the time I got back to the bar, the quaking had stopped and found the creature right where I'd left it. I pulled up the chair opposite the table and took a deep breath. I pulled up Alex in the crystal ball and watched the look of pure terror on his face as he watched me seizing.

Then I watched as the nurses once again, got my body to calm back down to a resting state and Alex, looking as if he couldn't handle anymore, walked out quickly. I continued to watch him as he made his way back to his house. I watched him sleep. As he slept, I couldn't tear my eyes away. I felt this deep longing to smooth his hair down or run the back of my hand over his cheek. I looked at his long eyelashes resting on his cheeks and his lips slightly parted, plump and inviting. I suddenly wondered what it would feel like to kiss those lips.

I gasped as I realized the thought that I'd just had. What was wrong with me. Was I really falling in love with Alex? He had been my best friend for most of my life. He'd always been there for me when I needed him, and even now, he was still being there for me after he'd bared his soul for the second time, and I'd trampled his heart. He was still trying to take care of me.

He said it was too late for us, that he'd moved on with Veronica. But what if it wasn't? I knew now that I had to tell him how I was feeling and find out if he really didn't still feel it too. I just hoped that he would come back after the way I'd acted. The fear that he wouldn't and that it really was too late tried to take me over. I couldn't stop watching Alex until I knew what he was going to do.

I continued to be glued to Alex as he woke up and called Allie. I listened to their conversation and was relieved that he would be coming back. Too bad he wouldn't be coming alone. Maybe though, I could find a way to get him alone for a minute. Maybe he wouldn't be able to bring in Allie at all. Or if he did, and I couldn't get him alone, then at least I could be on my best behavior so that he would have no reason not to come back again.

I watched him all day as he moved his stuff, bunching the muscles he hid under his shirt as he did so. I was totally captivated by it. I could see that he was still letting off some of the steam from the frustration he'd had when I'd acted the way I had before. Once he was finished for the day, and went to take a shower, it took everything I had to turn off the crystal ball and give him his privacy. Wow. I have fallen hard, I thought.

Getting up from the table, I made my way back to the bench to wait. I decided to give the mattress a little test drive, sliding off my shoes, and stretching out on my back. I laid there looking up at that unmoving solid orange sky and trained my breathing as I waited. I felt like my anxiety was threatening to make me jump out of my skin. Not too long after, I watched as Alex and Allie materialized in front of the bench.

———————

Allie hadn't been sure what to expect. Sure, Alex had detailed what the place Emily was trapped in looked like, but it was hard to picture when she'd never actually seen it herself. Her jaw dropped now as she took a big look around. There was no wind at all. No sounds of birds or insects or anything. And the sky, what was with that solid orange? It looked like something had taken an orange marker and just inked the sky.

Turning all the way around now to face the school, Allie looked down to see Emily getting up off a mattress that was just lying on the ground. The mattress that Alex had told her that he'd brought in for Emily. It looked identical to the one that Emily's body was lying on in the hospital. As Emily, finished putting her shoes on, and got to her feet, Allie ran over and gave her sister the biggest hug she had probably ever given her. Emily squeezed back just as tightly. They held onto each other for almost a full minute before loosening their hold and letting go.

Allie turned now to look in the direction that Emily was staring. She had been looking at Alex who seemed to be standing a few feet away awkwardly with his hands in his pockets. Allie's eyes followed Emily who walked up to Alex and looked him right in the eye. She told him she was sorry for how she had acted before. Allie had no idea what Emily was talking about and was a little curious as she watched Emily suddenly wrap her arms around Alex's middle.

Alex stood there for a few seconds as if he was unsure of what to do before finally giving in and hugging Emily back, although not as tightly as Emily was. He kind of patted her back awkwardly a few times before Emily broke the hug and took a step back.

Alex cleared his throat and said, "It's fine."

Allie took that opportunity to break the obvious tension. "So, Emily, this is what the inside of your head looks like. Lovely."

At the sound of Allie's voice, both Emily and Alex jumped a little turning to look at her. Emily rolled her eyes. "I know, I know. It's not ideal by any stretch. But it's what I've got to work with. Did Alex explain to you everything that's going on here?"

"You mean how you have to watch scenes from the past and figure out where you went wrong to wake up? Yeah, he told me about it."

"Well then, I guess, let me show you around."

"What is there to see besides the inside of the school? Believe me, even when I'm awake that's the last place I'd ever want to go." Allie said drawing back her mouth in a grimace.

"Well, there's more down the road now. The road only appeared about two weeks ago. It seems the longer I'm here, the more there is for me to explore."

"I hope that's not your mind's way of getting used to being here." Allie said crossing her arms in front of her chest and rubbing them with her hands.

"No. It actually seems to be the opposite I think" Emily replied. "The more I start to see how I went down the wrong path, the more things appear. Hopefully I'll have everything figured out soon and be able to wake up." Then Emily turned to Alex and said, "I think I may have it almost completely figured out now."

Allie turned to look at Alex whose reaction didn't seem to be much of one at all. Something in his eyes seemed to flicker for a moment but was quickly replaced by a shadowed look as he slid his hands back into his pockets. It was as if he were trying to hold something back, Allie thought. Things were getting more interesting.

Now Emily started walking down the road, and Allie walked alongside her with Alex following a few feet behind. She wanted to ask Emily what was going on with her and Alex, but he wasn't far enough away for her to not be overheard. Maybe she could ask Alex later after they'd woken up. They soon came to a large field on the left with a house set far back near the other end of it.

"What is that place?" Allie asked.

Emily had a strange look on her face that Allie couldn't quite decipher. "That's Jenna Thompson's house. She was a girl we went to high school with who also stayed at home to go to college. We went to a party there at her house once."

Sensing there was more to this story, Allie turned to look at Alex who had a look of shock, anger, and confusion on his face. Yep, there was definitely something else Emily had chosen not to mention. They walked on in silence passing the field. Allie could feel the tension pouring from Alex and she wondered if Emily could too.

A little further up on the right, was a little black, square building. It was hard to make out what it was until they were almost right up on it. "Oh, I remember this place!" Allie said excitedly.

Emily turned to look at Allie now, raising an eyebrow. "How do you remember it? We used to come here with our friends when we were still in college and play pool and sing karaoke."

"Yeah, I used to come here to meet college guys" Allie said. "Back when I was still young enough to date a college guy."

"Allie you're still young enough to go to college yourself if you wanted to" Emily responded.

Allie just rolled her eyes good naturedly and said, "I know, I know" letting Emily know that she should drop that subject before they got into an argument that neither one of them really wanted to have.

"Well, the bar just appeared here about a week ago" Emily said now. "It seems to be exactly the same as I remember it, not sure if it changed by the time you started going there."

Emily opened the door and took a step inside. Once all three of them were inside, Allie took a good look around. It took a moment for her eyes to adjust to the darkness. There didn't seem to be any electricity in the place. Everything seemed to be the same as what she remembered as well and she wondered if The Spot was one of those places that never changed, but instead just got grungier and grungier with each generation.

"Is there anywhere else to explore past this place?" Allie asked.

"No. Not yet. But I feel like there may be a few more places that will appear before this is all over with."

"I wonder if the pool table works" Allie said, walking over to it and picking up a pool stick.

"I don't know" Emily said. "I haven't tried it."

Allie watched as Emily burned a hole in Alex's back. He had walked around the back of the bar, and was looking into the kitchen beyond. "Well, let's see" Allie said, pushing in the quarter slide and pulling it back out. Nothing happened. "I don't have any quarters on me" Allie said. "Maybe if I get a chance to come back again, I'll bring one."

"How about this? If I wake up, one of the first things we can do together is go play pool."

"Don't say if" Allie replied. "I have to have faith that you will wake up so don't say if. Say when."

"Okay. When I wake up, we can go. Better?"

"Much."

"Allie, how are mom and dad doing with all of this?" Emily asked her now.

"You mean you haven't looked in on them at all? Yes, Alex told me you could do that too."

"No, I haven't really. I don't know why. I guess I just feel like it would be too hard to watch their suffering. Having a child in a coma can't be easy."

"Well," Allie sighed, "They are handling it okay. Or okay in the sense that nothing much has changed between them, so they aren't doing any worse. I mean don't get me wrong, they are both grieving. It's just that they are pretty much grieving separately, the same way they do everything else. I've kind of been taking care of mom when she calls. Which is a lot lately by the way."

"I'm sorry about that."

"It's fine. It's just the way things are right now." Allie said trailing off and looking down at the floor.

Emily decided to change the subject. "So how are things with you and Josh? I've watched you together a few times and I have to say, I actually think you made a good choice this time."

"Really? Thank you for saying so. That means a lot to me to hear you say that. I really like Josh and I think he really likes me too."

"That's just so wonderful" Emily replied.

Allie smiled uncontrollably and felt like she was glowing. She and Emily sat at a table and talked more about Josh and what a good guy he was for as long as Allie could think of things to say about him.

Eventually, the subject of Josh started to dry up and another thought suddenly occurred to Allie. "Do we need to walk back to the school to wake up?"

"Truthfully, I don't know. Alex just always happened to be at the school when he did wake up. But I wouldn't think so. It's not like it's a warp point or anything." Emily responded.

"Okay well the reason I'm asking is because I'm pretty sure it's actually getting close to the time that Alex set the alarm for to wake us up."

"No. Not yet" Emily whined at Allie in a hushed tone. "I kind of need to talk to Alex alone about something."

"Well look," Allie said, "Maybe I can get him to come right back in, you know, after we wake up. I can tell something is going on with you two. I mean, he hasn't really said a word to you since we've been here."

With that, Alex came out from the kitchen where he had previously disappeared. "It's time to go Allie" he said as he reached the place where the women were standing.

"I love you Emily" Allie said now giving her sister another hug. She felt lighter and could see her arms disappearing from around Emily's neck.

Once they were gone, I fell down into a nearby chair. That did not go how I'd hoped it would at all. First of all, when I'd apologized to Alex, he didn't seem to be very receptive. My heart had felt crushed in that moment, but there was nothing I could say with Allie standing right there. Then, when we were walking to the bar and Allie asked about Jenna Thompson's house, even though I didn't turn to look at

Alex, I didn't have to. I could feel him staring daggers between my shoulder blades. And now they were gone, without me being able to talk to Alex.

What was I going to do now? I knew it was almost time for Alex to leave again. Would he come right back after talking to Allie? Or would I have to wait another week? What if he never came back? I looked over at the table where the creature had been at before. It was now there again, as if it had just appeared silently upon the departure of Allie and Alex. I got up, walked back over to that table, and asked to pull up Alex.

They were just waking up as Josh turned off the alarm that had been set. Allie got up and stretched, then walked over to Josh, throwing her arms around him with a smile.

"It worked" she said into his shoulder as she laid her head on it.

Alex was getting up a little more slowly as Allie pulled back from Josh and looked into his eyes. "Josh, can you give me and Alex here just a minute alone. There's something I need to talk to him about privately."

Josh's eyes slid to Alex and then back to Allie's. "Sure, no problem. I'll be right out in the hall if you need me." With that, he placed a kiss on Allie's lips, walked up to Alex to shake his hand again, then walked out of the room.

"Alex, before we woke up, Emily told me that she was hoping to talk to you alone for a few minutes. I told her I'd let you know so that maybe, you know, you'd go back in before you leave town, and talk to her."

I watched as Alex sighed loudly then turned to look at Allie. "Honestly Allie, I'm not in the mood to talk to Emily. Maybe I'll come back next weekend."

"*Maybe* you'll come back? Alex, I know something is going on between you two. I saw the look on your face when you saw that girl's house that you guys went to a party at years ago. But whatever it is, don't let it keep you from hearing Emily out. Okay please? I just want her to have every opportunity to wake up..."

"Allie... I hope she does wake up. I don't really feel comfortable telling you about what happened at Jenna's house. And right now, I just need to get away from all of this."

I watched as Alex walked quickly out the door. I didn't continue to watch him then. I just couldn't. I felt my heart breaking as I asked the creature to turn off the image of Alex walking away.

Chapter Eighteen

I sat across from the creature for a moment in silence, trying to think. After all this time, and all the years that had passed where my best friend was totally and utterly in love with me, I had started to understand those feelings and even maybe reciprocate them. But all of a sudden, I couldn't get him alone long enough to talk to him about it. I now felt more than ever as if I were locked away in a cage, unable to get free.

So now I forced myself to stay calm as I thought about my choices. I could always go back to sleep and hopefully wake up in a week when, *hopefully*, Alex would decide to come back. But then, what if he didn't? I will have wasted a week just waiting for him. No, the best thing that I could do now, I decided, was to go ahead and watch the next scene from my past. So, without another moment to waste, I told the creature what I wanted, and the show began.

The scene opened with me and Samantha sitting across from each other at one of the tables here in this bar. We were not wearing our normal attire for going out to a bar, but were instead wearing nice, fancy dresses. Mine was a rose-pink color, that stopped just above the tops of my knees. It had fluttery cap sleeves on it. I had on matte gold-colored strappy shoes with a clunky two-inch heel. My brown hair, normally slightly wavy, looked as if it had been straightened and shaped to where it looked like it bobbed naturally, framing my face.

Samantha had on an emerald, green dress that also stopped just above the tops of her knees. It had quarter length sleeves. She was wearing black peep toe sliders with a wedge heel and her naturally blonde, curly hair, had been tamed down to look smooth and wavy. We were both wearing square graduation caps on top of our heads.

It was the graduation party that The Spot had thrown the evening after the ceremony. The same party they still continue to throw every year for every college graduating class from what I'd heard. We were sipping on free champagne to celebrate as all around us, everyone else who had graduated earlier that day were doing the same. We were laughing as the DJ made a joke about his surprise that some of the faces that he was seeing had managed to graduate from college.

Samantha's then boyfriend James came up to the table, a big grin on his face. He had already secured an engineering job which is what he'd just gotten his degree in. I remembered now watching the two of them in the crystal ball, that this was also the night that he had proposed to Samantha in front of all our friends. Of course, she had said yes.

Samantha had graduated with a degree in computer science, but she'd gotten pregnant with Tyler pretty quickly after her and James had gotten married. There was still some speculation by some that it happened before they were married. Not that it mattered. Samantha had been all too happy to become a stay-at-home mom and she and James seemed to be still madly in love today. That was all that truly mattered in my book because unlike Allie, if something were to happen between Samantha and James, Samantha still had a degree she could fall back on.

Soon after James made it to our table, so too had Alex. Both men were dressed handsomely in their dress pants and button-down shirts. Alex had already rolled his sleeves up over his forearms. It was amazing how handsome I thought he looked, when I hadn't even thought about it all at the time that this happened. Both men pulled up a chair around our table just as the DJ announced a toast. We all clinked our glasses with each other just as DJ loaded up his music que and the first song started to play.

For a while, Samantha and I had danced with each other to the faster paced songs and the line dances while James and Alex mingled with some of the other guys that had graduated. I remembered being so happy and having so much fun. I had also been completely carefree that night because I had already been hired as well to be a new teacher at the school that everyone except James had attended for most of our lives. I had liked the idea of going somewhere I already knew.

When the first slow song started to play, we made our way back to our table only for James to take Samantha back out to the dance floor. I remember watching them dance and thinking how glad I was for Samantha that she had found someone that made her so happy. Now as I watched myself watching them, I also watched Alex who had been still sitting at the table next to me. He was talking to some of the other guys, but every few seconds, I now saw him glance at my younger self. At the time, I hadn't noticed it at all.

Over the course of the night, we had all steadily sipped on cocktails and beer, not enough to get drunk, just enough to keep a good buzz. Several guys had asked me to dance, and I had obliged them all. Each time I watched myself dance with another guy, I also watched Alex to gauge his reaction. He seemed to have a look of torture on his face each time as he watched me out on the floor with someone else. Then after a few hours had passed, James had walked up to the sound booth and whispered something in the DJ's ear.

When the song that had been playing ended, the DJ said, "I have a young man here who has a very important announcement to make!" Then he handed his microphone over to James.

I watched as we had all looked on bewildered. James took a deep breath and started to talk. "As many of you know, Samantha and I have been together for three and a half years, for most of our college careers. We made it through college together by giving each other love and support when we needed it most. And now, because of this, we have graduated. And so, now with our labors complete, I would like to tell Samantha just how much I love her."

James, who had been looking around the crowd as he talked, now focused on Samantha. "Samantha, I love you more than you could ever know, and I would like to ask you to marry me. So, will you? Marry me?"

Everyone cheered as Samantha threw her hands up over her mouth in complete shock. She had gone completely red and had tears streaming down her face as she got up from her chair and walked over to where to James was standing. She took the microphone from him causing everyone to quiet down before saying, "Yes, I will marry you."

The crowd erupted once again as James slid the ring he had bought on Samantha's finger. Then they threw their arms around each other and kissed passionately. Finally, Samantha handed the microphone back to the DJ and they made their way back to our table. It had been such a great moment, and I was happy to be able to relive it seeing as it had not been caught on film. Too bad Samantha wasn't here right now to see this, I thought.

And now the DJ was congratulating the couple as I gave Samantha a huge hug and grabbed her hand to take a look at the ring. It was a simple round diamond on a gold band, but it was beautiful. Alex shook James's hand and told him congratulations as James turned to ask his now fiancé to dance. She smiled and took his hand as he led her out to the floor.

Then Alex stepped in front of me as I watched the happy couple and asked me to dance. I remember I had been taken aback a little and I guess he must've noticed the perplexed look on my face because he said, "We're celebrating."

I must've been satisfied with that answer, because I watched as my face relaxed into a simple half-smile and said, "Sure. Let's go."

I followed behind Alex out to the dance floor. He turned to me then and awkwardly put his hands on my hips. He kept a gap between us that was at least a few inches as I hooked my arms loosely around his shoulders. We turned slowly in a circle while the song played and I noticed now that I had pretty much been watching Samantha and James over Alex's shoulder as we danced, while he had kept his eyes trained on me. My heart fluttered watching the intimate look in his eyes and I wanted so badly to tell myself to look at them. That's all I would have needed to do. But alas, it wasn't to be, and as the song ended, we broke apart as he followed me back to the table.

"Thank you for the dance" I said to Alex as he took his seat next to me.

"No problem" he said turning to look at me with what looked like a forced neutral expression on his face.

Then he cleared his throat as James and Samantha came back to the table and took their seats as well. The night ended shortly after that with me and Samantha riding home together. As Samantha drove us home, we talked about the highlights of the evening with me telling her once again how happy I was for her getting engaged to James.

Then Samantha turned the subject to me and said, "So I saw you and Alex dance together tonight." She turned her head briefly to give me a raised eyebrow look. "Anything I should know about?"

I laughed. "Samantha, how long have you known us? We're just friends."

"Really? So, you didn't feel even the smallest hint of a spark while you were dancing then?"

"Not even a hint of one" I responded. "Why are you asking?"

"No reason" she said. "I just thought maybe something had changed and you know me, I want to hear all the dish when things happen."

"Well, there's nothing to tell" I said. "He asked me to dance because we were celebrating."

Samantha said nothing else, and the car was filled with silence as the scene ended and the image went black. I sat back in my chair now thinking about what I had just watched. How had it not been obvious, at least by that point, that Alex had asked me to dance because he wanted to get closer to me? I mean, he never asked anyone else to dance that whole night. But then, I hadn't been paying attention to whether he danced with anyone else or not.

But even when he asked me to dance, he could've asked any of the other girls at the party who didn't have anyone to dance with. I must've rationalized to myself that I was convenient because I had been sitting right next to him. He was also comfortable with me, I thought, because by that time, we already knew each other so well. There was no doubt about it now in my mind. I had unconsciously chosen to be blind to it all. Oh how we can deceive ourselves to the point of denial, I thought.

———————

Once Alex made it back to his truck in the hospital parking lot, he had started to feel better. He'd just needed some air. He'd had to hold in everything he was thinking and feeling the whole time he and Allie were visiting Emily. Now, in the quiet and stillness of his truck, he threw his head back against the headrest and shoved his palm against the steering wheel.

So, Emily had watched the first time that he'd told her he loved her. She'd watched how he'd made himself completely vulnerable while she'd passed out and missed it. Considering that the road leading to Jenna's house had appeared *before* he'd even shown up with the mattress, he was guessing that she'd already watched it by the time he'd gotten there. The thought that she had watched that moment and chose not to say anything to him about it at all made him feel so...so... angry!

Why wouldn't she have said anything to him about it when they were alone the night before? Is that why she got so upset for no apparent reason and told him maybe he shouldn't come back? Of course it was, he thought. It all made sense. She'd watched him pour his heart out all those years ago and thought maybe he was still holding that torch for her now. She couldn't handle that thought and pushed him away.

What a fool he'd been for thinking he could do something nice to help her. She'd read more into it than there actually was. That's why she tried to push him away. It didn't matter that he'd expressed to her several times that he didn't have those feelings anymore and that he'd moved on. It didn't even matter that he had a girlfriend who was waiting for him right now. The only thing that had mattered was that she knew he'd had feelings for her in the past.

But then, why did she apologize when he went back there with Allie? Maybe she was having second thoughts? Alex growled and shoved the steering wheel again. No, he could not let her get back under his skin that way. He couldn't sit here and wonder if she was changing her mind. He couldn't let her have that power over him anymore. He was over it. He had to be, for his own sanity.

Allie had said that Emily wanted to talk to him alone. She probably wanted to apologize for blindsiding him with the fact that she'd watched that particular moment in time knowing that he wouldn't be able to say anything about it in front of Allie. Well too late, he thought. She should've talked to him about it the night before, when she'd had the perfect opportunity to do so.

Alex didn't even want to wait until morning to go back to Maryland. The sooner he got back, the sooner he could talk to Veronica and tell her about everything he'd been holding back. He wasn't going to let his relationship get ruined over someone that didn't even want him.

He drove back to his house and quickly gathered his things. He loaded the last couch on the trailer that he had borrowed and brought it to the storage unit with the rest of his stuff. Next, he brought the trailer back to Brendan's, leaving it in his garage for him. Then, he headed back to the highway and back to Maryland.

Alex drove through the night hitting no traffic at all. He made it back in record time, not long before the sunrise. It was still dark outside as he made it upstairs into his apartment and collapsed on his bed. He didn't even bother to climb underneath the blanket first. He had barely bothered to take his shoes off, doing so as he walked to his bedroom. They were left strewn across the living room floor.

By the time he woke up, it was well after noon on Sunday. He checked his phone and saw that he'd had a missed call and a voicemail from Veronica. He pulled up the message and listened to it.

"Hey it's me. I just got home from a very long night working at the bar and saw your truck parked outside. I'm about to go to bed now but I'll be up at four if you want to come over and see me. Or I could come right over to you. Just let me know. Bye."

Alex had about an hour and a half to kill before Veronica would be up. So, he got up and made some breakfast and started washing clothes while he waited. Finally, a few minutes after four, he called her back.

"Good afternoon sunshine" he said when she answered the phone in a sleepy tone.

"Good afternoon" she replied while yawning. "What are you doing back so early? I wasn't expecting you till later this evening."

"Well, I decided to come back early. I've been spending too much time going back and forth and I missed you."

"I missed you too. Would you like me to come over or are you in the middle of anything?"

"No. Go ahead and come over whenever you're ready."

"I'll be there in ten minutes."

Sure enough, ten minutes later, Alex was cleaning his apartment when he heard the door to the apartment next to him open and close. Just a few seconds later, Veronica was knocking on his door just as he'd gotten there to answer it. When he opened the door, Veronica stood there leaning on the door frame wearing an oversized baby blue button up shirt and a pair of white boxer shorts that barely peaked out from underneath. She had walked over barefoot, with her toes painted a shade of pastel pink. Set against her bronze skin and dark hair, Alex felt absolutely powerless.

Veronica reached up, wrapping her arms smoothly around Alex's shoulders then pressed up against him, she gave him a deep kiss, sliding her tongue into his mouth. He shuddered as his brain turned to fog. She walked in, forcing him to walk backwards as she kicked out behind her, shutting the door with her foot. The sound brought Alex back to awareness and he eased Veronica's arms down off from him.

"I need to talk to you about something first" he said to her.

Veronica, undaunted slid her arms back up around his neck and said, "Shhh. It can wait."

Then she backed Alex up to his couch, pushing him down onto it. The next thing he knew, she was sitting on his lap, her knees pressed into the couch on either side of him, unbuttoning her shirt. When she unbuttoned his pants and reached down, while kissing him deeply once again, he lost all control.

Once I had finished watching our college graduation party, I was completely anxious. I felt like I couldn't move on to the next scene yet. I had to know what was going on with Alex. Was he still in town or had he chosen to drive back to Maryland already? I knew by now it had to be Sunday, but I had no idea how much time had passed. I took a deep breath and asked the creature to bring up Alex.

The crystal ball lit up with Alex's living room in his apartment. He and Veronica were standing just a few feet apart staring at each other with large grins on their faces. Veronica seemed to be pulling on some shorts underneath an opened button-up shirt which revealed her bra and torso. Alex was buttoning his jeans and had no shirt on at all. Oh my God! Had I just missed them having sex? I felt the stab of jealousy slice through me.

I was just about to shut off the crystal ball and metaphorically bleach my eyes out when Alex said, "Okay. Now I really need to talk to you."

"Alright alright" Veronica said. "You win. Well, you already won. But okay let's have a talk." Then she slid down into Alex's nearby recliner and sat back crossing her long silky legs.

Alex sat down on his couch and turned towards her. He said, "The thing is, I haven't been completely honest with you."

Oh no, he's going to tell her all about me now. This wasn't going to be good. I could just feel it. But now I couldn't turn off the image in front of me. I had to hear it for myself.

Alex continued, "It's not that I lied really. It's just that I haven't told you everything there is to tell, and I think I should."

"What is it?" Veronica asked, sounding a little wary. "I told you that you could tell me anything."

"I know... and I should have." Alex looked hard at her for a moment before taking a deep breath. "The thing is, my friend, the one that's still in a coma in the hospital? She's a woman. And... not only is she a woman, but she was actually my best friend in the world for most of my life until I moved here."

Veronica sat up a little straighter. "What happened?" she asked sounding anxious.

"The thing is, and it doesn't matter anymore, so please don't misunderstand, is that I was in love with her for a very long time. I guess you could say she was my first real love. I spent years wishing she would notice that I had feelings for her. But she never did and I didn't want to ruin what we did have by saying anything. When I finally did, she broke my heart. And so, I broke our friendship. I moved here to start over. To get her out of my head. And I did. I met you and you're great, I am very happy being with you."

"Well, if that's true, then why haven't you told me about any of this before now? I mean, we've been seeing each other now for almost two months. I just feel like maybe that's something you should've shared with me before now."

"Well don't get me wrong, it's not like I never dated or slept with anyone else. I definitely have. It's just that, before I met you, I never really liked any of those other women enough to tell them the things I'm telling you now. So, the reason I held off on telling you is because, I didn't want to lose you."

"But I would've found out eventually I'm sure, and then what would you have done? Because, the truth is, if I had found out from someone besides you, I think you would've lost me."

"So, are you saying I haven't lost you? That everything's okay?"

"Well, not quite. Tell me how your ex-best friend is doing? Is she getting any better or any closer to waking up?"

"Unfortunately, no. And the longer she is in that position, the more her physical health has started to deteriorate. If she doesn't wake up soon, there's a real good chance she may not make it."

"So, you've been going back and forth just to see her sleeping essentially and haven't even talked to her" Veronica stated.

"No. I haven't" Alex lied. "And that's another reason I'm telling you about this now. I promise you, my feelings for her in that way are completely in the past. They were in the past before I even heard she had been in an accident. I've only been going to see her as a concerned friend."

"Well, then here's what I think" Veronica said, uncrossing her legs and standing up. "There's no reason you can't just call from time to time to check on her progress. I think the fact that you felt the need to drive all the way down there says something different than what you're trying to tell me. Because of that, I think that you have done your due diligence as a friend, and I don't see any reason you should go back again. In fact, I would go so far as to say that if you really want to hold onto me, you will leave her completely in the past from now on, as a friend or otherwise."

Alex sighed and stood up himself. "I deserve your feelings of apprehension" he replied. "From now on, there will be no more trips back home. I am yours. I am all yours." Then he walked up to Veronica and pulled her into his arms.

That's when I asked the creature to cut off the scene. I had ruined my last chance with Alex. It was as I was thinking this that I started to feel the all too familiar quaking of the world inside my head.

Chapter Nineteen

Tables and chairs started falling over and pictures were falling off the walls. I ran out of the building in fear that it might collapse. After what seemed like forever but had in reality only been a few minutes, the quaking stopped. But not before it tore open the ground on the other side of the road. There was a massive rip that ran along the side of the road far off into the distance. What would've happened had I been standing there, I wondered. I shuddered at the thought. Would that have caused instant death?

I knew by now that the quake had meant that I'd had another seizure. This bothered me greatly. What if I still made it out of here and woke up with permanent brain damage? I pushed the thought away. I couldn't think about that now. I needed to push forward, I told myself. That meant watching the next scene from my past. No matter how much what I had just witnessed had hurt, and how hard it would be to push the image from my mind, I couldn't think about that now.

I took a few deep breaths and walked back inside the bar. The table that I'd been at with the creature was the only one still standing. So were the two chairs around it. I sat back down across from the crea-ture and asked it to pull up the next scene from my past.

What unfolded was an image of me in my classroom teaching a group of students. It wasn't the same students that I had right before my accident, but a group from my first year as a teacher. I watched as the bell rang and I had my students line up behind me. We were walk-ing down the hall when a man who had been walking the opposite direction, stopped me. It was Mike Garrison, the computer whiz that I had went on a few dates with.

"Hi, I'm here working on the school's computer systems, and I was just wondering if you could tell me where the main office is" he had asked me. He looked very sweet and innocent with his curly, light brown hair and thin, metal rimmed glasses.

He had kind eyes, I remembered thinking as I said, "No problem. It's right down the hall that way." I pointed him in the opposite direc-tion from which I had been walking with my class.

"Thank you very much Mrs.?"

"Ms. Bartlett" I finished for him.

"Oh a Ms., are we? Well in that case, you have a very nice smile *Ms.* Bartlett and I wonder if maybe you'd be interested in getting a cup of coffee with me. I'm Mike by the way" he said as he stuck out his hand to shake mine.

"Well Mike, that might just be a possibility" I said, taking that hand. Then I turned to my students and told them to continue single file to the cafeteria and that I would be watching them as they made their way down the hall. As they walked off, I looked back up at Mike. "Let me just give you my number" I said to him as I pulled a note pad that I kept on me out of my pocket. I scribbled my name and number down, tore the paper across the metal rings, and handed it to him.

Mike looked down at the paper examining it before looking back at me and saying, "I'll call you this weekend, *Ms.* Bartlett." Then he folded the paper neatly and stuck it in his shirt pocket, smiled at me, and went on about his way to find the main office.

The scene faded out and faded back in with me now sitting with Alex at one of our favorite adult bars, catching up with each other on the past week's events. Before everything that happened, we used to do that once a week followed by playing a friendly (or not so friendly) game of darts where we taunted each other the whole time about who was the better player.

My phone had started ringing as Alex was telling me about one of his physical therapy patients. I pulled my phone out of my pocket and saw that it was a number that I didn't recognize. I apologized to Alex and asked him if he could hold on for a minute as I answered the call. Alex seemed obliged to do so knowing it could be any number of people that I worked with at the school.

"Hello?" I said now scrunching my eyebrows in concentration as a group of people laughing loudly walked past us towards the pool tables.

"Hello, Ms. Bartlett? This is Mike from the other day at the school. I never did get your first name. I guess I was just flustered that you actually gave me your number."

I watched myself smile as I said, "Hi Mike. My name is Emily." Alex looked at me with a quizzical look on his face. He looked amused and curious at the same time.

"Alright Emily. Well, I was just calling to ask if you wanted to meet me for coffee tomorrow. Sometime around two?"

"Sure, sounds good. Where did you have in mind?"

"I was thinking maybe that little coffee shop around the corner from the school. I don't know the name."

"Yeah, I know the one you're talking about. It's pretty laid back. I can meet you there after three tomorrow. I can't do it sooner than that because of the whole teacher thing."

"Oh, that's right! Duh Mike. I'm sorry about that. I sometimes think I'd lose my head if it wasn't attached to my body."

I laughed at his self-reproach. "It's okay."

"Alright, good. Then it's a date and I'll see you after three."

I told Mike goodbye and hung up my phone. Alex was looking at me with extreme curiosity now as I slid my phone back into my pocket. "I met a guy the other day at school. He was there to work on our computer system or something. That was just him calling to ask me to meet him for coffee tomorrow. He seems like a sweet guy."

"Well… at least you're meeting him in a public place during the day. You never know about people anymore, no matter how nice they might seem."

I noticed that he'd had a look on his face that at the time, I'd mistaken for worry. But now, upon reflection, I could see that it had actually been jealousy.

"Oh Alex" my past self said slapping his arm playfully and rolling my eyes.

The scene faded out again and faded back into me now hanging out at a larger, cleaner, and more open bar than the one I was currently sitting in. This one sported a grill with pretty good food. Me, Samantha, James, and Alex sometimes frequented this place together to listen to live music, grab a bite, and just hang out with other adults. I was there with Samantha and James, who were sitting across from me at a table. Mike was there too sitting next to me. I remembered this night. It was a night out that I'd organized so that Samantha could meet Mike and give me her opinion.

We were all sitting there, enjoying our drinks and conversation, sharing an appetizer of fried pickles, and waiting for the local band that was playing there that night to start, when Alex came walking through the door. He was also with a date. The woman he was with, I had never met before. He'd known where I was going to be that night and with whom because I had invited him to join. Alex had declined my offer. So, when he walked in that night, I'd just assumed he'd changed his mind.

Alex caught my eye and walked right over to our table with his date who had perfectly straight blonde hair stopping midway down her back. She was slightly overdressed for the venue wearing a navy-blue shift dress and strappy shoes with a very thin heel. Me and

Samantha had both worn dressy jeans with boots and blousy tops while all three men were wearing jeans and button up shirts in various patterns of plaid.

"Hey guys" Alex said addressing everyone at the table.

"Hey Alex" Samantha responded with a curious look on her face. "Who's your date?"

"This is Heather. We've been out on a few dates and Emily said you guys were all coming out tonight as a group and invited me to join. At the time I'd said no, but then I thought, why not introduce Heather to some of my friends?"

Everyone looked at Heather who gave a half-hearted smile that didn't quite reach her eyes. She didn't seem so happy to be there. I remembered wondering at the time if Alex had even asked her if she'd wanted to go meet his friends before bringing her there.

"Heather this is Emily, Samantha, James, and what was it again? Mike?" he said last with his open palm out at my date and a look of apology on his face.

Alex had never met Mike before that night, so I didn't think anything of him barely remembering Mike's name. I could tell by watching now though, that he had had no problem remembering Mike's name and was pretending that he did. He had acted as if I had never mentioned Mike to him before in any meaningful kind of way. It was obvious that Heather was picking up on something, and I wondered if Mike had as well. I couldn't tell by the way he responded to Alex.

"Yeah, that's right. It's Mike. Nice to meet you Alex" he said standing up and shaking Alex's hand.

"Well, uh, why don't you join us, Alex?" Samantha said now gesturing for Alex to pull up two empty chairs from another table for him and his date.

Alex did just that, grabbing two chairs and placing them on one side of the table between me and Samantha who were sitting directly across from each other. He gestured for Heather to have a seat, and once she was sitting, he got comfortable in the other chair. Heather looked very uncomfortable, staring down at the table as Alex ordered a round of drinks for everyone.

Alex was friendly and boisterous the whole night, bringing up inside jokes that he, Samantha, James, and I had all shared over the years. I could tell now that he'd been trying to make Mike feel like an outsider. But Mike just went with it in stride, laughing each time Alex brought up a funny memory from our shared past. Alex was barely paying any attention to Heather who seemed to be getting more uncomfortable by the minute.

Eventually, the night was over, and I watched as everyone said their goodbyes and went home. Mike walked me to his car in the parking lot and opened my door for me before getting into the driver's seat and taking me home. Alex never went out with Heather again. At the time, I'd just thought that she was not very friendly, and they were just two very different people. Now I wondered what she would've been like if Alex had paid any attention to her.

The scene faded out and then faded back in on another night that I had been at that same bar and grill. This time though, it was just Samantha and James that were with me. Mike was nowhere to be found. We seemed to be having a nice conversation. I was talking about some of the things that the kids in my class tried to get away with, causing Samantha and James to both crack up with laughter.

Then a tall, dark, handsome man walked over to our table. He had a thick head of dark brown hair, dark brown eyes, and a cleft chin. It was the other guy that I had dated for a while, Dean Parker. I now knew that this memory was about a year after me and Mike had gone our separate ways. After that night where Mike had met Samantha and James as well as Alex, we met once for lunch during which Mike had told me that he had gotten a job opportunity across the country. He told me that he was taking it, to which I told him congratulations. He told me that he'd enjoyed the time he had with me and that maybe we could keep in touch as friends. I'd agreed with him that that would be nice, and we shared a nice hug before we'd left the restaurant. I never heard from him again, but I hadn't honestly expected to.

I wasn't heartbroken over it either. From my experience, relationships didn't really work out. And if they did, then both parties ended up pretty miserable. Samantha and James were just the very lucky exception. That's why, even though I hadn't really felt much for Mike beyond the fact that he was nice to talk to, I'd continued to go out with him up until he gave me the news about his job offer. Because he seemed to be happy with the relationship the way it was, and I didn't expect to find anything much better than that.

Then, about a year later, Dean walked into my life. I was watching now as he stood at the end of the table that Samantha, James, and I had occupied. He looked at me with those dark eyes and said, "I couldn't help but notice you from the bar. You seem to be the life of the party making your friends laugh so much. I wonder if they would miss you too much if I asked you to dance?" He turned to Samantha and James with an eyebrow up in question.

"Not at all!" Samantha said nearly slapping her hand down on top of mine and giving me a look that said I'd be crazy not dance with him.

"Well then, how about it?" he asked turning back to me. "I'm Dean."

"I'm Emily" I said putting my hand in his and allowing him to pull me up from my chair.

We walked out to the dance floor, my hand still in his as he pulled me close to him and we started to slow dance to the song that was already halfway through.

"You're a good dancer" I said as we swayed to the tune.

"Thanks. You're pretty good yourself Emily."

"So, what do you do Dean?" I asked.

"Oh, a little bit of everything. I work construction."

"Really? I wouldn't have pegged you for that."

"What I'm not rugged enough?" he asked causing me to think for a moment that I'd put my foot in my mouth. "Just kidding" he said now with a smile, causing me to feel a sense of relief. "Technically, I'm a foreman so I don't usually have to get my hands too dirty. So, what do you do Emily?"

"I'm a teacher. I teach fourth grade."

"You seem to be very suited for such a noble profession."

"Thank you. Anyway, that's why my friends were laughing. Because I was telling them about some of the things my students try to get past me sometimes."

"Kids will be kids" he said now with a smirk as he seemed to focus in on my lips.

I felt my breath catch and my heart start to pound and I wondered if he was going to kiss me. But then the song ended, and the spell broke. He stepped back and then turned to walk me back to my table. I remembered feeling kind of disappointed and chastising myself inwardly for such a thought.

Then he said, "Well Emily, I enjoyed our dance and if it's okay with you, I'd like to get your number."

On the inside I was jumping up and down. On the outside I said, "Sure. Let's walk over to the bar so I can get a napkin to write it down on."

"After you" he said.

After I handed him the napkin with my number on it, he walked me back to my table. As we stopped next to it, he took my hand and kissed the back of it, before saying, "Thank you for the dance." Then he turned to Samantha and James and said, "You guys have a nice night." Then he strode off out the door.

"Whoo-ee" said Samantha. "Dish girl. How was that dance?"

James groaned a little. "Do I really have to listen to your girl talk?" he said giving Samantha a puppy eyed look.

Samantha laughed. "At least you didn't get upset that I basically just made a reference to another guy being hot."

"That's because I trust you completely" James said with a look of love on his face.

"Thank you" Samantha said. "I trust you too." Then they smooched for the thousandth time that night. If I hadn't loved the sight of Samantha so happy, I would've been ready to puke by then. "Come on Emily" Samantha said getting up from the table now. "Let's go to the bathroom and you can tell me all about it there."

The scene faded out and then opened back up with me at my house. I was dressed up in a tight sleeveless black dress that had a short skirt. My hair was pulled up on top of my head and I was wearing black, pointed closed toe sling backs. I had some small gold hoops in my ears and a flat gold necklace. I seemed to be just finishing up my makeup when the doorbell rang. I went to open it and Alex was standing on my porch dressed in casual shorts and a t-shirt.

"Where are you going all dressed up?" he asked me.

"Hi Alex" I said letting him in. "I'm going on a date."

"Oh? Do I know him?" Alex asked casually.

"No actually. We've only been out once before. But what's up?"

"Well, I came over because I was just taking a walk around the neighborhood and saw your lights on. Figured I'd see if you wanted to hang out, maybe catch a movie. But I see you're about to be otherwise occupied."

"Yeah, sorry. He should be here any minute." The doorbell rang. "Speaking of..." I said as I went to open the door.

"Hey Emily, you look very nice. Are you ready to go?" Dean asked looking handsome in a black leather jacket, dark dress pants and dress shoes. His hair just as thick and good looking as ever was greased up on top of his head. He looked past me then and saw Alex standing behind me a few feet away.

"Oh, this is my friend Alex" I said turning towards Alex. "Alex, this is Dean. Alex was just leaving. Weren't you?" I asked Alex with a forced smile.

"Yeah. I was just leaving. I'd just stopped by to see if Emily wanted to hang out and see a movie or something but she's busy. We're really good friends."

"I see" Dean said eyeing Alex speculatively. "Well, if you'll excuse us, I don't want to be late for our *date* reservation. We are going on our *second* date. Technically our third if you count the dance we had the night I met you" Dean said looking into my eyes and smiling at me. Before Alex could respond at all, Dean said, "Nice to meet you, Alan."

"It's Alex" he responded to Dean as we all walked out the door. "Talk to you later Emily." Alex said as he turned and started walking back down the street.

"What was that about?" I asked Dean once we were in his car driving towards the fancy restaurant that he had brought me to that night.

"What was what about? I'm sorry but your friend doesn't seem to get the message that you're just friends. And frankly, it makes me wonder how you feel about that."

"What? No, we are just friends. We've just known each other for a very long time. Think grade school. And no. You read Alex all wrong. He was just being protective. I mean with your dark, handsome good looks, could you blame him?"

"I don't know. I've never been just friends with a woman if you know what I mean. But if you say so, then who am I to argue?"

The scene faded out and then faded back in. It was midday, and I was sitting with Alex. We were again catching up with each other, at the bar we liked to play darts at.

"I don't really like that guy you went out with last night Emily" Alex said to me.

"He's harmless" I said to Alex with a smile. "He seems kind of dangerous, but really that's all just an act."

"Well, I just didn't get a good vibe from him" he said. "I'm just giving you my opinion."

"Your opinion is duly noted *dad*" I laughed. "Don't worry. I promise he's really okay."

The scene faded out and I thought, wow, I really never paid attention to any of the signs, did I? Now I thought about why things had ended with Dean. When he'd danced with me that first night I'd met him, he was like a mysterious stranger. Normally I didn't go out with guys like that, because he was the type that knew he looked good. That type always broke women's hearts. But that night, I'd been in kind of a funk watching Samantha and James be all lovey dovey and when Dean walked up, I suddenly felt like I needed a little excitement.

Then after Dean had called me, and we went on a few dates, I realized that I had no real attraction to him. Even that day when Alex had told me what he thought of him, I already knew that I didn't see Dean and I in a long-term relationship. I knew I needed to break it off. It wasn't fair to have Dean bringing me out and spending money on me when it wasn't going to go anywhere. But I also hadn't wanted to share those feelings with Alex, hence my deflection and sarcasm in that last scene that I'd watched.

Now, my thoughts of Alex and what I'd seen right before my last seizure caught back up with me. The image of him and Veronica getting dressed like that flashed through my head and I suddenly felt very weary and exhausted by it. I needed an escape. I knew I needed to keep going with the past scenes, but I just felt like I couldn't. I wasn't even sure it mattered anymore if Alex wasn't going to come back. I decided to walk back to the mattress that Alex had left for me and go to sleep.

Allie got the call that Emily had had another seizure the next morning. Her phone ringing had jarred her awake from a fitful night's sleep. She had tossed and turned all night thinking about her visit inside her sister's head. In a panic, she quickly threw on the first decent looking thing she saw and took off for the hospital. Up in Emily's room, a nurse was standing over her bed, writing something on Emily's chart as Allie ran in, out of breath from running all the way through the hospital.

"Hi" Allie said taking big gulps of air as the nurse looked at her with a startled expression on her face. "I'm her sister" Allie continued glancing in Emily's direction. "As you can tell, I came literally running as soon as I heard she had another seizure. How is she doing?"

"Well," the nurse said glancing down at the chart in her hand and back up to Allie, "Honestly, her vitals aren't looking too great. But I really shouldn't be the one to talk to you about it. Let me go get her doctor."

Allie thanked the nurse and waited patiently for the doctor while she took a closer look at her sister. Emily was starting to look so pale, that in her opinion, it was a wonder she was still hanging on. Allie imagined that her life force was just slowly slipping away. Was it all truly hopeless?

As she sat there, feeling helpless to help her sister, the doctor came into the room. He explained to Allie that this seizure was a lot stronger than the last one Emily had experienced and that it had left Emily's breathing and pulse weaker. He was afraid that if she had another one, that she might not live through it. He apologized to Allie for his bad news, before leaving her to go check on another patient.

Allie sat there in silence for a few moments before pulling herself together to call her parents. Brenda answered and confirmed that she had also gotten the call that morning. She couldn't make it down there however, because Bob had taken off once again, and while they had two vehicles between them, Allie could hear Brenda slurring her words as she explained that she couldn't drive there herself.

Disgusted with her parents, Allie hung up her phone. She took a minute to calm her thoughts before taking a deep breath and calling Alex. It rang so many times that Allie was preparing to leave a voicemail when Alex suddenly answered.

"Hey Allie. Look, I think I need to tell you that I can't come visit Emily anymore. It's just not helping anything for any of us. You shouldn't call me anymore."

"Can't or won't?" Allie asked eliciting a loud sigh from Alex in return. "*You* look Alex. I know something else is going on between you and Emily that I don't know about, and I know you don't want to talk about it. But I also know that Emily had another seizure this morning. Alex, it was worse than the last time and the doctor says that he's afraid if she has another, she won't make it."

"Well, what do you expect me to do about it Allie?!" Alex asked in frustration. "I've done everything I can already."

"The thing is, I'm wondering if maybe her seizure isn't related to whatever other problem you weren't talking to her about yesterday."

"That's crazy Allie."

"Maybe. Maybe not. This is her second seizure. The first one happened right after the first time you visited her and left angry. Now this one happened the morning after we left her without you having said more than two words to her."

"Well, if that's your logic…" Alex trailed off. "I've visited her several times Allie. But not only did she not have a seizure after those other times that you *didn't* mention, but of the two times you *did* just mention, one was immediately after the visit, and one wasn't. I'm sorry but your argument doesn't hold up."

"Are you really going to be able to live with yourself if she dies and you didn't visit her as much as you could to try to help her? I wish I could help her. But no one can visit her without you. Alex, there must be a reason for that."

"I thought so too Allie. But I don't anymore. She's not getting any better. If anything, she's getting worse. That can only mean one of two things. Either my visiting her hasn't made a difference one way or the other, or my visiting her is actually hurting her. And by your own theory, it's actually the latter. So maybe it's best if I just stay away."

"I didn't mean that I thought you were causing her to have seizures. What I meant was that maybe it's when you leave in such a way that causes her to have to wonder if she'll ever see you again, it causes her so much pain, that outwardly, it manifests as a seizure. I don't know, it's just a theory."

"The night before I brought you to see her, she was the one who told me to leave alright?" Alex took a deep breath and let it out before continuing. "I only went back with you because I had already told her, and you for that matter, that I would. The reason I didn't talk to her while you were there was because she didn't even want me to come back."

"I wonder why? She told me right before we left that she was hoping to get you alone to talk. Maybe she wanted to apologize. I don't know why she told you to leave Alex. By the sound of it, you don't either. Maybe you should come back and find out."

Alex snorted into the phone then. "Whatever, I'm done with Emily, okay? I'm at peace with the fact that she may not survive. I've done all I can do. I visited her several times Allie. It didn't make a difference. And I've got a life here in case you haven't noticed. I need to get back to focusing on that."

"Wait Alex" Allie said now. "Please. Please just think about it."

"Allie, I really can't. Please don't torture me with this."

"Alex, if you really care at all for Emily, even just a little bit, please, just think about it."

Alex sighed. "I'll think about it."

Chapter Twenty

Alex slept well that night. He made sure of it by taking some melatonin as soon as he was alone. After his very much enjoyed start with Veronica, and their subsequent conversation, she had gone back to her place next door in order to shower and change so that they could go out and spend the afternoon together.

It was while she was gone that Allie had called. Allie never failed at getting to that raw nerve, he thought, as he argued with her, hoping to God that Veronica didn't come back before he was able to end the conversation. Luckily, Veronica took her time next door, allowing Alex to get off the phone with Allie and still have a few minutes to compose himself before she came back.

They'd spent the afternoon walking around the city, with Veronica stopping here and there at her favorite stores to try on new clothes and model them for Alex. He'd pushed himself hard that afternoon to keep his attention focused solely on Veronica, not allowing his thoughts to stray from the here and now with her. He commented appropriately with every outfit she tried on, and the ones that she bought, he carried for her in their bags from store to store. He did the best job he could at being the dutiful, doting boyfriend.

By the time they'd parted ways, Alex was exhausted. At Veronica's door, she told him that she'd had a wonderful day and that she'd miss him while she slept. Alex was not oblivious to the fact that she was hinting that she wanted Alex to stay with her. But Alex just felt like he needed the night alone. He used the excuse that he had to be up early for work, which was technically true, before kissing Veronica deeply to reassure her and heading back to his own door.

The next day however, his doubts about whether he was doing the right thing started to return. No matter how hard he tried to push the thoughts out of his head, they just kept coming back. He blamed Allie for calling him like that and pushing him to come back. Even though he'd told her he'd think about it, his intention had been purely to get her off the phone.

But it seemed his mind just wouldn't let him off the hook. The longer the day went on, the more he thought about Emily lying there in her hospital bed and the more guilty he felt for not going back in after waking up with Allie. He tried to tell himself that he had no reason to feel guilty. After all, it was like he'd told Allie. She was the one who had wanted him to leave.

Emily was the one who'd carelessly tossed his feelings aside as if they didn't matter. She'd watched the scene where he'd first confessed his love, and still, it meant nothing to her. Less than nothing. It had obviously made her feel uncomfortable for him to even visit her as a friend. She'd told him to leave. Then she'd told him that he shouldn't come back. What was he supposed to do? He wished he knew.

He was tired of feeling like such a fool. By the time he left work that day, he was so riled up in his anger that he just felt like he needed to do something to get it out. He was never happier for Veronica to be out working than she was that evening. He went home, changed into some running shorts and an old t-shirt, and ran all over the neighborhood surrounding his building. Even when his muscles ached for him to stop, he pushed on, punishing his body until he couldn't anymore.

By the time he got back home, it was dark outside. By the time he made it into his apartment, he could barely walk. He didn't even make it to his bed. He threw his shoes off, turned off his living room light, and collapsed on the couch. A few hours later, he awoke and realized what had happened. Then he limped to his bed, made sure to set his alarm on his phone, and passed out again.

When his alarm went off in the morning, he groaned as the pain in his limbs slowly started coming back reminding him of the evening before. He was sorely tempted to call in sick, wanting nothing more than to just sleep through the day. In the end though, he made himself get up, take a shower, and go to work. His patients needed him more than he needed to stay home.

This day was a continuation of the thoughts that plagued him the day before. He couldn't get away from them, no matter how hard he tried. By the time he left work that afternoon, he'd decided that the reason he couldn't stop thinking about Emily was because he was just so angry with her. Holding in his anger was causing this and he was going to have to go back and tell her how he felt in order to purge himself of those feelings.

But how was he going to explain it to Veronica? He could only imagine how she would take it if he told her how he was feeling. And really, did he need to put her through that knowing it would be the last time he'd ever go back? But if he kept it from her and she found out where he'd gone, he knew she'd never forgive him.

He spent the next day debating whether he should tell Veronica that he needed to go back. He hadn't told her about his mysterious sleep connection with Emily because there was no way she would believe it was true and because it would probably make Veronica doubt that he was over Emily no matter what he might say to the contrary. That was definitely better off being kept to himself, he thought.

Then he came up with an idea. He called Brendan and asked him if he would be willing to go along with calling Alex at a time when Alex would be with Veronica. He wanted Brendan to tell him that he needed Alex to come back to sign some paperwork that he'd missed in regard to the selling of his house. It would be paperwork that had to be signed in person, not faxed or emailed back and forth. Surely Veronica couldn't get too upset about that. He would go back Friday night, confront Emily with everything he wanted to say, and come back early Saturday, allowing himself to still have more than 24 hours with Veronica before the work week started all over again.

That evening, he was out to dinner with Veronica when Brendan called. Alex relayed what Brendan had said while they finished their dinner and waited for Veronica to respond. She took a moment, sipping her wine slowly, before setting her glass down and coming up with an answer.

"Well, as it happens, I asked off from the bar this weekend in order to spend it all with you. After all, this was supposed to be the first weekend you haven't left in over a month. So why don't I just go with you? You could show me around the place you grew up."

Internally, Alex thought, what do I do now? To Veronica he said, "It's going to be so boring for you. It's a small town with not a lot going on. I'd just be going for the evening to get those papers signed and then I'd be back early the next day. Honestly, it wouldn't be worth it for you. Let me just get this taken care of and I'll be back before you know it and we can still have almost the whole weekend together. In fact, why don't you make plans for us to get out of town and stay somewhere Saturday night together? Anywhere you want."

"Well," Veronica said now looking down at her plate as she pushed food around with her fork, "There is a nice romantic hotel not too far from here that I read about in a magazine recently."

"Perfect." Alex said almost too enthusiastically. "You set it up and I'll pay for it, and we'll have a nice evening away all to ourselves."

Friday afternoon, Alex went to his apartment straight from work, packed a small overnight bag, and booked a room at a decent hotel back home. Then he called Allie to let her know that he would be coming back, just for that night, for one last visit. He wanted to make sure that she could keep her parents away while he was there.

"Oh, that's no problem." Allie responded. "They only visit in the mornings and only a few times a week."

"Okay that's good. I mean it's not good that they only go a few times a week, but you know what I mean."

"Yeah, I get it. My mom won't go without my dad and my dad for the most part acts like he's trying to pretend it isn't real. I think maybe it's too hard for him. It's a change though for sure. It was always mom that denied reality growing up you know. Drinking it away instead of getting angry at dad for just leaving the way he does, sometimes for days at a time. And then when he does come back, he always expects things to be just like he hadn't left. He still expects dinner on the table every night. And she still just goes along with it."

"I know you've already told me all about that, and I still have a hard time believing it. I can't imagine growing up with that Allie. My parents were so good to me. It must've been hard not knowing from one day to the next what was going to happen."

"At least I had Emily. She was the most stabilizing person in my life. But she didn't have that the way I did, you know, because she's the oldest. I don't know how she managed to be so solid. I wish now that I'd tried harder to be like her."

"She's not gone yet Allie. There's still time. We don't know what's going to happen."

"I'm having a harder and harder time believing she'll be okay Alex. She's just been asleep for too long. How could she possibly wake up and not have some brain damage or something after this long?"

"I don't know Allie. All you can do is continue to hope that she'll wake up and be just like she was when you visited her in her head last weekend. Honestly, I think as long as she is undamaged there in that place, there's a chance that she'll be undamaged when she wakes up as well."

"*If* she wakes up."

"Right. *If* she wakes up."

With that, Alex got off the phone with Allie and made his way back south. It was pretty late by the time he made it to the hospital, first having to stop at the hotel to check into the room he'd booked. He made his way up to Emily's room and pretty quickly fell asleep. The first thing he saw once he was back inside her subconscious world was Emily, asleep on the mattress he'd left for her. Everything else looked about the same and he wondered how long she'd been asleep. He remembered her telling him that when she slept, it would be for days and when she'd awake, she'd have no idea what day it was or how much time had passed.

He wasn't sure he should even try to wake her. He watched her for a few minutes, debating on what he should do, before deciding that he needed to at least try to wake her because he absolutely had to leave in the morning, and he had to get out the things he wanted to say. She was lying on her side, so he knelt down beside the mattress and gently shook her shoulder. She slowly started to come awake and open her eyes.

———

It sounded like someone was calling my name from somewhere very far away. So far away that I could barely hear them. The voice sounded muffled even though it also sounded like they were hollering. Suddenly I felt like I was being jostled around by an unseen force and the voice that was calling my name was getting louder and clearer. And then everything stopped. Someone was touching me. Someone was shaking my shoulder.

I opened my eyes, and it was Alex. His lips were formed into a thin straight line and his eyebrows were slightly creased as his blue eyes bore straight into mine. They were dark like the ocean. I practically jumped out of my skin as the realization that it was Alex right here in front of me dawned. I was on my feet in less than two seconds causing his upper body to pull back like he'd been burned. Then he got back up on his own feet.

Now I started to think about all the things I wanted to say. I needed to tell him about the feelings that I was starting to have towards him. I needed to explain to him how I just didn't understand before about how much he'd loved me. I needed to tell him how watching his confession when we were alone at that party melted my heart and how when I watched him get me home and put me into my bed that night, I'd wished afterwards that he had been here with me.

I needed to tell him these things now because, even if it was really too late for us, even if he was really in love with Veronica, it just may be what was keeping me from waking up. And I knew, I might not get another chance. Just the fact that he was here now, was a miracle. But how was I supposed to start? He looked so angry.

"I'm so happy you came back, even if you're upset with me." I said nervously. "I have so much I want to tell you. But I'm going to be quiet first and allow you to say what you came back to say. I'll listen, even if it's hard to hear. All I ask is that, when you're done, you don't just take off and disappear without listening to me as well. Because I really need to say some things. And I know I may never get another chance." I said this while feeling the force of tears trying to escape from my eyes. I willed myself to hold them back and thankfully I was successful in my efforts.

"I don't even know where to start." Alex said as he threw his hands up in the air and let them fall, slapping his thighs loudly. "I tried to do something nice for you and you tell me to leave. And this, *after* you watched my confession at that party that night and chose not to tell me. And *still*, I came back with Allie, for *you*."

"I'm sorry" I said now. "Watching that scene was still just so fresh in my mind when you showed up with that mattress... I wasn't ready to talk to you about it."

Alex continued, "I don't know who I'm angrier at, me or you. I'm angry at myself because I should have known I couldn't just do something nice for you, without you automatically assuming I still want to be with you and pushing me away. I was just trying to make amends for being blind to the things that were really going on with you our whole lives. I wanted to do that so that I could move on and know we left off on a positive note, whether or not you ever woke up from this place."

"I know. I know you were."

"That was stupid of me." Alex continued as if he hadn't heard me. "And I'm even more stupid for coming back now just to yell at you. It's really just a big waste of my time. But I just, I had to get it out because otherwise, I was always going to feel like you just thought I could not get over you, and honestly, my pride can't handle that. I know that sounds like a chauvinist attitude, but there it is."

Alex who had been pacing as he told me these things stopped now, and momentarily looked at me as he pushed his hand through his hair. I walked up to him quickly now, as I had been standing a good five feet away the whole time he was talking. I needed to make sure he didn't take off before I got to say what I needed to. I was terrified for sure of saying the words. But I was even more terrified of never getting the chance again.

As I got within just a few inches of him, he suddenly turned away from me. "Alex." I whispered, causing him to cinch his shoulders up and start walking fast in the opposite direction.

"Alex" I said a little louder now.

"What?" he asked as he continued walking without faltering in the slightest.

"Where are you going?" I asked him as the pitch of my voice started to rise.

"I don't know. I don't know where I'm going!" he yelled back as he continued to walk.

"Alex!" I said louder as I started jogging after him. "I still have some things I need to say to you. Please."

Alex continued on without a word. As I reached him, I grabbed his arm, causing him to swiftly turn around, staring at me with such an angry intensity. But there was also something else that I could see in his eyes behind the anger. I could almost swear it looked like heartache. Could that really be right? Did he really still feel something for me?

Our faces were just a few inches from each other. He was breathing heavily with his lips slightly parted as if he'd been running. Even though my heart was pounding in my chest, and I felt completely unsure, I did not move away. I stared back at him, holding his gaze, as I felt his breath on my face.

After what felt like forever, staring at each other in silence, something started to shift in Alex. I felt the intensity between us slowly begin to change. I could feel his anger slipping away as it was replaced by something that I couldn't define. The look in his eyes began to soften as I continued to hold his gaze. What was he thinking about? I couldn't have looked away if I'd wanted to. I could feel anticipation starting to build inside of me.

His face started moving slowly closer to mine now, never breaking eye contact. It happened so slowly that it felt like time was freezing incrementally. Eventually, he stopped moving closer, letting his lips linger just a fraction of an inch from mine. I could feel his breath on them, and it seemed as shaky as my own. My heart was beating frantically, but in a good way. Was he going to kiss me? This was my friend Alex. But all I could think about at this moment was how much I wanted to feel his lips on mine. I felt my eyes start to close and my lips start to part of their own volition. I had no control. The need to close the gap between us was very overpowering.

Then out of nowhere, he pulled away, gasping loudly as he started to fade away. I wanted to yell out, to tell him to come back, but I couldn't find the words. It all happened so fast, that even though he hadn't actually kissed me, I still felt the electricity on my lips.

Chapter Twenty-One

The suddenness with which Alex had been awakened caused him to burst up out of the chair he'd been sitting in while he slept. The force of this caused the chair to fall over with a loud clatter. He looked around wildly for a moment as if he wasn't sure where he was, and it took him a moment to get his bearings. He only had a few seconds to take in the room around him before he saw that Veronica was there. She swiftly crossed the room now to where he was standing, stopping right in front of him.

"What the hell is going on?!" She asked angrily. "What are you doing here? You told me you weren't going to come back to see her again." Veronica said, pointing a finger into Alex's chest.

Alex, still stunned by this rapid turn of events, was having a hard time focusing on the situation. "Wha...what are you doing here?" was all he could manage to say.

"I followed you back here from Maryland. I had a feeling you were lying to me the other night. It looks like I was right. It just seemed so strange to me that you were trying to convince me that I didn't want to come with you. So now I'm going to ask you again, what are you doing here?"

"How did you know what room to come to?" he asked, trying to stall her while he tried to figure out what to say.

Veronica paced angrily as she relayed her story. "I told you, I followed you here. I mean literally. I followed you on the highway, and then I followed you through the hospital. I watched you come into this room. I waited for you to come out for an hour, but you never did. I was going to confront you out there, but I got tired of waiting. So finally, I came in here to get it over with and I see you sleeping with your head on her leg while holding her hand!" She stopped suddenly as she finished, turning back to stare daggers at Alex.

"I...I'm sorry Veronica" Alex said trying to absorb everything she'd just told him while still reeling over what had almost happened with Emily only a few moments before. "I really can't explain now. I know that's not what you want to hear, but this is just really the absolute worst time for this conversation. Can I please just talk to you in a few hours? I can meet you somewhere a little more private."

"More private than what?" Veronica said looking around the room. "We are the only ones in here. Unless you count her." Veronica said gesturing forcefully in Emily's direction. "She can't hear a damn thing. I think this is the perfect time for this."

Alex knew he could not have an honest conversation with Veronica unless he was first able to go back to Emily. He needed to find out if what he thought had almost happened, had indeed been the case. Had Emily actually been about to let him kiss her? Or had he imagined it? And if she had wanted him to kiss her, what did that mean?

On the other hand, did it even matter? He wasn't supposed to care about how Emily felt about him anymore. He had Veronica right here, and he already knew for sure that she wanted him. Didn't he want her too? He'd thought he did. Now he felt completely torn, and he hated that he'd had to lie to Veronica.

"Veronica, I just need a few hours to sort everything out. I'm just so confused right now. I'm sorry. Please just give me a few hours."

"You told me you'd moved on and that you wanted to be with me. Are you telling me that you're not sure about that now?!" Veronica yelled in a loud, shrill voice.

"I don't know what else to say. I'm sorry Veronica, I need some time…"

"You need time?!" Veronica cut Alex off. "You should have thought about that *before* you decided to sleep with me and make me think we actually had something together! I'll tell you what, either you leave with me right now and forget all about this bitch, or we are through. Do you hear me?!" Veronica screamed just as Emily started to seize once again.

As soon as Alex disappeared, I took off for the bar. I ran faster than I had probably ever run in my life. I had to know if he understood what had almost happened between us and if he even cared. I got to the bar, my chest heaving for air. I pulled the door open and ran over to where the creature was still sitting at the table near the stage. I told the creature to pull up Alex as I gasped for air and collapsed in the chair on the other side of the table.

Alex appeared in the crystal ball standing in my hospital room. He looked completely wide-eyed and pale as Veronica stood right in front of him screaming. He'd apparently lied to her in order to come back to see me. She was trying to make him leave with her. Please God, don't let him leave with her I prayed silently. Then I started to hear that familiar rumble.

Everything started shaking, more violently than I had ever seen it shake before. Plaster from the ceiling started to come down on my head as I ran for the door, wrenching it open to escape. I got about 20 feet from the building before I stopped to look back at it. I watched as it actually started to collapse. Was this the end? Was it time for me to die now?

I ran back along the road, still tired from running to the bar in the first place. I was trying not to fall as the ground shook hard, causing it to rip open across the road behind me. As I passed the field and Jenna's house, it too started to collapse. It was all so terrifying to see. I made it up over the hill that blocked the view of Jenna's house from the school. Then I continued on to the bench in front of the school. Then I watched as the school also collapsed into a gigantic pile of rubble.

Alarms started ringing loudly seemingly from everywhere as four nurses and a doctor ran into Emily's room. Emily was seizing again. The medical staff forced Alex and Veronica out into the hall, slamming the door behind them. Alex immediately ran to the window on the door, plastering his face to it, trying to see what was going on.

"Are you coming with me or not?!" Veronica said angrily from behind him, hands on her hips.

Alex turned to look at her, incredulous that Veronica could ask him that after Emily had started seizing again that way. Even though Emily was a complete stranger to Veronica, and even though Veronica saw Emily as a threat, he felt like that was no excuse for the way Veronica was acting. He had made his decision.

"I can't go with you Veronica. I'm sorry. I think it's over."

"You son of a bitch" she screamed now, raising her hand as if to slap him.

Alex caught her hand in midair and held it tight as she continued to scream. "Please calm down. I don't want to fight with you."

"I came all this way for you." She said, her voice starting to wobble as she lowered her arm.

"I'm sorry for that. I should've been more honest with you. I wanted to move on from Emily. I really did. I just can't I guess."

"You used me!" Veronica yelled, her voice cracking with a shrill sound. "You used me as a rebound! You asshole!"

"I did, I guess. I wasn't really thinking of it that way but now I see that I did. I'm sorry. I am an asshole. But I never meant to be. So please calm down." Alex saw that he wasn't getting through to Veronica by being calm, but he wasn't sure what else he could do.

"Why should I?" she yelled back as she once again tried to slap at Alex's face.

This time she was using both hands and Alex had to shield himself with his arms. Then, from behind Veronica, a burly looking security guard came running up, putting himself between her and Alex, one hand on each of their chests. "Is everything alright here?" the guard asked Alex.

"Well, I guess I just broke up with my girlfriend and she's not taking it too well" Alex replied. "I'm here visiting a friend of mine that's dying."

"I'll show you not taking it well!" Veronica screamed, trying to get around the security guard. Alex backed up instinctively.

"I'm sorry miss" the security guard said to her. "You're going to have to leave the hospital right now and I'm going to have to walk you out." He put his hand around her upper arm to lead the way.

Veronica continued to fight the security guard, screaming and cursing at Alex as the guard forced her down the hall. It was only once he had gotten her onto the elevator, and the doors closed, that peace was once again restored in the hallway outside of Emily's room. Alex turned to look at the nurse's station where only a single nurse was left to man the desk. She was older and had a no nonsense look about her with fluffy white hair, cat eyeglasses and a frown upon her face. She had been watching all of the commotion and in fact, had been the one to call the security guard.

Alex's face turned red as the nurse continued to frown at him. "I'm sorry for all of that" he told her. "It was my fault and it'll never happen again."

"Let's hope it doesn't" she responded in a dull tone. "Or we might have to kick you out as well."

Not sure of what else to say, Alex turned back to the window on Emily's door. He hoped that Veronica would decide to just go back to Maryland now. But in case she didn't, he was going to have to watch his back when he inevitably left the hospital. He hoped she hadn't decided to go find his truck and slash the tires or something. But if she did, he couldn't say he didn't deserve it.

He watched the doctor and nurses still fighting to stabilize Emily. It had never taken this long before. What if it was too late to go back? Alex sent up a silent prayer, begging for another chance. After another few minutes, the door finally opened, and Alex moved aside to allow the medical staff to pass.

The doctor took Alex aside for a moment. "I know you want to go in and see Emily, but I think she needs to rest now. Unfortunately, it might not be too much longer, and I don't want her to have another seizure with guests in the room like that. It makes it harder for us to help her when we first have to get people out of the room. I wouldn't want us to have to waste precious time."

"Please," Alex begged the doctor. "I'm the only one here now and I just really need to be with her. I promise, if anything else happens, I won't get in the way." The doctor sighed and was about to say something when Alex continued. "You just said yourself that she could go at any time. If you're sure she's not going to wake up, what's the harm in letting me see her?"

"Patient care is our number one concern. Even though I do not believe at this point that she is going to make it out of here, it is still my duty to ensure that when she does pass, it happens in the most comfortable way possible." The doctor stared hard at Alex's anguished face for a moment before sighing loudly. "Okay. How about this. You can go back in for now. But, if anyone else comes to see her, I only want one person in there at a time. Understand?"

"Yes, I completely understand. Thank you." Alex said, running his hand through his hair.

"I'm going to go notify her parents now that she has had another seizure. Don't forget what I said." With that, the doctor turned and walked off down the hall.

———————

Once the shaking stopped, I took inventory of this place around me. All of the buildings that had appeared since I got here were now in heaps on the ground. The ground was split open into giant slits, making it so that I'd have to step carefully in order to move from the spot I was now standing in, the spot where I first started this journey, right in front of the bench. I was scared to death. If I move, would the ground crumble beneath me?

The last thing I'd seen before everything collapsed was Veronica in my hospital room letting Alex have it. If past experiences here had been anything to go by, I was now guessing that Alex had not under-stood what was about to happen between us before he woke up and disappeared. He must've decided to leave with Veronica, I thought. That must've been why I'd had another seizure. If that was the case, then this really was the end. I felt overwhelming sadness start to en-velop me.

I collapsed down onto the bench and started to cry. There was nothing else I could do. Alex was gone. I'd missed my chance to change things. I was going to die. After a long time of trying to recon-cile myself to this inevitability and being unable to do so, I slid down, lying on the bench in silence. Time passed slowly as I just stared out into that sun-less orange horizon.

A while later, I suddenly started to hear something. It sounded like a quiet scraping sound coming from behind me. I whipped my head around to look for the source. There had never been anything here that made any kind of sound before besides Alex and Allie. Or that creature. What if that creature had come to tell me my time was up?

About twenty feet away, with one of those giant slits in the ground separating us, was Alex. He had his hands in his pockets and was looking down at the ground and then back up at me, absentmindedly scraping his foot in the dirt. When he saw that I had noticed him, he stopped scraping his foot, and just looked at me in silence. I stared back for a moment, frozen in place, stunned by his appearance.

Alex had come back! This realization slowly registered in my brain as we continued to stare at each other. Then, as if jolted by lightning, I unfroze. I couldn't seem to get on my feet fast enough now. I realized how limited my time was as I started running towards him, dodging carefully around the edge of that slit between us as I went. I was just so happy that he had come back. Nothing else mattered in the world. I had another chance. It wasn't over yet. I couldn't believe he had actually come back.

I plowed straight into him when I reached the spot where he was standing causing him to make a loud oomph sound. I just hadn't been able to slow down fast enough. He felt sturdy and warm as I wrapped my arms around him and squeezed as hard as I could. The smell of his cologne was so inviting. I drew in a big whiff as I laid my head on his chest. He continued to be silent as I did this. But he didn't push me away.

After a few blissful seconds, I stepped back, and looked up into his eyes. The look on his face said that he was unsure, and he didn't want to make the wrong move. So, I reached up, and slowly and silently took his face in my hands. Then I stood up on tip toe, placed my lips on his, and closed my eyes. His lips were soft and warm. I felt a zing of excitement and desire run through me at the feeling of those lips on mine. It was the best sensation I'd ever felt.

He didn't pull away. Instead, he wrapped his arms around me, pulling me as close as he could. We were pressed together with no air between us, and it was a heady feeling. We both let the kiss linger for a few seconds before parting. I lowered my feet back to the ground as I slowly dropped my hands from the face of this man. I stared into his eyes and felt a strong sense of wonder and amazement.

He was staring right back at me with a look that I could only describe as a look of complete desire. Seeing him now, I couldn't believe that this was the same Alex who had been my friend since we were small children. Where I had once only seen him in that way, I now saw him as a man. A strong, masculine man who was in love with me and who had always been there for me. True he had his faults, mainly getting angry about me seeing his vulnerability because of pride, as well as jumping not only into a new relationship so quickly with Veronica but jumping into bed with her as well. He had let his hormones mixed with his wounded pride control his decisions in that regard. But in the end, he was all mine, and he always had been.

I wanted so much to kiss him again. The pull was so strong. It must've been the same for him because he suddenly lowered his head and planted his lips back on mine. This time the kiss was harder, deeper, and more passionate. I could feel myself starting to get lost in the sensation as my brain started to fog and I started to feel a little dizzy. I had to drag myself back out of that fog before it went too far, reminding myself that I still needed to tell him everything. I ended the kiss and was just about to start talking when the ground started shaking again.

"It's going to be okay Emily" he said to me now, grabbing me and holding me as tightly to him as he could.

I could feel the fear pouring off him and I knew that at any moment, he was going be ripped awake again by my seizing. So, I looked up into his eyes and yelled as loudly as I could over the sound of the loud rumbling around us, "No matter what happens, I love you, Alex. I just wanted you to know."

The look in his eyes was one of complete distress as he yelled out "No!" and started to fade away from me again.

———————

Alex woke up with a start as Emily's body was shaking beneath his head. He jumped up and moved quickly to the corner of the room as the doctor and the team of nurses came rushing back in to help. He watched silently from that corner as his eyes filled with tears. Was it really too late for them? She'd told him she loved him. How could it be too late? Please God, don't let it be too late, he begged silently inside his head.

It seemed like forever before Emily's seizure subsided. The nurses looked grim as they slowly left the room. The doctor could do little more than to tell Alex how sorry he was that they couldn't do anything more for her. He left Alex alone in the room to grieve. Alex sat back down in the chair next to Emily's bed, took her hand, leaned his forehead against it as he held it, and began to shudder with tears.

Alex had disappeared and I was left alone to once again try to run and dodge the holes in the earth that were now widening as new holes also began to form. What was the point of even trying to dodge the holes now? I had told Alex I loved him, and we kissed. I had experienced that feeling that others describe as having your heart soar. I had never felt that with anyone else before. And it turned out that it wasn't the answer that I'd thought it would be. I must've been wrong all along. Turning down Alex hadn't been the reason I had ended up here. That thought quickly drained me and sent me into complete despair.

I stopped moving now, deciding to wait for the ground to just open up beneath me. I guess I was just meant to die. I was scared to death but too tired to fight it. I sat down and pulled my knees up to my chest closing my eyes and putting my head down, waiting for the end. After several minutes of sitting there in complete fear, the shaking slowed to a halt. When it was over, I wasn't sure what to do, so I kept my head down and my eyes closed. After another minute or so of silence, I started to feel air moving over the surface of my arms. I slowly opened my eyes and lifted my head. There had never been any kind of breeze before.

What I saw now had me in complete awe. I stood up slowly, dusting myself off as the world that had previously been around me was completely transformed. The sky was blue with light, whispy clouds and there was a sun that was warm and yellow. The ground everywhere was completely covered in grass and different colored flowers. Gone was the road and all of the crumbled buildings. There were trees here and there all around me and I could hear birds singing in them. I could feel that cool breeze blow by me again and the air smelled fresh. It was wonderful.

A short distance away, I saw a beam of beautiful light shine down from the sky, forming a circle on the grass. Somehow, I knew I was supposed to walk into it. Was this the end, or was I going to wake up now? There was only one way to find out.

I slowly walked towards it, taking one last look at this beautiful place around me before stepping into the circle of light. I immediately had the sensation of weightlessness as I was lifted up from the ground. Then suddenly, I was shooting through the air. I was moving so fast, so quickly that now I couldn't see anything around me. It was all a blur. But somehow, I wasn't scared.

The feeling of moving so swiftly lasted for several minutes before suddenly slamming to a stop. This left my limbs feeling very heavy. Everything around me was now solid black. I couldn't see anything, including my own body, but I could hear something. It sounded like someone crying. As I listened, the sound became clearer and more defined. It sounded like a man crying. It sounded like Alex.

I became more aware of my body the longer I listened to the sound. I started to feel as though my eyes were closed, although, I wasn't sure why. I tried to open them, but like the rest of me, they were very heavy. Over the next several minutes, I continued trying to force them open. Eventually, I could feel it starting to work. I saw a sliver of light starting to form and it slowly got wider and wider.

Everything in that light was fuzzy and out of focus. The longer I stared at it though, the clearer it became. I saw movement on the right side of the light, and I forced my eyes to shift in that direction. The thing that was moving came into focus. It was Alex, from the torso up. That's all I could see. His eyes were closed as he held someone's hand up to his forehead. Tears were streaming down his face.

I realized that it was *my* hand that he was holding as I started to feel his hand holding it. Was I awake? "Alex..." I tried to say, although what actually came out was completely unintelligible. My throat was so dry that it was hard to make any sound at all. "Alex" I tried again, this time making noise sufficient enough to cause his eyes to pop open.

I was now bombarded with thoughts of everything that had happened in the last 24 hours. I'd almost kissed Alex, before he was ripped away by Veronica. Then everything started collapsing and I worried that he was gone forever. But he came back, giving me renewed hope. Then we did kiss. Twice. And it was the best thing that had ever happened to me. Then he was ripped away again, and I thought for sure it was my time to die. But it turned out that it wasn't, and now I was awake after several months of being lost in a world inside my own head. It was a lot to process.

Now Alex was looking directly at me like he was unsure of what he was seeing. "Emily" he said after a few moments. "Yes. It's me, Alex." He started to smile and then he started to laugh in a slightly hysterical manner. "You're awake. Oh my God, you're awake!" Then he started crying again but this time it was out of happiness. "Hold on, let me go get the doctor."

"Alex" I said again as he jumped up out of his chair and started heading for the door. He stopped for a minute and turned back towards me. "I love you."

His grin broadened even more as he said, "I love you too" and then turned back to the door.

Epilogue

Everything was beautiful in the small chapel. I'd found the perfect little place, just small enough to feel intimate but still large enough to accommodate everyone who had RSVP'd. It had a vintage feel about it, with old wooden whitewashed pews. It was perfect, and it was situated on a few acres of open land with perfectly green grass and gently sloping hills. It was a beautiful day outside.

As the song that me and Alex had agreed on began to play, my bridesmaids in their full-length violet dresses and violet and cream flowered crowns started walking up the aisle with their groomsmen counterparts. It was a small wedding, with only three bridesmaids and three groomsmen, but we didn't need a lot of people to celebrate this momentous occasion.

First, it was Jenna Mitchell (formally Thompson), walking down the aisle with Alex's friend Brendan. It seemed only fitting that I should reach out to Jenna since it was at her party that Alex had originally shared his feelings with me. Then it was Samantha, my best friend, walking down the aisle with James, and finally, it was my maid of honor Allie, walking down the aisle with Alex's best man, Josh. Brendan had pitched a slight fit over not being the best man, but Alex had decided that it was only right to have Allie and Josh walk down the aisle together. After all, they were next in line to get married.

The walls of the chapel were white, and it had a wood plank bolstered ceiling. Bouquets of violet and cream flowers were attached to the walls between every gothic style window. The pews each had their own bouquet of flowers attached to the inside ends as well. The entire floor was made of an old hard wood, and a long train of cream-colored flowers was strewn up the aisle for the wedding party to walk on.

Now I hear the music die down, and the first chords of the wedding march begin to play. Without seeing it, I hear everyone in the pews collectively stand as I walk from around the corner outside of the chapel into the doorway and start up the aisle. This was the best day of my life.

Although I had a troubled history with my father, I allowed him to walk with me. The only thing that really mattered was that I was here, marrying Alex. My father looked the best that I had ever seen him in his nice new tuxedo, with his hair combed back and a genuine smile on his face.

We made our way slowly up the aisle, and my father held tight to my arm. It had only been a few months since I'd awoken from my coma. I'd had to work hard to get used to walking again. But I had the best physical therapist in town to help me and I was about to marry him right now. What better motivation could there be?

I saw my mother, Brenda, standing with the rest of our family, all of whom I didn't know all that well. But they came to my wedding and for that, I was grateful. My mother had tears in her eyes as she watched me pass by with my father. She'd cleaned herself up as well, wearing a nice plum colored dress to go with the color scheme while still standing out from the bridesmaids. There was no sign today from either of my parents that they were going to cause any problems. Today was a day of peace.

On Alex's side of the church, he also had distant family that had come from all over the country. His parents had originally come from two different places causing this scattering of aunts and uncles and cousins. And although Alex's parents had both passed, we knew they were looking down on their son today.

Finally, I got to the end of my long walk, and I looked first at the priest and then at Alex. I could feel the love pouring out of his eyes as I locked my eyes on his. It was the most wonderful feeling to be loved that way. I listened to Alex's calming tone as he repeated the vows the priest had set forth for us. Then it was my turn. I repeated after the priest as the swelling of emotion threatened to take control. I managed to make it through the vows before the floodgates released a few tears of joy.

And then it was time to say those two little words. First Alex and then me. When the priest pronounced us husband and wife and told Alex that he could kiss the bride, Alex did something completely surprising. He took me in his arms and dipped me as he leaned over me and laid an amazing kiss on my lips. As I gave into the sensation by wrapping my arms around his neck and closing my eyes, everyone began to cheer.